THE GRASSLAND GAMES

THE GRASSLAND GAMES

Chitta Ranjan

Vitasta

Published by
Renu Kaul Verma
Vitasta Publishing Pvt Ltd
4348/4C, Ansari Road, Daryaganj
New Delhi - 110 002
info@vitastapublishing.com

ISBN: 978-81-19670-43-7

First Edition 2024
MRP ₹395

This novel is entirely a work of fiction. Names, characters, events and incidents are entirely imaginary. Reference to real places, actual regions, institutions or community practices has been made in a fictitious manner. Any resemblance to actual persons, living or dead or actual events is purely coincidental.

Edited by Seema Nambiar
Typeset & Cover Design by Rohit Gautam
Printed at Chaman Enterprises, New Delhi

Chapter 1

Day 1 (Afternoon)

Raj had gotten used to it—the odd sensation when the whole body resonates with the vehicle's shaking, traversing the bumpy gravel roads in and around the park. The SUV tunnelled through a patch of elephant grass as it turned from green to a surreal orange, glistening in the afternoon sun. Tyres spluttered pebbles from the edges as he pressed the accelerator, leaving behind Village 8, a minuscule brown dot of *frustration* in a vast expanse of greenery.

Phew! He had never toiled so hard with his persuasive and diplomatic skills. Looking through the dusty windscreen at the narrow dark path ahead, hands steadying the steering wheel, tight fists absorbing the vibration, he reminisced the unproductive interactions with the stubborn settlers. The coolness of the steady breeze rasped against his face. The sun went down further on the horizon, now casting a halo of melancholic redness on the grasses. He wanted to turn the car around and head straight to his quarters. It had been a long day of counselling a group filled with scepticism, ingrained or fuelled by outsiders—he was not sure.

The headlights shone fleetingly on the animals of twilight, the hares, civets and barking deer, all clamouring for cover. Days are short in January in India's northeast, the region receiving the morning sun's first rays when the rest of the country is still engulfed in hazy darkness.

Another day went by without achieving any new line of sight.

The SUV's body rattled following a sudden grinding sound, and before Raj could realise it, it stopped moving despite his frantic pressing of the accelerator. The shadowy grass swayed lazily on both sides of the road. His car had broken down many times before in his four years of posting at that place. It had often happened inside the national park's core area, in the wilderness. He always had someone, his driver or deputy or an armed guard or one of his anti-poaching crack force members. There the dwellers of the forest always behaved predictably for some reason, but in the fringe areas, near the park's boundary, the conflict zone of men and animals, he had seen both behave edgily. Trying the ignition again, he gave up as the vehicle showed no signs of starting. A sigh escaped his lips as he scanned the locality devoid of any human presence. The undulating grasses on his right merged with the protected woodland; the patch on his left gave way to a tea estate's manicured carpet of green.

Should he try asking for help from the estate people? Where are they?

He made another attempt at turning the key, only to hear just a persistent spluttering sound. Taking a deep breath, he crouched and got out of the car. No point trying to check the snag by lifting the bonnet; in the receding light, he would not be able to do anything. The fuel meter read full. He had filled the tank the night before and driven straight to the village. The whole day, he had talked with the villagers about the rehabilitation package. His SUV had stood under a banyan tree while the urchins circled it. Raj glanced at the time; it was still a couple of hours to the meeting. Cursing himself for agreeing to Vijay's suggestion of the venue, he locked the car and started walking as the last of the sun's crimson radiance went down on the western horizon. Wisps of fog over the leaf-carpeted path added unhealthy dampness to the chill. In the air filled with the ever-increasing sound of cicadas and calls of the night birds, he sensed a nameless dread floating as he walked the narrow lane. The blades of grass brushed the rough fabric of his half-vest jacket and cargo pants. The swaying grass seemed hungry, as if he was prey to be swallowed. Wrapping the muffler around his head to protect himself from the cold, he dug his hands deep into the pockets, missing the metallic coldness of his 9 mm pistol; he hastened his pace.

Vulture Hill's cliff appeared before him like a dark monster rising in the mist. From the base, an unpaved, winding path through the grassy slope led to a nondescript anti-poaching patrolling camp—his rendezvous point with the informer, under the shadow of a silk-cotton tree with its branches reaching out like long arms. The road went straight ahead and then took a sharp right, skirting an expanse of the water body. The river breeze from the Brahmaputra flowing a few kilometres to the north, mixed with the dank stink of hyacinth-clogged wetland lying in front of him, touched his face.

A fork of branches loomed high over the camp, like the two extended arms of a witch, reminding him of the stories he had heard from his department colleagues of guards committing suicides and villagers practising weird and secretive rituals. Before they built the house, the spot under the tree had been a site of various shadowy activities and animal sacrifices by those believing in witchcraft and other superstitious practices. People reported finding many human remains, including decapitated bodies, near the hillock. The thoughts made him shiver as darkness engulfed the area. The evening light seeping through the branches played with his senses.

Where are the guards?

With two long hours left to go for the meeting, Raj hoped the informer had some worthwhile leads for him. His mobile did not show any signal bars. No way was he going up; let the men return, he decided. An eerie mist had gathered above the swamp in front of him, the park's deepest water body where the water level remained at least a dozen metres deep even during the dry winter months. The bulbous stocks with the purple flowers stirred a slow refusal to give away their secrets. Hundreds of flying foxes out for the night's hunt blocked the strands of fading lights. Raj sat down on a flat white stone; it felt ice-cold, despite his trousers' thick fabric. Whining mosquitoes around his head formed a cloud as he turned his gaze to the rectangular concrete water tank behind the house. A dark-faced macaque sitting on the corrugated sheet covering the water tank mocked at him before vanishing into the thicket behind. Smoke billowed from the factory; at least some people were working nearby across the lush green carpet of the undulating tea garden behind him while the shadowy woods on his right hummed with uncanny noises.

Another long sigh escaped him as the day passed into tarry darkness. He walked up the hill to the tin-roofed camp, searching for the key in his pocket. A distant noise, more like a rumbling hubbub, drifted to him. An orange halo appeared on an otherwise pitch-dark night, a few kilometres away on the same road he had traversed.

What is it? Is it a group looking for stray cattle? Is it a group of protesters demanding some compensation?

Raj pushed the door open, his head still turned to the left, looking into the distance. From the number of flickering torches, he worked out that it was not a bunch of individuals; it had to be a hundred-plus crowd or an entire hamlet. They walked parallel to the park boundary. The mobile still did not show any signal bars.

Rushing inside and switching on the first room's light, he came across two unkempt beds that still had their mosquito nets drawn. The familiar odour of damp bedding, unwashed clothes and *beedis* assailed his senses. A calendar with the picture of Lord Ganesha jostled for space with a Bollywood heroine's poster on the wall. He trod through the middle room with a single bed, the room doubled as a kitchen, taking care not to trip over the stacks of utensils kept on the floor, towards the last room with the walkie-talkie: his resting room ahead of the meeting.

A cold gust hit his face; the back door was ajar. Muttering curses at the guards, he groped for the switch. The room filled with light. She lay on the bed—an angelic face with high cheekbones, rosy cheeks, full cherry pink lips and kohl-lined eyes. The face emanated serenity, a silver ring on the slightly flat nose accentuating her sensual beauty. She wore a floral white T-shirt and a short blue skirt. Her long black hair was waist length. He noticed her ivory white hands with manicured nails. Her unsoiled feet seemed to have never touched the ground.

The camp's transceiver set was missing from the table. His phone had no signal. He shuddered taking stock of the surreal situation: the marching villagers with their hostile and inflammatory shouting, coming straight towards him at an even quicker pace than before; the missing guards; the out-of-range mobile network; a broken-down vehicle; and a dead girl.

★★★

Chapter 2

Day 1 (Evening)

Raj shivered in cold sweat as he walked down from the high point of the water tank. A faint glimmer of orange halo varnished the dense foliage across the path, skirting the base of the hillock. On the other side, softly blowing winds created slight ripples over the leafy tea bushes to lull the estate to sleep so that it wouldn't see what was going to unfold. The only witness, an owl, a soft feathery ball with curled-up talons, hooted as it flew past the moonlight-splashed trees of the garden.

Raj hastened his steps and returned to the room, closing the door, heart still pounding. Cold air seeped through the cracks. Minutes later, he felt the ominous turbulence of shouts and the restiveness of the angry shadows—the mob had arrived. This feeling of dread was something he had never experienced before, though he had been working in a place the BBC had dubbed as the park that shoots people to protect rhinos, and he had faced hysteric hordes before. Even during his earlier postings in the lesser-known wildlife sanctuaries, he had warded off armed gangs of land grabbers and poachers. This time, it was different; he didn't have any firearms or the company of his anti-poaching sharpshooters. It was sinister and surreal, the young woman's glistening nose ring and the sudden appearance of a dark mob.

Their screams broke Raj's thoughts as he peered through the gap of the wooden planks of the bitumen-painted front door. The spots of colour on the men's faces grew darker and angrier. Heat rose in his cheeks as someone amongst the crowd screamed, 'Hey ranger, come out!'

The ghostly congregation of animosity gathered at the hillock's base, and the scream hit him in his face. There was no babu, sahib or sir—just an impudent 'hey ranger'. Raj took a few deep breaths in, waited, removed the latch and then pushed the door open.

The frenzied mob's faces emanating menace under the shadow of their flickering torches resembled a cackle of hyenas. Their eyes shone with murder in the darkness; they stood on the road, still giving him some space. They would not push their luck too far too soon, unsure of the manpower and the firearms capability of the camp. They kept looking at him; their excited murmur continuing.

Raj estimated about a hundred people in the charged group as the shadowy mass swayed and emitted venom in their incoherent shouts. Country liquor acted as a huge incitement for the simple village folks. They had waited, delaying their climb up to the cottage; perhaps still mustering the last-minute resolve despite the intoxication and incitement, needed to launch an assault in an anti-poaching camp of the country's most well-protected national park. They carried bows and arrows, spears, sticks and dozens of drawn swords. Some had jerry cans of petrol for the final carnage.

Was it just a cheap, locally brewed spirit that made villains out of unaffected villagers? The same lot with their folded hands and sad faces, their scrawny children clinging to their bodies, had pleaded with him for redressal of their numerous grievances and demands during the day. They listened to him like meek students as he went through the modalities of the relocation process.

Raj scanned the crowd while they mouthed profanities. It was dark, but still, in the light of the torches, the ringleaders stood out as an unfamiliar lot. The five of them had similar features: well-built bodies made by hours of pumping iron in the gym, so unlike the bony build of most of those who accompanied them.

The vocal instigators exhorted the flock to get started. Their impatience—heads shaking, hands moving—bordered edginess. The second and third files consisted of the docile genre that would never cross any words with the department. The grim expressions on their faces said none of them had much clue why they had come marching.

'Hey, what's happening? Why are you all here?' Raj found his voice. Undoubtedly, the pack members were from the settlement he had visited during the day.

'Somebody abducted one of our girls,' one of the goons said.

'Why have you come here? Go to the police,' Raj said without wavering, scanning the faces. 'You didn't tell me of anyone missing when I was with you all.' Beyond the hostile pairs of eyes, beyond the row of the thugs, stood the schoolteacher with a vacant gaze; he was the one who had acted as his aide to make his people realise the benefit of relocation. Many like him, the silent majority with doubts over their bearing like shadows, stood behind.

'Master babu, why didn't you tell me about the missing girl before?' Raj directly addressed the man with his raised voice.

'Hey, talk to us. What does he know?' One of the ruffians shouted. Even if the teacher had replied something, it was lost in the crowd's din as a tall man from the group accosted the leaders. Raj recognised the jeep-safari guide as an argument ensued between the man and the ringleaders.

Raj addressed the villagers, 'If you all are thinking I am linked with the girl's disappearance, why don't some of you come up and check my quarters?' He realised it was time. 'Why don't you send master babu? There is nothing here. And you five, why are you inciting all these people who have always cooperated with us?' Raj pointed to the brawny brutes to set them apart from the crowd.

Master babu, the shaky, shrivelled-up, bespectacled teacher of the local school, came forward, and the guide joined him. After talking to each other, he signalled two others to accompany them. One of the adamant ringmasters said he also wanted to search the camp. So, five men with burning torches and all but two carrying various weapons walked towards Raj. The thug passed him fast, his face red and flustered, followed by the beefy tour operator, a moustached man with a neutral expression, dressed in his army fatigue jacket. The teacher and the other two just scurried past him, avoiding eye contact.

The remaining four troublemakers continued to spew their venom. Raj rushed inside the house to find the men in an animated conversation. The guide admonished the instigator in his booming voice, who stared at Raj wide-eyed, his mouth agape. He was about to say something when a sound startled them. Raj's mobile rang; he stood on that sweet spot where weak signals showed up.

'Are they on their way?' Raj nodded his head.

Pause.

'I want the police battalion also,' Raj said, burying the confused murmur of his sister from the other side. By this time, master babu, the nervous old man, turned into an angry, trembling teacher castigating the ringleader for bringing them on a diabolical mission to attack government property.

The ringleader with beads of uneasy perspiration showed on his bald head, kept looking at the bed, shaking his head. A floral bedsheet, without a crease or any folds, covered it. Master babu and the two villagers had already left Raj to join the rest who were drowned in excited murmurs and protestations. The group, preparing to march back to the village, hurled abuses at the ringleaders.

The remaining instigators urged the crowd not to go. 'She will be in that house. We will find her. We can't leave her here.' They started climbing up one by one, their swords glistening in the lights of the torches, their bulky bodies heaving in excitement, or was it nervousness?

'Listen, tell your men to back off.' Raj cracked his knuckles. 'I have had enough. If you don't want me to press charges against you for trespassing on government property, stop right there.' He paused for a moment and faced the thug. 'I will not do anything if you ask them to go back!' Raj looked down at the man, his pointed finger almost touching the man's sweaty forehead.

Seeing the remaining goons coming towards the camp, the guide rolled up his sleeves as if he would take all the sword-wielding men with his bare hands and bombarded them with the choicest swear words. 'Go back, you idiots. We have checked the place and didn't find the girl. There must be some mistake. Ranger babu is not involved in all these things.'

The eyes of the four shell-shocked goons queried, 'What the hell did you do with her?'

★★★

Chapter 3

Day 1 (Night)

Trip Advisor describes Kolkata as crowded and polluted, but invigorating as a daily festival of human existence. It is simultaneously noble and squalid, cultured and desperate, futuristic, yet splendid despite its decay. Amelia readied herself for a crushing sea of humanity, but she found the swanky airport quite empty. The only passengers were the sleepy arrivals from the Silk Air flight.

A friendly Indian family joined her in the immigration queue. The man, who seemed to be in his thirties, was wearing a cap backwards like a teenager. The woman in trendy jeans and a T-shirt, with her arms covered with bright red bangles, had sharp features and confident poise. She had her silky brown hair tied in a loose bun. The couple's cute twin girls dressed identically in pink were cranky and sleepy. The man courteously asked Amelia to stand ahead of them and enthusiastically conversed with her; the wife busied herself, calling various relatives to announce their arrival from the US.

After a long session with a grumpy officer at the counter, Amelia collected her blue suitcase and then waited. Most of the passengers had retrieved their luggage and left. The number of bags in the intermittently stopping luggage belt had dwindled.

'Madam, are you looking for this?' A tiny man in a starched white uniform asked, pointing to her box on which he had kept his foot. Must be a customs officer, Amelia guessed.

'What is inside this?' The man bent his head, poking his ear with a finger.

'Raincoats.'

The man raised his brows. 'What are you going to do with them?'

'I am giving them away,' Amelia said.

These crazy foreigners with their charity ideas—he shook his head, yawned and took his foot off the box.

Amelia pushed the trolley hard through the passage marked as the green channel to step out of the building. A gust of humid warmth replaced the AC-induced coolness. A few men stood on the sides of the steel railing, their eyes hungry while they shouted, 'Memsahib, taxi! Air-conditioned taxi!'

The extended arrival area with many numbered gates was deserted. No other flights had landed since she arrived. As Amelia reread the message, she scanned the surroundings for anyone holding a placard with her name. She did not have

Dev's phone number, as they were in touch only through Facebook Messenger. There was no point in sending him a note; he appeared offline.

The friendly man of the US-returned family saw her. 'Still here?'

Amelia thought of telling about her dilemma. In the meantime, the beautiful wife nudged the man, beckoning him to pick up one of the sleepy twins. Before she could speak to them, a horde of relatives surrounded them. Moments later, the engines of two cars roared to life, and the vehicles zoomed away with the family.

Amelia summed up her scenario: no one was waiting for her; she did not know her host's contact number; all the decent-looking people had vanished from the terminal building. Despair clutched her stomach in a cold grip; her excitement on reaching her destination had disappeared.

'Absolutely it's really up to you,' Dad said when she had mentioned her India trip for the first time. 'We had a horrible experience. People never arrive on time. Misplaced luggage, cancelled bookings, we faced everything.' As she remembered her father's consternation, a message blinked on her screen. 'Hi Milly, I hope you reached your hotel in Kolkata. Call if you can.' She checked the time; she still had not adjusted it to the local time. It was five in the morning in Sydney. His day was about to begin. She did not want to spoil it. 'Yes, everything is alright, Dad,' she replied, pressed the send button, and instantly regretted it.

Amelia regarded the men leering at her from the other

side of the road. Were they closing in on her? Amused murmurs came from the group. Was there a sly exchange of smiles amongst them? Some kept on shouting if she needed a taxi. A few advanced towards her with the cards of hotels and their rates. Weighing up her options, she tried hard to stop her legs from trembling. Even if she took a cab, where would she go? Kolkata was an unknown territory for her. Dev had promised that his man would pick her up on her arrival and drive her to a guesthouse for an overnight rest. He would bring her back to the domestic airport the next morning and hand over the journey ticket.

Why did I depend on him?

That was when the duo appeared from nowhere. One man carried a placard with her name written as 'Amelia Brown,' and the other ambled behind him. A rush of elation overwhelmed her. The first man—a portly guy in a crumpled red t-shirt with a heavy gold chain around his thick neck, pushed through the crowd of touts and taxi drivers.

'Welcome to Kolkata, madam. My name is Sujol!' He greeted her as his smile revealed a row of stained teeth. 'Take the trolley,' he growled at his companion—a lanky man with a shabby appearance, standing next to him wearing a servile attitude.

Once Amelia scrutinised the two men, her initial euphoria disappeared. She was unsure. 'We are sorry, madam. The traffic here is terrible.' As if to placate her, seeing her beguiled expression at the mention of congestion at that hour, the man added, 'It is deserted here. In the city, there are a lot of cars. All the young people are out, going to nightclubs and discos.' A sly smile appeared on his face. 'You do disco?' He shook his body. The man was not all fat. His tight muscular body had a bulging waistline due to excesses.

Are they Dev's NGO members?

She had only seen her host's photo. 'Who are you both? Who asked you to collect me?' Amelia searched her phone to see if Dev had appeared online.

'Your host asked us to take you to a comfortable place for the night's halt,' Sujol said, glancing all around. Soon after, Amelia found herself inside the rear of a strange, box-like, spacious yellow car with the burly man at the helm and the assistant sitting next to him with a weird grinding sound; the man adjusted the rear-view mirror, from which hung a photo of an Indian goddess with a flickering red tongue. Amelia appeared in the mirror view. She wanted to move to the other side to check whether the man would adjust the position again. The men talked in hushed tones as they traversed to a deserted road from the parking spot. 'How far is the place from here?' Amelia asked. Neither of the men answered.

'Excuse me, can you guys please reply? Where are we going, and how long will it take?' Amelia was surprised to find her voice, her anger more directed towards Dev for sending such uncouth men to receive her. The driver switched on the stereo, and it sprang to life, emitting red and blue lights while a Bollywood song filled the space. Amelia shook her head; she had chatted continuously with Dev till she boarded the flight. It had never occurred to her to get his number.

The taxi gained speed; a strong gust of wind hit her face. She let the cool breeze soothe her frayed nerves, stealing a glance at the mirror; his eyes were on her. The man wiped the sweat from his forehead. He switched off the loud music and turned around. 'We will reach in half an hour.' He tried hard to sound reassuring, but Amelia sensed a sinister undertone.

The car screeched to a halt near two uniformed men waiting on the roadside. One man leaned against a motorcycle, and the other man with a potbelly poked his head through the front window. Amelia could not understand a word they said, but she realised it was a police checkpoint; she heaved a sigh of relief.

The pot-bellied policeman came near the rear door; he had an avuncular face. 'Where are you going, madam?'

Amelia had a strong urge to tell him she had no clue where they were taking her. Instead, she said, 'To Assam House.' The policeman's kind face contorted into an angry one, directed to the front occupants. He shouted something aloud to them, and both the men jumped out of the vehicle in seconds, trembling and bowing with hands folded.

The policeman said to Amelia, 'Madam, do you know these men? They said they are taking you to some lodge, and you say you are going to Assam House.' He turned and spoke to the other officer, a young and handsome man with a lean, taut build and chiselled facial features. His spotless white uniform glistened. His hands were clasped, fingers pressing his lips. From his vantage, the young police officer's steady gaze was on her.

'No, I don't know them. They said my host sent them.'

'What is your host's contact detail?' The policeman's brows creased, but he still leaned on the bike. He glared at the two men, his face reflecting scorn. Amelia regarded the pair. What if they were doing their duty and their only fault was that they appeared unsavoury!

'I don't have his number. I got a message from him saying someone would be waiting for me. These two came for me.'

The young officer relaxed. 'Did they wait with a placard with your name?'

'Yes.'

'You said you are going to Assam House; these people are taking you elsewhere.'

'I don't have any preference. I need to spend the night. My host might have fixed the place.'

Both the policemen conversed, and the men gaped at each other. The pot-bellied officer passed a thick register through the window. 'Madam, please write down your name, email ID and your address during your stay in India.' After Amelia wrote her details and handed over the notebook, the policeman gestured the driver and the assistant to get into the car. The young officer's intense gaze was still on her, but he was lost in some deep thought as he waved his hand, urging them to move on.

The two men murmured as the vehicle gained speed. Amelia felt silly for being suspicious; she relaxed for the first time. Her eyes closed momentarily, only to be woken up by the fluorescent white glare on a blue signboard. It said,

Thank you for visiting the Kolkata Metropolitan region. She realised that they were going away from the city. The lanky assistant turned around towards her, his hand growing in length, saying, 'Welcome to India.' A sweet-smelling cloth was stuffed over her nose, and a shroud of never-experienced-before drowsiness descended upon her.

***

Chapter 4

Day 1 (Night)

The fat, silver moon sank below the leafless trees jutting from the meadow with grass as high as an elephant; grass that sustained the life of those who belonged there and hid the gory deaths of those who intruded into the sanctum sanctorum, the inviolate core zone of Kaziranga. Raj touched his forehead; his hand slipped over the pearls of sweat despite the chill. The life of a ranger was fraught with dangers; he knew it. However, this was not what he had signed for when he joined the eastern range, one of the many ranges of the sprawling park, around four years ago.

He walked out of the room to come under the starlit sky. The shadowy crowd had melted into the darkness. The water body on his left was bereft of any swells; no waves played with the moon. Instead, a thick floating jungle clogged every space of the lake, choking the life out of it. A damp, wintry gust from the wetland made him shiver. The booming sound of watercocks hidden in the tall stalks of water hyacinth added to the eeriness. There was still no sign of the guards; a nightjar flew in an incessant circle. He waited for some time and then retreated inside, closing the door behind him and making sure that it was correctly bolted. One single bar of the mobile network appeared. He tried his deputy Vijay's number, but the call was not received. Next in line was his boss, divisional forest officer Roy and then the park director, Ajay Sir, but the feeble signal had vanished by that time. He slumped back into a chair, his head reeling in confusion as he scanned the messages. There it was, the last one, from the informer.

Dear Ranger Sir,
We will meet at the place you mentioned, at 7.
PS: Please don't call me. I beg of you, as it may endanger my life.

Raj checked the time. It was eight. Another false lead, he sighed, playing the whole sequence of events in his mind again and again, scanning the images on his phone. Somebody was banging on the door, but Raj's eyes and mind were transfixed on photos of the girl lying in a state of divine bliss. He hadn't thought about it; he had simply clicked the pictures.

When he, at last, heard the frantic knocking, it still didn't register that he should let them in. How his hands slid under her well-rounded buttocks and back as he lifted her. Strangely, the icy cold body gave him warmth. As her sweet scent wafted to his nostrils, he didn't think about the marching belligerents. What if she opened her eyes and cried out in horror on being carried by a stranger whose mouth almost touched her forehead. He tried to remember if her neck slanted downwards, sort of hanging freely. She seemed so peaceful, with no tell-tale signs of injury on her body.

Loud shouts interspersed with persistent knocking on the door brought Raj back to the present. 'Sir, Sir, it's us!' The guards shouted from outside. He pushed the door open; the pungent miasma of country liquor coming from the men hit him. Rahman and Ronald saluted, blabbering some apologies. 'I am sorry, sir. I asked them to go,' said Vijay, Raj's mild-mannered deputy, a veteran forest officer in his late fifties with his trademark well-oiled hair parted in the centre, dressed in his starched and khaki uniform, his eyes casting a curious glance. Without his 303 rifle, which he used as a support at the moment, he resembled more a wily clerk in a government office than a forester.

'Where were you?' Raj scanned Ronald, the stocky one with small eyes. His cheeks were swollen and red; either a wasp had bitten him, or he had too much of the hooch. Behind him stood Rahman, ruthlessness personified with his bandit-like moustache and a protruding goitre, his demeanour sterner than usual.

'Sir, we went to the Riverside camp,' Ronald said.

'How come you are here?' Raj checked Vijay, who appeared sober.

'I told them to go there. I totally forgot that you had

the meeting here. Later, when I realised my mistake, I tried to contact them. I could not. I could not get you also. So, I decided to come. I reached there sometime back.' He still leaned on the rifle for support, his breathing laboured, but his usual aura of efficiency restored. 'The tea garden people told us about a mob coming here. Why did those bastards come?' Red-eyed Rahman held an INSAS light machine gun—the authority's latest acquisition after years of petitioning with the government for a weaponry upgrade. Raj regarded the guard; his handlebar moustache on the lean, dark face accentuated what Raj knew about him, that he was one of their most daredevil guards, one who always shot to kill.

'What took you so long to reach here if you heard about the mob?' It would be terrible if a sharpshooter like Rahman was compromised.

'When they saw all those people coming towards our camp,' Rahman pointed to the distant shed-like structure of the garden factory, 'They tried contacting us here; on not getting anyone here, they called the Riverside people. Unfortunately, we didn't take our cycles today. We had to run.' The trio was panting. Vijay ambled to the door from his resting place, the rifle now placed on his shoulder. His eyes were downcast, his breathing heavy, most probably because of the sudden exhaustion of rushing from the other camp, especially at his age.

'They came looking for a missing girl. Some people instigated the villagers to suspect our place,' Raj said, eying the three of them.

'What girl are they talking about? Do they think we are deprived demons who will abduct their girls? This is my fifteenth year in this range; nobody dared to raise a finger on our people. How did they gather the courage to charge us? That, too, when they knew you camped here. Let's get reinforcement and teach them a lesson.' Ronald's round face was about to burst due to excessive redness. With his eyes as large as saucers, Vijay kept a steady stare on Ronald as he was combing his slightly dishevelled hair on both sides of the partition. Raj retreated a few steps as the pungent stench from the guard's mouth hit his senses.

'Sir, we have to go to them tonight! Now! Otherwise, they will get bolder.' Rahman's restlessness soared as he still held on to his INSAS, his eyes burning bright like an angry tiger and breathing slow and laboured, suppressing the rage within him.

'Wait! You guys shut up. Sir will say what to do,' Vijay rebuked his two assistants, his lower lip wobbling.

Raj regarded the guards with their frayed tempers under the influence of alcohol, thankful for their absence when the mob had arrived. Ronald changing into his underwear as if it were a summer day, fiddled with his mobile. No, he would not give away the truth about the girl to the trio.

'The wireless is missing. You people kept the back door open.'

'I am certain we had locked the back door.' Rahman paused, taking a deep breath to press home his point. 'We talked to the Riverside camp people using the set.'

Vijay went to the last room and then headed towards the backyard. Raj heard the hand pump; he hoped his deputy would not remove the sheet over the tank.

Soon, Raj, with his head heavy with sleep, after trying to call various numbers unsuccessfully, was on the bed. He switched off the light, closed his eyes, and let the darkness grow around him as his thoughts wandered to the girl. The dark and not-so-handsome faces of the men conditioned by decades of existence in a hostile swampy savannah region came before his eyes. There was no way that she, with her rosy cheeks and those beautiful upward-slanting eyes, could be someone from that place.

She had to be from the hills. He moved his hand over the sheet; goose bumps rose on his skin. He had not changed it. He could sense the girl's purity, not the coldness of her death. He smelled a slight hint of a fragrance, a remnant from the maiden, wondering how she had come in. Or rather, who had brought her here? Who murdered her? Why kill someone so beautiful? Why in this camp? Why, when he was there?

He took another deep breath, struggling to slow his heart rate as questions swirled in his sleepy head. Turning on his belly, he buried his head into the pillow. It still carried her sweet scent. Her head did not reek of cheap oil; instead, he breathed a whiff of shampoo and conditioner, much better than the stink of the country liquor coming from the fast-asleep guards, their snoring rising to a crescendo.

The forest outside became quiet. The only movement was that of the floral curtain on the door as it rose and fell languidly to the breeze seeping through the crack of the door. The cold gust brought Raj back from his reverie. He pulled the blanket over his head; a shiver ran through his body as the image of the lifeless girl in the cold water tank flashed in his mind. Tears stung his eyes. Has her flawless fair skin started turning wrinkly and dead white? What is happening to her hair? Does the hair float while the body sinks? With a heavy sigh, he got up from his bed. He sat for a moment on the edge of the bed, grasping the bedsheet with both his hands. As the three men slept, he tiptoed through the back door out to the backyard. One single signal bar became fleetingly visible on his mobile.

He climbed the steps to the water tank, stood at the hillock's highest point, and dialled a number. His heart started hammering in his chest—what if he had killed an unconscious girl by throwing her into the basin?

★★★

Chapter 5

Day 2 (Morning)

Raj woke up with a slight throbbing headache. He was surprised as he had never expected to fall asleep. A glimmer of light sneaked through the top ventilator window. The room was silent except for his heartbeats. A sense of restlessness engulfed him wondering when the police would turn up.

Arjun was always prompt in such matters. When needed most, he appeared only at the last moment, far too late for comfort, but he invariably did come. Taking a few deep breaths, he said to himself, Arjun will come. What would be the guards' reaction when they see the body? Why did Arjun forbid him to say anything to anyone? They would find out anyway once he turned up with his force.

Raj removed himself from the bed, tottered towards the back door, and opened it. The crisp morning air bit his face. The stems of tea shrubs in the garden immersed in a mist appeared like hundreds of dark, ungainly serpents rising from the ground. He shifted his gaze to the right, to the concrete water tank. There she lay at its bottom, so close and yet so far. He thought of the guards, their snoring sounding like rapid thunder. It took a while for him to realise that somebody was banging on the front door. How come he did not hear the cars arrive?

Raj rushed to the first room where the men slept as the knocking got louder. He switched on the light. Rahman got up, his eyes still red, the muscles on his face taut. Ronald, still in his underwear, slept like a baby. Raj unlocked the door. The police inspector Arjun's portly frame stood at the doorway, a slight frown on his round face. His short crew-cut hair was ruffled; there was no smile below the thick, full moustache that almost covered his upper lip. He was in his uniform, but it was crumpled as if this was another errand in his long list for the night.

Despite the policeman's unenthusiastic arrival, Raj felt thankful. The man had never let them down—the national park authorities, rangers, foresters, game watchers, when it came to back up even at the most inopportune moment. A sigh of relief escaped him, thinking of what all they had done together. There were numerous ambushes by poachers. They had broken the nexus of wildlife traffickers and smugglers, and thwarted encroachment attempts in the park's various proposed additions. They had also faced the occasional wrath of the higher-ups for their heavy-handedness. However, never ever had a girl, dead or otherwise, been involved.

Arjun, his eyes bloodshot and dark bags showing under them, craned his neck beyond Raj and shouted at the guards. 'You two get into the jeep. A poacher needs to be identified.' He poked his staff at Ronald's rising and falling belly. Rahman fumbled to put his uniform on while Vijay joined them, his hair dishevelled, eyes blinking in confusion, already dressed in departmental khakis, saluting Arjun a few times in a sycophantic frenzy. With another thundering shout from the policeman, Ronald—the puffiness of his face had subsided considerably now, clambered to find some clothes to cover himself. Both the guards, with a reluctant Vijay, were bundled into a waiting vehicle before long. Arjun took a deep breath, his chest swelling, and he stretched his arms. 'Tell me again, from the start. Your voice broke up yesterday.' Raj narrated the whole incident again.

'Have you ever seen the girl earlier?' Arjun's forehead was creased in a frown.

'No, never. Did anyone lodge any missing person complaint?'

Arjun shook his head; the furrow on his brow deepened.

'How will you retrieve the body? You sent your men away.'

'You don't want to be seen with the dead body of a girl. Not even your deputy—that slimy bastard, should know.' Creases of irritation appeared on his puffy cheeks.

They walked the moss-covered, slippery path to the water tank. Raj's feet sank into the moist, soggy soil. The grass was wet even though it didn't rain in the night. He removed the corrugated metal sheet. He leaned over the side to peep inside, a wave of adrenalin rushing through him, but the rectangular basin was empty. A stoic-faced Arjun stared at him.

'Wait a minute.' Raj ran to his room to fetch a torch. He shone the beam into the tank; an involuntary shriek of horror and disbelief escaped his lips. 'This is impossible! How is the bottom dry? There is no water or body!'

'Not there?' Arjun raised his brows.

Was there a tinge of amusement? 'It was here! I dumped it myself.'

Arjun's face shed all its hues. 'I don't see anything. This means you didn't dump anything here. You didn't find anyone dead here. Alright?' His tone was strange and unmoved.

Raj was not sure. He could understand the mystery around the bodies of poachers killed inside the park's core area, away from the glare of the ever-intrusive media. But why hide the killing of a beautiful girl?

'What do we tell the bosses?'

Arjun's small eyes almost disappeared as he contemplated. 'They will anyway come to know about the mob attack, but if you tell anyone about the body, it will spread.' He shook his head, biting his lower lip. 'You are being set up. It is as simple as that.'

'When did you remove it?' Raj asked, accustomed to the antics of the maverick officer.

'After you called. Man, it was a bloody hell of an effort.' Arjun shook his head.

'Any idea who she is?'

'It was dark. Had to act fast. I had some photos taken.

The girl can't be from the village.' Arjun stopped as a man rushed to join them. 'Thapa, let's go!' Arjun said. 'Are you coming?' he asked Raj.

'Yes, drop me at the workshop. I will need a replacement vehicle till my car is repaired.'

The driver brought the engine to life as his senior and Raj walked down the slope. Arjun sat in the front while Raj slumped back in exhaustion in the backseat, mulling over the happenings. Arjun, his eyes straight ahead on the road, was not in the mood to talk in the driver's presence.

Raj leaned back and sighed deeply. Somebody wanted to kill him for sure through those villagers. If it were the wildlife traffickers and extremists nexus, why didn't they ambush him as they had tried so many times in the past? He was alone and unarmed. They took the trouble to murder a girl, plant her body in the camp to implicate him and then take care of him either through mob frenzy or through police custody. Someone wanted him to be gone, and he was not sure if it was the handiwork of the motley unorganised poaching groups.

Safari jeeps appearing through the fog wheezed past them, all in a hurry to get a front position in the queue as dozens of vehicles entered the wilderness with the tourists. In their monkey caps, there were expectant elderlies, ladies with their shawls covering their heads and upper bodies, and the young ones with cameras strung around their necks.

They would not know that some bastard had killed a beautiful girl.

Soon, they entered the municipality area accommodating

the offices of the Director and the Divisional Forest Officer (DFO) of the park to whom all the rangers like Raj reported. Raj peered through the tinted window of the vehicle. The town was shedding its stupor of the wintery morning as the business outlets opened their shutters. Jeeps full of tourists continued to hit the highway. They came from the side alleys, from the various private resorts and homestays that had mushroomed in the region. The forest guards and the tour guides were having tea at the roadside stalls, all gearing up for their morning duties, the patrolling and for escorting the sightseers. Some visitors not joining the morning trips gathered around the shops to buy souvenirs.

'Where do I drop you?' Arjun turned around and spoke after a long time as Thapa stopped the car in front of the emporium shop. A life-sized yellow-varnished rhino stood outside. How unsightly and poorly crafted, Raj wondered.

'Yes, you can stop here. The shop will open at any moment.' He did not want to lengthen his friend's trip seeing the man's sleep-deprived, droopy eyes. It was another twenty kilometres to his range office from the place.

Raj walked to the only workshop in the town. A small boy popped up from a tyre lying on the ground. His face was blackened with grease, and his thin arms showed through his tattered clothing glistening with engine oil. 'Where is your babu?' Raj shouted to him. The teary-eyed boy pointed to a shed covered with advertisements for car service parts, behind a row of cars in various stages of repair. The workshop's owner cum manager greeted him and ordered a worker to get Raj a replacement car. Soon after, he sat in the driver's seat of a brand-new SUV, savouring the warmth of the sunshine. The boy inside the tyre was not to be seen anywhere. Where had he seen the kid before, he wondered? Despite the circumstances, he found himself whistling a cheerful tune as he sped through the tea gardens interspersed with shady trees and green patches of deciduous forest. First, it was going to be a few hours of sleep, followed by a simple lunch prepared by Daju, his trusted Nepali cook who understood sahib's moods and whims too well. Afterwards, he would update the bosses about the mob attack—no, not about the girl.

Cruising on an empty highway stretch, a thought buzzed in his head. He braked and parked the car on the side of the road, almost touching a tea garden's fencing. He took out his mobile and read the message from the informer.

'Please don't call me. I beg of you as it may endanger my life.'

He dialled the number anyway.

***

Chapter 6

Day 2 (Morning)

Raj's hands clenched the steering wheel hard, almost hurting his knuckles so that he did not fall asleep. The crisp morning sun shone from the eastern sky as foggy air drifted to the hills. It carried the whiff of firewood smoke rising from the small bonfires lit by roadside huddle of crouched bodies.

During winter, the highway's stretch did not have a speed limit, no need for the animals to go to the highlands crossing the highway. He pressed hard on the accelerator; oblivious of the animal corridors; the shanty eateries; the upmarket ones with various luxury cars lined up in the front yard, and the old thatched *dhaba*s with goods-laden trucks parked haphazardly in the courtyard; the numerous bylanes leading to a growing number of resorts crawling towards the park boundary, almost gnawing at the wilderness; and tea gardens dotting the sides of the highway now and then. A sigh of relief escaped him when he took the left turn, a small side lane branching off the main road. The vehicle jumped up and down on the unpaved pothole-ridden track to his range headquarters, a sleepy cluster of tin-roofed houses bathed in smoke and remnant morning fog. He stopped in front of the bamboo boom barricade; it was down. Two guards manning the guardhouse came out. They hesitated a bit, seeing an unfamiliar car, until they saw Raj sitting inside. Saluting, they raised the pole and then pushed open the iron gate as the small wheels squealed over the rail. Raj entered the campus and made a circle in the empty patch of land between his official quarter and his office, announcing his arrival, and he parked the SUV at the portico of his modest two-bedroom house. A door flung open in the distant kitchen as a drooping old man rushed towards him. Daju greeted him with his toothless smile.

'First, a cup of hot tea. As for lunch, make it simple.'

With his trademark Nepali cap, the old man nodded, smiling. Raj assured that Daju had understood his need for comfort food, got out of his car and walked towards the quarter's veranda. The phone in his pocket buzzed. He took it out as the cook ran back to the kitchen, throwing instructions to his helping hands.

Raj, go to the police station immediately. Important.

A message from the director—should he call back to check why? It was just four months since the new director joined. Raj had started liking the man with no-nonsense yet polite mannerisms. He had been a breath of fresh air in comparison to the earlier incumbent. The previous boss was not bad, but he was not as dynamic as Raj wanted him to be.

If Ajay Sir had told him to go immediately, why waste time calling anyone? Had Arjun mentioned the dead girl to his senior? A long sigh escaped him as he started the car after sending the director a 'Yes, sir' message to head towards his destination, Daju's warm meal forgotten.

Within an hour, he walked into the tin-roofed, unpretentious police station. Arjun, his mood sombre, face stoic, sat on his chair behind his desk with a mess of untidy paperwork and his gleaming 9 mm service pistol. Dev sat opposite him; something was amiss. The NGO chief's boyish face wore a frown, his characteristic beaming smile was missing.

Arjun held his gaze for some time, silently instructing Raj not to mention a word about the dead girl. He gestured Raj with his eyes to take a seat. Raj settled on a chair next to Dev as he regarded the surroundings.

'We need to go to the airport to receive someone. Your director suggested you should come with me. She is Dev's guest. He is also coming.' Arjun did away with the small talk.

Dev said, '*Dada*, I hope you remember our raincoat distribution ceremony.'

'Yes, it's tomorrow, isn't it?' With every passing minute, Raj's restlessness increased.

'The tourist who was supposed to arrive with the raincoats had an incident.' Arjun's smallish eyes almost closed as if he was in deep thought as he spoke. 'The Kolkata police found her unconscious inside a taxi, a kidnapping attempt.'

'So why am I here?' Raj asked himself. 'Why was she kidnapped?' Raj stretched his arms, suppressing a yawn.

'The police is looking for the kidnappers. The men fled, leaving her in the car when they were stopped the second time. She had given Dev's resort's address when police stopped them the first time. So, they contacted us.'

Soon after, Dev, Raj, and Arjun sat quietly in Arjun's jeep as Thapa belted out the latest Bollywood songs from the crackling sound system. Arjun snored; Dev either worked on his laptop, his fingers typing frantically, all the four digits adorned by rings with various gemstones, or fiddled with his collection of phones—Samsung, iPhone, Vivo; he had them all. While still trying to make sense of the situation, Raj's thoughts drifted to the first meeting with the firebrand activist after getting posted in the park. The young man had already acquired a legendary reputation. He was on the front line of everything: making a huge civic outcry when poachers killed a rhino, stopping trucks of illegal loggers, confiscating dumpers of the stone quarry mafias, exposing corrupt forest officials, filing public interest litigation in the national green tribunals or courts. Raj regarded the man who for a change, looked a bit grumpy, wondering where he got this unbridled energy from.

Did he ever sleep? Not everyone in the department loved him though. He was one who sniffed conspiracies against nature in every step of the authorities. Some of his colleagues warned him not to get too cosy with the wildlife warrior. Was it Roy? They had various names coined for him: rich brat, armchair conservationist, strike master, and management guru. A smile touched his lips as he recalled another name, given by Arjun to the party-loving NGO chief, his favourite, 'wild night warden.'

Here he was, sitting with the 'wild night warden' on the way to the airport to pick up a girl he had never met. Arjun woke up and turned to the back, a long, weary whistle followed by a feigned mischievous smile. 'Why do you create trouble by inviting all these beautiful foreigners?' Dev pretended not to hear.

'She was your guest. Why didn't you go to receive her in Kolkata?' Arjun prodded.

'I can't run to the airport to pick up all the visitors who come to my place.'

'She is a special visitor donating something through your NGO. You should have gone or sent someone responsible,' Arjun persisted.

'It is peak tourist season. Otherwise, I would have gone myself. What do I do if those idiots can't reach there on time?' Dev turned to Raj, looking for some support.

The vehicle screeched to a halt in front of a roadside restaurant for lunch. All three got down from the car. Raj stretched his frame, inhaling the crispness of the outside air. The smell of tandoori delicacies wafted to him from the eatery. Dev gestured for them to carry on as he went away to talk to someone on the phone.

'What did you do with the body?' Raj turned to Arjun.

'I made a report that we found a dead body in the woodland across the bridge. I despatched it for post-mortem to the north bank,' Arjun said, sipping a hot cup of tea.

'Why there?'

'Why create a circus here? The media here is obsessed with Kaziranga; they never get enough of rhino-poaching stories. A dead girl in one of your forest camps would be an eyeball-grabbing news item for the TV channels. Man, who do you think they would proclaim as the perpetrator?' Arjun raised his brows in quick succession. 'Send me the photos you clicked of the girl. Mine didn't come out that well.' Arjun stopped as Dev joined them at the table.

They drove nonstop after lunch and reached the airport when the electronic display blinked, notifying the Kolkata flight's landing. The trio got down from the vehicle and rushed to the arrival lounge. A surge of passengers came down the escalator. Arjun and Raj waited together while Dev wandered around, as usual, talking on the phone. A few local city policemen loitered around. One of them, perhaps an old acquaintance, greeted Arjun warmly. Arjun introduced the man to Raj and then pointed him towards Dev. 'Chief of Rhino Warrior is also with us.' The policeman shook hands with Raj; it was a cursory shake. He beamed, noticing Dev, who was busy on his phone. 'Ah, the famous Dev of Rhino Warriors! Have heard a lot about him.'

A crowd had gathered in the arrival area. Among the passengers collecting bags from the belt, a white girl stood out. Tall as she was, she pulled an oversized box on to her trolley and then waited for her second baggage. She was in jeans and a light green T-shirt, as her golden-brown hair tumbled over her shoulder. She collected her bag and, effortlessly hanging her purse and a leather jacket from her hand, walked towards them, pushing her belongings.

'Is she the one?' Raj wondered, looking at the girl, her sunglasses resting above her forehead. Is she someone from Hollywood? Raj forgot about his surroundings as his eyes remained glued to the girl. She radiated a smile; he had never seen such dreamy blue eyes and a set of dazzling, angel-white teeth as she stopped to say something to someone who accosted her.

★★★

Chapter 7

Day 2 (Afternoon)

How could she miss thanking the man, that tall, lean police officer in shining white? If he had not suspected something was amiss, she would have been dead, dying, or something worse. Amelia shuddered involuntarily at the thought, becoming aware of her co-passenger on the aisle side, who continued staring at her with the intent to start a conversation. Amelia busied herself, looking for something in her purse; as the pilot announced imminent landing, a sigh of relief escaped her. Peering down through the plane's window, she marvelled at the sight of the unknown land she was going to. Velvety white clouds hovered on the hills below; there were some red and brown scars on the green blanket. The small plane finally touched the runway; the airport resembled an airstrip of some tropical remote region in Papua New Guinea. A yellow and black striped wall surrounded its small compound; the windsock hung limp.

A draft of moisture-laden stifling air hit her as she stepped out of the plane. She picked up her luggage and the box of raincoats, and headed in the direction of the arrival lounge, a riot of gaudy advertisement signboards and chaos of numerous people milling around. A life-sized statue of an Indian rhino with wart-like bumps covering its upper legs and shoulders, almost giving it a living appearance, greeted her. The nasal horn, back curved from the colossal head, was not as pointy as she imagined. She turned her head around, scanning the numerous faces, some almost gawking at her. Apart from the passengers, numerous armed security personnel milled around. She pushed the trolley with wonky wheels towards the exit; a well-built, pot-bellied policeman stood with a placard, 'Amelia Brown', near the door.

'Oh no, not again,' she muttered under her breath.

'Welcome, madam! I am from the state police department.' She regarded the officer with a round face and thick chevron moustache. His smile was reassuring, his eyes small and puffy.

Amelia smiled back. 'Thank you very much. Is there anyone from the Rhino Warriors—my host in Kaziranga?'

The man again beamed warmly. 'Yes, he is here.'

Dev is here. She scanned the only two persons not in uniform, standing behind the policeman. 'Hi Amelia, so happy to meet you. Apologies for all the trouble you went through.' The young man exactly matched his Facebook profile picture—bespectacled, youthful, and intelligent-looking with a friendly face and eyes hiding the traces of the activism he nurtured. She wanted to punch his beautiful face for almost making her regret the decision to ignore her parent's advice not to come to India.

'Poachers killed a rhino the day before yesterday. It was the oldest bull in the central range. Now it is the peak tourist season here. I also must manage our resort. Hence, I could not go to Kolkata to receive you.' His voice was deep and rich, so unlike the one you would expect, seeing his boyish face.

The anger gave way to comfort, a warm feeling. The day which had sown the seed for this trip, flashed through Amelia's mind. Dappled sunlight filtered through the window onto her bedroom at her parents' place. She loved being back in her old room after leaving her parents' home on turning twenty-one. It was still bright and sunny outside, although it was six in the evening.

Pulling down the blinds and jumping on to her bed, she flung open her sleek Lenovo laptop. She powered the computer to life and opened her mailbox. Detesting all the junk flooding her inbox, she started deleting them. Many were her own doing or her dad's. For the ones like adopt an orangutan, this Chitwan rhino calf needs your help, that Sumatran baby tiger is for you, she pressed the 'select all and delete' buttons.

Amelia took turns squeezing a small stuffed grey rhino, chatting with friends on the phone, and scanning her emails. She had treasured the soft toy for more than a decade, and her mother, thankfully, had not given it away with the other toys since she moved away. Her mind drifted to the hot and humid day in Singapore Zoo, around fifteen years back, and the tantrum she threw to make her father buy the toy. Amelia was seven or eight years old when she fell in love with rhinos. Her father suggested the name Kifaru, and she readily agreed. Later, she learned that the word meant rhino in Swahili, and that her Kifaru was a one-horned rhino from Asia.

The zoo visits ignited Amelia's interest in wildlife. When she turned twelve and got her email ID, her dad sent her an email asking if she would like to adopt an orphan rhino in Nepal. She agreed excitedly and started getting regular updates on her adopted baby while dad paid the money through his credit card. She received a few photos of 'Mohan' growing up initially. The periodic news on Mohan's whereabouts eventually thinned out and was replaced by occasional letters from WWF asking Amelia to contribute more.

The email updates became less about Mohan and more about adopting a tiger in Russia, or an Oryx in the Arabian Peninsula, or about fostering a nursery of sun bears in Vietnam. Most of them started going to her junk mail. One day, she read news about poachers killing a rhino in Chitwan, taking advantage of a storm and heavy rain.

The criminals fled with the horn and tail and left the animal in a pool of blood. Was it Mohan? She cried that day. But then amid uni, a boyfriend (now ex), and moving away from her parents—Amelia forgot all about her adopted rhino. Nevertheless, the emails continued. Mohan's memory came back to her, on her coming back to her parent's place.

Was dad still paying WWF for Mohan? One subject line caught her attention; it was not from WWF.

'The rhino does not need your support.'

She opened the email. If that's the case, why send junk to clog my inbox? She read it anyway.

Hello,

Greetings from Kaziranga National Park!

Our park harbours the world's largest concentration of one-horned rhino. Our pachyderms are in constant threat from the poachers. Some ignorant people in Southeast Asia believe that the rhino horn has high medicinal value. If only they knew the horn's chemical composition, which they buy for thousands of dollars, is the same as the hair they cut and throw at the barber's shop.

Now, coming back to our rhinos, yes, they don't need your support. The most dedicated team of forest guards in the world protect them. These valiant men patrol the park day and night to ensure our rhinos stay alive. The rhinos still get killed. The poachers are ruthless, and our guards are human. They work with meagre resources to fight the ruthless bandits armed with sophisticated weapons.

Kaziranga, situated in central Assam, endures a long wet season. The conditions in this place become hellish: incessant rains, floods, wild animal depredation, and intrusion of the merchants of death into the park. However, our warriors don't let their guard down.

Why does it not come to the point? Amelia was about to delete the mail and move on when an image blinked saying, *See the conditions under which they work.* On clicking it, an album loaded. She clicked on the first thumbnail. It took a while to shed its graininess. It was a picture of a group of Indian men in uniform carrying guns.

They stood in front of a ramshackle green vehicle. The second photo was of a single guard standing close to a giant one-horned rhino. She scanned the animal's armoured body, its tough and leathery hide and plated pelt with round balls near the rear end, that looked so different from the smooth body of Kifaru. The man was unafraid.

His eyes reflected care and concern for the vulnerable beast he protected from the bad guys. The third photo had a forest guard in a torn uniform, drenched in the rain. He wore a handlebar moustache on his thin, dark face, his gaze undeterred; he clenched one rifle in his hand. The images ended, and Amelia returned to the text.

Yes, our rhinos don't need your money or support. The brave guards, working day and night to keep them safe from the poachers, need your help.

We are a front-line NGO operating in the park's periphery to ensure our animals stay safe. Our focus is on the men who protect the rhinos. The forest department's sanctioned posts for this nine hundred square kilometre area park are one thousand guards. Only six hundred men are patrolling this area. You can imagine the workload on these poor, overworking men spending weeks away from their families in the wilderness.

Our NGO seeks out supporters like you to get raincoats for these brave warriors to equip them better to face the impending rainy season's challenges. If you would like to become a part of our efforts to help, please contact the undersigned.

Warm regards,
Dev from the Rhino Warriors

She cuddled Kifaru; the vision of the moustached guard in a drenched uniform came back to her—how he stood there, resolute!

She typed Dev Rhino Warriors on Google; it didn't take long to reach the Facebook page. The picture was of a young man in a casual outdoor waistcoat and cargo pants with binoculars slung around the neck. The bespectacled face had a charming persona. Amelia checked Dev's profile, after her friend request was promptly accepted, to find that it had an impressive news feed. Protest rally for stone quarrying near some national park, memorandum to the minister asking for modern firearms for the wildlife protection guards, attending biodiversity week programme in a remote village, welcoming the representatives of the IUCN rhino specialist team, and many more. All the posts had one thing in common: Dev. The cute activist was the centre of attraction. After exchanging a few messages, she decided to go to India with a hundred and fifty raincoats.

'I am sorry for all you have gone through,' Dev's voice

brought Amelia to the present.

'Hi Dev, it's a pleasure meeting you. It's all right. Don't worry about the incident. It is not your fault,' Amelia said as she saw the second man standing next to Dev. He was tall, well-built, with a broad forehead and sharp cheekbones, and interestingly long curly hair like a rock star. He looked at her with his warm brown eyes. Or was it an unabashed stare with his mouth somewhat agape?

★★★

Chapter 8

Day 2 (Evening)

Raj tried to quickly glance away, but not before the beautiful foreigner caught him staring at her. His hand unconsciously went to his face, touching the stubble; he realised he hadn't shaved. He extended his trembling hand when the girl said, 'Hi, I am Amelia.' The handshake was shy and awkward; of course, he was still baulking. 'Welcome to, umm, India,' he mumbled; this time, his left hand went over his shoulder, pulling his curls. Before he could blabber in his nervousness, Dev came to his rescue. 'Kaziranga is divided into quite a few ranges. All under daring rangers like him.' Dev smiled; he had found a new spark.

Soon after, Amelia found herself in the rear seat of Arjun's jeep, sandwiched between Raj and an enthusiastic Dev who queried her about Australia, her hobbies, and if she liked Indian food while Raj remained quiet. Arjun sat in the front, half-sleeping, half-awake.

An effusive Dev asked, 'When are you going back?'

'Not sure. I am yet to confirm the return dates,' Amelia replied. She said something about going to some other places.

'Once you visit Kaziranga, there is nothing much to see in the other smaller national parks,' Dev said.

She smiled but did not say anything. The sun went down on the western horizon, vanishing in the heart of the human habitations behind them. Raj did not realise that he might have slept for a considerable amount of time. Dev and the girl were chatting now and then, with Dev repeating 'pardon me' after almost every sentence to understand what she said. She spoke English, but her accent was so different. After some time, the green, fluorescent signboards appeared, declaring they were nearing a UNESCO World Heritage site. She scanned the countryside; the roadside shanty dwellings gave way to the forested highlands on the right and a vast spread of the misty savannah on the left. The last trace of daylight died around them, and soon they tore through a tunnel of darkness with the flickering lights of thousands of fireflies.

Dev's hand touched her, shaking her a little. 'Tired? We are almost there. Are you alright with the distribution ceremony tomorrow? Do you want to postpone it for a day?' Perhaps the girl too had dozed off despite the jolts and the jerks, or was she trying to avoid facing her host's barrage of questions.

'We can do whatever you like. We just have to tell *Dada*,' Dev said, pointing to Raj.

'I am fine! Of course, we'll go ahead! Let's get the raincoats to the guards,' she said, blinking herself out of her stupor. She turned to Raj and tried to gaze into his eyes; it was too dark. 'If it is all right with umm—'. 'I am Raj.' He introduced himself again to his co-passenger as River View Resort's arched gateway emerged in the dimness. After four hours of the journey, which Raj felt passed too quickly, they got down from the car.

Dev led his guest through a winding path, crossing many round cottages standing high on stilts, with Arjun and Raj following. Each of the conical huts had guests. The resort was reaping the benefit of the peak tourist season. The guests sat, sipping drinks and munching snacks in the small balcony where a dim light shone from the natural bamboo-made lamp-shade. The meandering path through various accommodations was bordered with trees and shrubs covered with colourful fairy lights. The bean-shaped pool reflected moonlight, and the patch of lawn around it had groups with glowing faces gathered around a bonfire.

Raj mulled over the two facets of wintry evenings in Kaziranga. On the one hand, you had the bonhomie of the happy tourists around the blazing bonfires. On the other, it was the huddle of the forest guards around the smouldering log fires in their anti-poaching camps to ward off the chill. Drowned in the cacophony of myriad creatures, their ears strained to hear the one dreaded sound that would break the cosy huddle into a frenzied flight towards the source: the boom of gunshots. The tourist season operated during the dry winter months, whereas the macabre industry of shooting rhinos and chopping of the horns, and to top it all, killing bears for their gallbladder, capturing slow lorises for their cuteness, lynching of leopards for their pelts, poisoning tigers for their bones, catching pangolins for their scales—happened all year round. If only the fire's warmth or the dazzling smiles could remove the dread of foresters on a night like that. Nevertheless, Raj was happy, despite the long, tiring day, until Dev caught the girl by the hand and almost dragged her towards the resort's boundary, away from the guest accommodations. The moon shone dimly in the sky, and he could make out a sizeable shadowy structure ahead.

'This is your place.' Dev pointed to a cottage at the far end. Unlike the other round huts they passed, the house was a bigger rectangular one, and seemed to float in the air. Raj recognised Dev's private residence.

'Do you own this place?' Amelia asked, enthralled.

'Our NGO owns it. All our staff is from the surrounding villages. All our food comes from nearby fields. The only things we receive from the outside world are visitors like you,' Dev declared with glee as his guest regarded her surroundings.

'This is my office cum residence. I only give it to exclusive visitors like you,' Dev gushed. The rickety bamboo bridge connecting the cottage to the shore creaked as they walked on it towards the cottage's veranda.

Raj wanted to stay for some more time; the girl's golden-brown hair shone in the place's muted light. However, he felt as if the bones of his legs would melt, and Dev's sightseeing tour did not show any signs of finishing. He ambled towards Arjun, who shook his head with impatience.

'Let's go, man.' Arjun's face reflected disgust and edginess; it seemed the man had many things going on in his head. They left soon after; Dev and the girl were too engrossed in conversation to notice them depart. 'Our warrior is definitely smitten by the girl; what do you think?' Arjun said as they headed into the darkness, leaving the resort bathed in a glow of bonfires and garden lights.

The question pulled Raj out of his reverie, and he let out a long sigh. 'Thinking about her? Isn't she beautiful? How old would she be?' Arjun asked, his generally hidden mischievous self emerged through his tired eyes.

'No, I am not.' Raj gazed into the blackness as the car traversed the bumpy road, wondering why the director insisted that he go to the airport to receive her.

Arjun turned, his small eyes still twinkling. 'It was not a bad trip, was it?' He then lowered his eyelids, indicating to wait for the unsaid. 'Thapa, take us to the police station first. Sahib needs to collect his car,' Arjun said to his driver. Raj got the message; Arjun wanted to speak to him alone. It made sense; the area around the park, with each pachyderm carrying a million rupees worth of horn, was a veritable bed of mistrust. No one knew who colluded with whom, including police personnel and forest department employees. Reaching the police station, they changed the car. Raj sat in the driver seat and Arjun by his side as they cruised towards the eastern ranger headquarter, piercing the tarry blackness.

Thapa trailed them separately.

'The girl in the camp, had you ever seen the girl before yesterday? The darkness hid Arjun's face. Raj's hands clasped the steering wheel hard as his eyes peered ahead; the low-mounted, high-intensity yellow lights were unable to penetrate the fog that blanketed the road.

'No, I have never seen her earlier. I just hope...' Raj stopped. A passing truck in full beam shone on their faces, almost blinding them.

Raj reminisced the moment before the goons arrived. It was a miracle that he had been able to lift her so easily. As if she wanted to make things easy for him. He remembered carrying his father's body on his shoulder as one of the pallbearers. His frail father, who had lost half of his body weight before he died, had been heavy as a rock. That night, the beautiful girl with an hourglass figure and a full face weighed like a feather in his arms. Or was he possessed by a supernatural being enabling him to carry her to the top of the water tank, climbing the slippery, muddy steps? The challenging part, to topple the body over into the tub, required superhuman strength, and he somehow acquired it at that time, as if some shadowy spirit from the silk-cotton tree guided him.

Raj returned to the present when Arjun asked, 'You just... what?'

'I hope she was dead before I plunged her into the tank.' Raj took a long breath.

'They had killed her before you arrived. They would not leave an unconscious girl behind to spill the beans.'

Arjun bit his lower lip.

The car slowed down. They reached the eastern ranger headquarters. It was a sleepy cluster of tin-roofed houses bathed in the flickering yellow light. The arrival of ranger babu, followed by a police vehicle, woke the colony up from its slumber.

'Try to get some rest.' Arjun got down from the car and headed to his jeep. 'Tomorrow, I will get in touch with Kolkata to learn more about this Australian girl's incident.'

Raj nodded and ambled towards his quarters, weighed down by confusion and exhaustion. Half a dozen sleepy figures, heads wrapped in shawls, gathered in his veranda and a flurry of activities started in the distant kitchen, seeing his return. A few insects buzzed around the lone light hanging from the ceiling. Stepping inside his home, he switched on all the lights until he reached his bedroom. A neatly made bed exuding warmth awaited him. The bookcase, with its burgeoning load of new additions he had bought in the successive book fairs, made the place even more comforting. He sat on the bed, leaning against the headrest with a pillow. He pressed the softness of the mattress and thought of the hard bed he had slept on the day before.

An image of the girl lying on that cot flashed in front of his eyes. His hand flinched spontaneously from the soft depression of his bed. There was a light knock on the door. Raj rolled his sleeves, heading towards the door in anticipation of Daju and his attendants with food casseroles. The knock on the door was repeated; it was an urgent one. Raj muttered under his breath as he hurried out of his room and flung open the door.

It was not Daju with his dinner. 'Sir, just now we found a carcass.' It was Vijay waiting in the portico, his face undecipherable under the shadow of his cap.

★★★

Chapter 9

Day 2 (Night)

'What is it?' Raj asked in trepidation, hoping it was not a rhino. The tally in his range was still zero.

'A tiger, sir; claws and teeth removed, totally skinned. They even cut the tail,' Vijay blurted out, his tone bordering edginess.

'When did you find it?' Tiger, was it the new love of the killers? A feeling of dread and frustration flooded him, one that had almost become a regular feature in the last few months.

'Just now, before you arrived. It was killed somewhere; they threw the carcasse near the gate.' Vijay sounded exasperated, and the other men, standing at attention with their grim faces reflecting cluelessness, remained silent.

As Raj walked to the back of the office building, the usual place where the unsavoury official acts took place, all the traces of his sleepiness vanished. Two guards hurried before him and switched on a light hanging from the roof of a temporary shed. The creature's wretched red and pink remains resembled a skinned dog, only slightly bigger. It was a juvenile which had been killed and not one that had died of old age. If it was poached, why did they leave it like that without getting the bones? 'Bastards!' Raj swore under his breath when the raw odour of the rotting carnivore hit his nostril. A crowd had gathered around the carcass. 'Dispose of it right now.' This was a first: a killed tiger, skinned and discarded at the range campus' entrance—a gauntlet thrown at him to curb his enthusiasm. Or was it to remind him of the helplessness of the foresters of the park, who came and went, and things remained unchanged.

Daju led a retinue of servants rushing to his master's quarter with the casseroles of food. Raj found himself sitting on the passenger seat of his official vehicle, which had been retrieved from the wilderness, his edginess manifesting in fingers tapping the door through the half-open window. The engine roared to life, and the surprised and confused faces of his men stared at him as the car passed through the open gate just an hour after he had come in.

'What was the problem with my car?' Raj asked. 'Sir,' the driver hesitated. 'They found water in the fuel tank. They drained it out. Luckily, it didn't damage the pistons as you did not drive long.' Raj didn't say anything; his mind was fogged up. He didn't even remember whether it was he or someone else who had filled the petrol that day. Did the engine rattle when he had started it that afternoon? The driver slammed the brakes in front of a two-storied wooden bungalow, interrupting his thoughts. The director's office area was a hub of activities during the daytime.

The official residence was next to the office, but located far behind a gated complex with tall hedges of hibiscus. He lifted the massive iron triangle that kept both the gates together, made a gap and sneaked through, walking over the cattle grid after closing the gate. The guard's house was empty. It was quite a walk to the sizeable residence of Ajay Mathur, the new director of the UNESCO-inscribed World Heritage Site park. The mansion, which could comfortably house a family of a dozen, was immersed in darkness, caressed by a swirling mist descending from the hills behind the building.

Raj stopped halfway to the bungalow. He grimaced, thinking about the unearthly hour he chose to come. Though Ajay sir was a man of easy charm and relaxed manner, would he welcome Raj at this hour? Should he turn back? A tiger was gruesomely killed and skinned, and somebody impudently threw it in his compound. Some rascals in Kolkata almost abducted a girl coming to the park with raincoats. And the dead body in the camp! He needed to see the director. Raj dialled a number, and the call was received after two rings.

'What is it?' Ajay sir's voice reeked of irritation.

'Sir, I want to meet you now. I need to discuss an important matter.'

'Can't it wait till tomorrow?'

'Poaching case, sir. I am waiting outside your home.' He retreated a few steps backward to give an impression of just crossing the cattle grid if someone saw him from inside.

'Okay, come in then,' the voice softened. The lights were switched on in the building. Raj reached the doorstep and pressed the bell. The veranda was covered with a thick metallic wrought iron grill, so he waited on the steps leading to a wooden door with mesh. It was a long wait. The new director believed in doing most of the household chores himself. The cooks, gardeners, and other helpers worked during the day and left the campus by evening, leaving just the two of them—the man and his wife.

The door swung open, and the aroma of expensive cologne hit Raj's nostrils as the friendly demeanour of Ajay Mathur, the oval face with a toothbrush moustache, greeted him with a broad smile, and then it turned sombre. 'What is it? Where? Come, come inside.' The tall North Indian man with a well-built frame, though shorter than Raj by a couple of inches, dressed immaculately in ironed trousers and a blue t-shirt with a small crocodile logo led him to the lounge room.

Ajay sir sat on the soft single leather sofa, behind which was a painting of the park—a water hole surrounded by savannah grassland with its most famous denizen, the Indian rhinoceros. The brightly lit room with many photographs, souvenirs collected from the places of his earlier postings and a well-stocked bookcase dispelled any doubts that had crept into Raj's mind when he approached the house.

'My wife is not keeping well,' Ajay sir volunteered. 'I was about to give her some medicine when you called. Sorry to keep you waiting.' There was not a hint of irritation. His eyes sparkled with curiosity while his fingers tapped the sofa's handle. 'Tell me.'

'Sir, we found a tiger carcass near my range office.'

Ajay sir's eyes bore into him for a while, and then a frown came. 'Three tigers in six months. Second, since I joined. You didn't find this one. They made sure that you see it.' He sighed. 'What did you do with the carcass? Has the news spread?'

'I asked them to dispose of it in my office campus.' Raj tried to remember the gathering. All were from the department. Or were there a few from the villages who sneaked in under cover of darkness? He had heard Vijay shouting, 'No cameras, no photos, anyone.'

'I think only my people know. I have not yet talked to Roy sir or the police.'

'We need to brief them. This is not normal.' Ajay sir sounded tense. 'Make sure the story does not spread. No point in creating an unnecessary media circus. What is the solution? It can't go on like this.' His eyes probed Raj for some answer. If only he knew. It was indeed a new menace, tiger poaching had never been an issue in the park. Stringent habitat protection for the flagship species, the greater one-horned rhinoceros, the pride of Kaziranga, created a haven for the royal Bengal tigers, whose population multiplied over the years due to the abundance in the prey base. The killing of the rhino attracted a tremendous amount of attention, so the poachers' focus shifted to other fauna. The irony was that

India's national animal had become their new favourite.

'Sir, I am not sure. They must have a local mastermind here, maybe someone from our department. This one is also a poisoning case. With no guns fired, it is becoming difficult to seize them. Somebody must be feeding them with information about the waterholes frequented by the tigers. After taking away what they wanted, they could have just left the carcass in the forest. We may not have found it.'

'But then they decided to throw the remains at your doorstep?' Ajay sir completed what Raj was about to say. 'They didn't even bother to take the bones. I am a bit worried because of this throwing of the body in front of your office.' He sounded ominous, and then he shifted his tone.

'Listen, we have to ensure there is no repeat of the incident. We are a tiger reserve. NTCA will be after us, and so will be our emotional public. Be discreet about today's event and do whatever is needed to stop any such case.' Ajay sir glanced at his watch. 'Otherwise,' he paused for some time and said, 'There will be political pressure to take action. Our people will end up becoming the scapegoat.' His eyes closed in thought. 'These Rhino Warrior people and Dev, they don't know yet?'

A sigh escaped Raj. 'It does not take long for them to find out. Those guys are everywhere.'

Ajay sir clasped his palms, his forehead creased. 'But they don't make any hue and cry when they hear about tiger poaching.' He turned his head towards the dining room.

'They are all about rhinos, aren't they?' Ajay sir smiled, his eyes probing Raj.

Dev and the Rhino Warriors, true to the name, were only concerned with rhino poaching. Raj nodded. 'Yes sir, that's what gives them the most publicity.'

Ajay sir bit his lower lip, checking the time on his mobile as he stood up. Raj realised his senior wanted to end the meeting. It was late and he was yet to broach the issue plaguing him. 'Sir,' Raj hesitated, gathered courage, and then asked. 'Why did you send me to the airport?'

Ajay sir sank back on the sofa, regaining interest in the conversation. 'The girl is our guest. She is bringing all those raincoats from Australia. Somebody from the department should go to receive her. By the way, how is she? There was an incident with her, wasn't there?'

'Sir, there was a kidnapping attempt.'

'Arjun did mention that to me. Kolkata is a notorious place. Single women travellers should always be careful. We don't know what heroics this Australian woman attempted.' He shook his head. 'We have to take care of her. Just imagine what a huge embarrassment it would have been for our country if something untoward had happened to this girl despite all this incredible India shit.'

Ajay sir kept talking, his gaze steady on Raj. 'Do you think her kidnapping has anything to do with her trip to this place?' he asked, his eyes probing in a way Raj had never seen before.

'Not sure, sir,' Raj said, thinking of the tourist girl. He hid his smile; of the four rangers in the park, the director chose him to receive her.

'By the way, why did you go to Vulture Hills? I asked Arjun to arrest the miscreants as soon as possible.' Ajay sir's stare on Raj was unwavering.

'Vijay arranged for me to meet an informer. The place was near Village 8, so it was convenient.'

'What did you learn?' Ajay Sir sounded keen.

'Nothing sir, he didn't turn up. Even if he did come, he may have left seeing the crowd.' Raj paused; and took a deep breath. 'Sir, I will make sure those people relocate. Somebody is instigating them not to accept our package. We need to acquire that place.'

Ajay sir nodded. 'Yes, that's a key habitat. Keep engaging with them,' he said, glancing again at his watch. 'We have got the fund allocated for relocation.'

A pang of guilt hit Raj, that of holding back the kind man, with his doubts and fears while he had to attend to his wife who was not keeping well. Soon after, Raj ambled towards the exit, and the lights in the lounge room, where he sat moments ago, were switched off, engulfing the bungalow in darkness again.

As he neared the gate, a heart-rending shriek emanated from the house—the wail of a distressed woman under the stranglehold of a monster. A scream that quivered through the air long after it had ended. He turned back, and the window of a room on the upper storey lit up.

A frail-looking woman with dishevelled hair pressed against the metal grill, her hands holding and shaking the metallic rods, face jutting out through a square opening.

Within seconds, a strong pair of hands caught hold of the frail body and pulled it away with brute strength.

Raj did not see it, but could almost visualise the hands hurling her inside like a mannequin. The room became dark, and he stood over the cattle trap his feet shaking, beads of sweat on his forehead.

★★★

Chapter 10

Day 3 (Morning)

Raj felt rejuvenated as he pulled the curtain to peer at the outside world, a streak of dawn filtering through. He was surprised that he had slept soundly. His men were out and about; it looked like a typical day. Things could have been worse: losing colleagues to gunfights with AK series armed poachers, character assassination by a merciless media, attacks by ungrateful villagers, and vindictive transfers by spiteful seniors.

The sense of thankfulness was short-lived when he realised that nothing like this act had happened before. It was too blatant an act to throw the body of a tiger at a ranger's doorstep. He opened the window to let the morning breeze in; it still carried that biting chill. He inhaled the dampness wafting in the air, reminiscing about the night before, how sleepy and dead tired he had been as he dragged himself to his bedroom, his body stiff and limbs like jelly.

He stretched his arms in the cushiony comfort of his king-sized bed, remembering the hard mattress in the camp that still had a hint of the girl's scent. It was not the cold smell of death. It had the fragrance of a maiden who played with butterflies and flowers; the aura of a young woman getting used to the city's polishes and perfumes, without overwhelming a hill maiden's raw aroma, which was innate to her. How peaceful she had seemed in death. He drifted to sleep, thinking of Ajay sir's shrieking wife, how she was suffering.

'How is she to look at from close quarters?' Raj wondered. He had seen them together, mostly when they got into the car to go somewhere. The husband's tall frame always hid the dainty lady who would quickly get inside the vehicle with dark tinted windows. Oversized sunglasses would cover half of her face.

Those fleeting glimpses left an impression of exceptional beauty from the tinsel world. It was like one of those images of a movie star from a distance; you think she is beautiful, but you don't know how beautiful she is.

'Now she is a vegetable,' someone said in the office, or was it Roy himself?

'Why do you call her that?' one man asked.

'What should we say? Hot chilli? Ripe tomato?' Roy became irritated. 'After a hard day's work, our boss goes home to his better half, but all he gets is a few blinks from her otherwise lifeless body.'

'But in the daytime, she moves,' the man persisted.

'That's the issue. The wife does not move when the husband wants her to. This has been going on for years. What a frustrated man he would be!' Roy shook his head, his countenance reflecting the pity he felt for the director. Raj remembered that sly smile as his senior turned to him. 'So, the moral of the story is that you shouldn't marry a beautiful woman. They are not worth it. They give you all sorts of trouble. Don't ever go for a beauty queen,' the man concluded, winking at Raj.

Raj shook his sleepy head to bring himself to the present as he picked up the newspaper and started browsing through the headlines to see if any reports had been printed related to the park or the forest department, both recurrent punching bags for the media. There was nothing that day. The four-day-old rhino-poaching incident was already stale news, having adorned their front pages with pictures of clueless guards with the hornless body of a rhino. There was no story on the encounter near the river shore, no speculation regarding the intruders' innocence. There was nothing about any tiger carcass, and there was no mention of a female body discovered near the bridge.

Daju, with sunken eyes, wearing his timeworn cap, came ambling in with a cup of tea. Raj thought of harnessing the gossip from cooks and servant's networks. 'Do you know the cook in director sahib's bungalow?'

'Yes, Sir, he is a distant relative of mine.' There was a sparkle in Daju's dull eyes.

'How does he like it there?' Raj knew very well that the storyteller in Daju just needed a cue like this.

Daju hesitated a bit. His teary eyes, burnt by the smoke of kitchen firewood, pleaded to Raj. 'Sir, he is facing a problem. Before he took up the bungalow job, he worked in a resort. After all the cooking was done, he used to stay in the place. This sahib does not want him to live on the campus. He must finish all his work before dusk and go back to the village. In the morning, he needs to be there at five. You know how it is in the winter.'

'Why does Ajay sir not want anyone with him at night?'

Daju shrugged and shook his head with his characteristic frown, 'Who am I to cast aspersions on the department's babus?'

'What does he say of the madam?' Raj knew he should not be going there.

'He says she is beautiful, like a Bollywood heroine.' Daju's weathered face broke into a giggle, revealing his toothless gums; he was just getting started, 'But she is never happy. She gets angry easily. Sahib takes care of all her needs. One day, he saw...' Daju paused with an unsure look.

'What did he see?' Raj asked casually, pretending to eye the headlines.

'Sahib was bathing her. She was naked.' He burst into laughter, followed by a cough, covering his mouth. 'Do you know...?' Daju started again when he stopped coughing.

'Ok, tell them to get my car ready. I need to go to the police station.' Raj had to stop him. 'Send another cup of tea for me.'

Raj went inside his quarter, and after gorging on his favourite breakfast prepared by Daju, he changed into his department uniform. He stood before the mirror, loving the department's green and red logo with the glistening stars on his shoulders. Touching his rockstar-like curls, he smiled, recollecting how worried he had been during his teen years that his natural curly hair would straighten in adulthood. They did not straighten out. Initially, he did feel odd—most of his batch mates in the rangers' college had crew-cut hair, but then he got used to it. His sister told him that quite a few of her friends pestered her to introduce them to him. He brushed her off pretending total nonchalance, even though he did wonder who the girls were. The smile stayed on him as he put his cap on and donned his Ray-Ban sunglasses. He liked what he saw.

After visiting Arjun, I will go to the resort to check on the Australian girl. As Raj's SUV whizzed past the director's bungalow, he experienced a pang of guilt. What if Ajay sir came to hear about the dead girl somehow? How would he face the man if he learned about the body later? It didn't take much time for him to reach Arjun's station as he drove the car unmindful of the surroundings, lost in thoughts.

A restive crowd, mostly of women and elderlies, gathered outside the dull, yellow-painted tin-roofed house. Raj climbed up the steps and went straight ahead through the corridor full of perplexed villagers sitting on both sides on wooden benches. He stepped through the centre courtyard of the rectangular complex to enter Arjun's office at the rear of the premises.

'Good timing,' Arjun said with a beaming smile. 'They are all locked up. You want to see them?'

Raj nodded. He wanted to see them, all five of them, especially the one who had shouted, 'Hey you ranger, come out.' The ringleader who gave him a death stare in the end, and the other three with their drawn swords. On reaching the lock-up room, he found that the police had collected all five of them. Crammed inside the small cell, their eyes teary, it seemed as if their pumped-up muscular bodies had shrunk. It took him a while to recognise the faces as they stood clasping the iron bars. Yes, they were the same men, but something was different. They resembled overgrown crybabies.

Two constables came out of the cell hyperventilating and swearing, massaging their knuckles. Raj realised what it all meant. All those angry, spiteful men were now wretched and pathetic, crying for mercy; they must have been beaten and butted with the rifle stocks, and the latest police-work was visible on their faces with bloody, flattened noses.

On seeing Raj, the arrested men shouted in unison, 'Ranger babu, please save us. We never had the intention to attack the camp. We were searching for a missing girl. We are not poachers. Inspector sahib has put all those charges against us. You must tell him. We didn't touch a hair on your head.'

Raj eyed the men. *What would you have done if you had found the girl's body?*

'I think I got them all. Let's go to my room.' Arjun pursed his mouth in a self-satisfied smirk.

'So, what did they say?' Raj asked. 'Who sent them there?'

'This is what is bugging me. These bastards are telling the truth. I grilled them individually after a thorough thrashing. They are quite sure that the girl was at your place.' Arjun sounded exasperated.

'She did not seem to be from the village. You saw those people.'

'No, not the girl we found,' Arjun almost whispered. 'Don't even think of her. She is gone, and you had better forget her. There is another girl in their village, she is missing.'

★★★

Chapter 11

Day 3 (Afternoon)

Raj braked in time to avoid running over an agitated crowd: a motley group of people with towels wrapped around their heads, students, mostly boys, some still wearing their school uniform, from the local schools, and generally anybody with some free time on their hands. A few lanky forest guards stood with the burly police battalion personnel as they tried to half-heartedly restrain the restive crowd from spilling over to the centre of the road. It was an all too familiar sight in that part of the country. There were raised hands, banners, and placards.

The year had just started; what was the protest about—job reservation, land rights demand, the vexed foreign national's issue, Raj wondered. A thunderous roar filled the air. 'Hang the poachers. Forest department down down.'

Raj discerned the crowd. Many of them were Rhino

Warriors members and its village recruits, gathering in front of the director's bungalow. It seemed the director was inside, having gone from his office for a lunch break. The bunch was worked up, and they were unrelenting with their sloganeering. 'What's going on?' Raj asked a guard who saw the group from a distance, wearing the same bored expression. They knew that despite the staged aggressiveness, the demonstrations were benign, organised for the media's benefit. All those jostling and shouting against the park authorities was to get the attention of the numerous news portal camera people hungry for breaking news.

'They are protesting about some letter our director sahib wrote to the minister,' the guard said, leaning on his stick.

'Now what?' Raj wondered. 'Is Dev there?'

The man, with a smirk on his face, pointed to the congregation's centre. Dev stood on an elevated platform with a stern face, his fist raised, exhorting the gathering to shout, 'Save our rhinos, save our park.'

And then he saw her, the Australian girl with golden-brown hair burning bright in the wintery sun. With an unwavering gaze directed towards Dev, she was spellbound. Her face reflecting awe at the raw passion oozing out from one of the most firebrand conservationists of India. Dev's baritone voice boomed out from the public address system. 'We will ask the director to take back his suggestion to the government. How can he advise against the addition of the riverside area to our park? Lack of manpower! Is that an excuse?' He waited for a dramatic effect, scanning the gradually thinning congregation. 'Recruit more guards then.'

Raj was not looking at Dev; he eyed the alluring girl in a lemon-yellow dress, her long hair cascading down her narrow back, ending just above the full hips. She continued looking at her host even though perhaps she hardly understood any of what he said. Raj realised that the issue they were protesting was Ajay sir's pragmatic decision to increase the national park area only after recruiting more field personnel. Incorporating a northern range comprising of the river islands without infrastructure would affect the existing ranges as the guards would temporarily be deputed to the new entity to carry out patrolling. With the paucity of funds and lax political will, temporary could mean a few decades.

For a change, the action of his superior made sense to him. Dev's argument alluded that the authority was indifferent to provide more protection to the northern side so that poaching could go on unabated and unnoticed. He exhorted the immediate creation of an extra range. It would mean losing one-third of Raj's men, as they would be sent to patrol the new area.

After some time, the sloganeering stopped, and the crowd trickled out. The people hired for a fixed amount of time left as soon as they reached their promised quota. Dev and half a dozen of his core team members remained; he climbed down from the makeshift podium and waved at Raj. The young wildlife warrior walked towards him with a sense of gratification on his face, a 'mission accomplished' like expression.

'Are we ready for tomorrow's ceremony? Will Ajay sir do the distribution or Roy sir? Or is it you?' Dev asked with a broad grin, his face red with excitement and beads of sweat on his forehead.

Wow, man! One moment you exhort a thousand-strong mob to shout anti-director slogans and the next, you want him to grace your function.

'Hi,' a radiant smile with sparkling teeth brought Raj to the present. The girl, Amelia, stood between him and Dev. 'I wanted to discuss the raincoats,' she bubbled with enthusiasm. He had dealt with many foreign tourists—American, Australian, French, English, German, but he had neither seen anyone from such close quarters, nor anyone so beautiful. 'We'll organise the ceremony tomorrow at ten in the morning,' Raj said, spying the flowing curl caressing the tinge of rose of her ivory skin. He took a long breath, those piercing blue eyes carried so much warmth. He needed a distraction; he tried to discern the Rhino Warriors members milling around them. So many unfamiliar faces gawked at him.

From where had Dev managed to recruit all these new people?

'I need to go,' Dev said in his busy bee tone. 'Are you coming?' He turned to Amelia.

'I will stay back for a while. I will join you later if that's alright,' Amelia said.

Raj could hear his heart beating loudly.

'*Dada*, can you please drop her at the resort?' Dev requested Raj as he proceeded to leave.

'Oh, sure.' Raj took a deep breath to rein in his thoughts. 'Dev, just a sec, you knew about the management's position. I thought you also agreed in principle that there is no point uselessly expanding in size if we don't augment the manpower and infrastructure first.' Raj's eyes asked why then the street circus. 'Sometimes, the official stand can be different from your personal belief.' Dev gave a wink, followed by a broad smile and was about to head towards his car when he changed his mind and came back again to Raj. 'No, seriously, I am aware of the poor state of funding of the park and the constraints under which the department operates. I agree that it does not make sense to add one more range to what we have under the present circumstances.

At the same time, we all know that the habitat must be increased. We reached the carrying capacity of rhinos long back. Lack of funds can't be an excuse for not expanding a world heritage site,' he said aloud in English and gave a disarming smile, his most potent weapon, to Raj and rushed to his SUV with the crest of a rhino head and cross spears painted on the body.

Has he heard about last night's tiger poaching? It was doubtful that he would not know about it with his vast network of informers, Raj wondered. Amelia had confusion writ over her face. Raj realised that she didn't understand most of what was going on. 'Do you want to come to my workplace?'

'Oh, sure!' she smiled, revealing two lovely dimples on both cheeks.

Raj kept a steady gaze on the road. He was unsure whether he would ever get a chance to meet the girl. And here she was sitting next to him as he headed to his home turf. A flurry of movement heralded Raj's SUV's entry into the eastern ranger headquarters complex, the core of his kingdom that spanned more than a hundred sq. km. As Raj got down, followed by his guest, all the personnel froze like statues, their eyes shamelessly glued to the memsahib who accompanied their ranger sir.

'You stay with your family?' Amelia gazed around while seated at the small dining table. Daju had laid a warm lunch before them.

'I live alone.'

'Umm, married?' her eyes moved fleetingly across the room.

'No.' Raj smiled, and before he could ask her anything, his phone rang. He disconnected it and sent a message. 'Your host has already called twice.' Raj hid his irritation.

'Dev? He is so sweet and caring, so full of energy.' The afternoon sun coming through the window moved across her radiant face.

A sheepish nod, that's all that he could manage. 'How long have you been working here?' Raj was snapped back to the present by another question.

'I have been in the park for the last four years. Before that, I was in another sanctuary for three years.' He resisted the urge to ask how old she was—it would be very rude, even though he was sure she wouldn't mind disclosing her age. She must be around twenty-four, Raj guessed, intentionally going for a higher number to reduce the gap between their ages.

Raj's mobile phone rang, and a picture of a girl flashed on the screen till Raj picked it up. His sister grilled him again about about why he didn't visit them during the festive season. He cut short the call and kept the phone in silent mode.

'Sorry, I had to take it. It was my sister.'

'It's alright. Your sister, she is beautiful.'

Raj smiled, running out of conversation topics. 'You want to see my family photos?' He sheepishly said as he fumbled, scrolling the picture gallery of his phone.

'Sure! Why not?' Amelia politely leaned towards him as the most recent photo he had clicked came up on the screen.

'Is she the one? Oh my God, she is so beautiful!' Amelia smiled; her eyes were curious.

Raj flicked his finger to remove the photo from the screen. 'No, she is someone else.'

'Can I see her, please? Girlfriend?' For the first time, Raj had someone smile at him that way. He handed her the phone. 'I think I have seen her before,' Amelia said as she fixed her gaze on the dead girl's picture.

At first, it didn't register; then, a chill ran down Raj's spine.

★★★

Chapter 12

Day 3 (Evening)

Amelia's blue eyes were filled with curiosity, her brows creased. 'I don't know; she looks so familiar. Did you take this photo while she was sleeping?'

Raj's phone buzzed yet again. The call was from Dev. Relieved; he answered the call.

'Let's get going. Dev is quite worried about you. I told him to relax. I said I will take you back to the resort. Hope it is all right with you.'

Amelia nodded; her eyes sparkled with warmth, giving her a girl-next-door kind of beauty. As she settled on the passenger's seat, Raj, overwhelmed with her sweet perfume, shuddered at the thought of what the abductors could have done to her. What if she had been killed like the girl on his phone? Raj took a deep breath. 'When those thugs came to receive you at the airport, you didn't suspect anything?'

'Honestly, I didn't expect to see them. I thought Dev would come to pick me up in Kolkata. I got a late message from him saying that he would send someone else. They didn't appear to be very friendly. However, I'm not judgmental and didn't think anything was wrong. They had my name written on a placard. I was tired and sleepy, so I jumped into their taxi. The next thing, I knew was that I was on a sofa surrounded by many cops in that old police station,' Amelia said, her smile still filling her face.

Raj's cheeks turned hot. Dev should have handled it properly, especially when such a dainty guest came on her own to an unknown place. 'He could have gone himself. Or sent someone reliable from his resort. After all, you had all those raincoats with you. For a single traveller with so many things.' Raj shook his head.

'It's my fault too. I didn't have his phone number with me. Can you believe it?' Amelia shook her head at the incredulity of the situation.

'I do admire your courage, coming all alone to India and then getting yourself freed from those thugs.' Raj shuddered; what sadistic intent the abductors could have had!

'Come on, Raj, it's nothing,' her exuberant protest brought him back to the present. He dabbed the sweat from his forehead.

She called me by my name for the first time.

'A young girl like you decided to come all the way to distribute raincoats to forest guards whom you have never met. You are brave.'

'No,' Amelia protested. 'You guys are amazing, working under such difficult circumstances to save the rhinos.'

'We are still in our native place amongst the people we know. I would not dare to go to an unknown place if I were of your age.'

'I think it was a one-off thing. Those men saw me alone and sprang into action. I guess I am lucky.' Her radiant smile showed her glistening upper teeth while with one hand, she pushed the strands of hair falling on her face.

Does she really believe it to be a one-off thing, or is she trying to play it down?

Raj took his eyes off the road and glanced momentarily at her. 'You said they had a placard with your name on it.' He took a deep breath. 'The abduction was organised by someone who knew you were coming. How did you learn about Dev and his Rhino Warriors?' Raj asked, shadows of doubt clouding his thoughts.

'Internet!' she said in a matter-of-fact way. Raj pressed the accelerator, seeing little traffic on the road. 'Dev, he is all over the net,' Amelia continued. 'I saw an appeal from him. I became Dev's friend on Facebook, and it just took off from there.'

'So, you guys were in touch for some time before coming here?' His curiosity had not yet abated.

'Oh no, maybe just a few days,' she shrugged.

'You met someone over the net and then embarked on a journey like this?' His gaze stayed longer, spying the insanely cute dimples on her cheeks. 'Maybe western girls are like this,' he surmised mentally. Luckily, it was an empty stretch of grey highway.

'That girl's photo. Can I see it again?' Amelia asked.

Raj's heart started pounding again. He slowed down the car and parked it on the side of the road. He handed the phone to Amelia. She scanned the photo, enlarging it and then again shrinking it with her deft fingers.

'Yes, I am fairly sure I have seen her. She is beautiful! Are you sure she is sleeping? She seems to..., Amelia didn't say anything further.

'Where did you see her?' Raj's voice rose above the roaring sound of a truck whizzing past them.

'Are you on Facebook?'

Raj shook his head.

'Just wait,' she fumbled to take out her phone and tapped the blue icon. 'Dorothy, is she the one?' she said, holding a photo for Raj to see.

Yes, she is the girl.

'Are there more photos?' Beads of sweat appeared on Raj's forehead as his heart slammed in his chest.

Dorothy's album had dozens of pictures, all similar, of a beautiful girl with a dazzling smile in a hilly backdrop. The profile read: a free bird who loves life, the sky, and nature.

'How did you become her friend? Surely you didn't know her?'

'Of course not! After I came to know of the Rhino Warriors, I went to their Facebook page and went through the pictures. I liked the page and commented on some photos.

The girl might have seen me there and sent me an invitation.'

'Invitation?' Raj was getting confused.

'Maybe the girl was already Dev's friend, and when I became his friend, she saw my name as a possible new friend suggestion for her. She sent me a request. I saw her profile picture. She had long silky hair, small eyes, and an oval face. She resembled the girls from Bali or Thailand, but her details indicated that she was from Assam, India. I didn't know that an Indian girl could look so different, so Asian. I accepted the friend request.'

Raj's mind fogged up. 'So, the girl is known to Dev?'

'I think when I checked on her before accepting the request, Dev came up as a mutual friend.' Amelia went to Dorothy's profile and clicked on her friend's list. 'Wait, let me check. Hmm, his name is not there now!'

'What do you mean?'

'He is not on Dorothy's friend list.' Amelia's brows creased. 'I am sure he came up as a mutual friend once I became her friend. I think Dev might...' before she could say any more, Raj touched her hand lightly. 'Listen, keep this information to yourself for the time being, about you knowing the girl,' Raj said slowly.

'But why?' her deep blue eyes were as confused as he was.

'She is dead, murdered a day before you arrived. The police is investigating. The photos I showed you were taken after her death. Please don't mention anything to anyone. Not even to Dev.' Amelia did not look sure. Raj continued gazing softly into her eyes. 'Did you talk to her?'

'We chatted a few times. She was quite insistent. She also pestered me to give her my email ID, saying she had something important to write to me. I can take you through our chats if that helps to unveil something. She was an interesting person.'

'What did she say?'

'When I told her that I was planning to come to Assam, she started getting chatty. She said that I should visit the hills as it is quite scenic. When I mentioned my Kaziranga visit and told her that I would be distributing raincoats to the forest guards, she became quite curious. I asked her if she knew anyone here. Her replies were a bit obscure and confusing. She once mentioned she knew some people. Later, she retracted, saying she did not know anybody. She sounded somewhat hesitant.'

'What do you mean?' Goosebumps rose on Raj's skin. The photos flashed in front of his eyes; the same girl, alive and radiant on Amelia's phone, cold and distant on his.

'I really don't know. Dorothy wanted to tell me something, but she was not sure at the same time. She asked me who I would be seeing and where I would be staying. I told her that I would meet the park director and stay at Dev's place. She sounded a bit worried. Or perhaps I misjudged what she was trying to say.'

Raj listened carefully. 'What did she say, exactly?'

Amelia scrolled through the chats; her forehead creased into a frown. 'No, she didn't say anything about Dev or your director.' Her deft fingers kept scrolling the messages.

'She said she had to warn me about someone,' Amelia said, looking lost.

Raj's heart skipped a bit. Amelia knew the girl murdered in the camp, and she was not done yet.

★★★

Chapter 13

Day 3 (Evening)

Amelia remembered that day vividly. How annoyed she had been with her parents' suggestion to cancel the trip! There was an insinuation that the appeals for donations and charities were scams in that part of the world. She was irritated and surprised, finding how quickly her parents got into the mode of controlling her just because she had returned to their place for a few days.

A surge of anger arose within her.

Is it worth trying to make my folks understand? Should I leave right away and extend my trip from one week to one month?

Facebook photos of Dev in army uniform photographing a bird; standing proudly with the apprehended poachers; attending some international conference looking dapper;

and some plain ones with that sweet disarming smile flashed before her. It would not hurt spending time with that guy, she thought while retreating to her bedroom upstairs.

Her last overseas trip, an exorbitantly priced African safari with her fly-in-fly-out ex had been two years ago. The whole experience was too touristy. Wildlife sighting during the safaris was bountiful, but it was along the expected lines, and there were no surprises, everything seemed too well managed. She wanted it to be different this time; she did not want that upmarket intensive wilderness escapade.

It would be all about meeting the park rangers and mingling with the locals. There would not be a fixed itinerary this time as she longed for surprises. She jumped into her bed and opened the laptop. The message icon showed one unread message. It was from this girl, Dorothy, saying, 'I need to warn you about someone. It is important. You will be meeting him when you come here. Can we chat?'

Her status was online.

"Sorry, busy. I will talk once I am there. Bye. Cya, xo," Amelia typed before pressing the send button. She had heard enough warnings that day and was not in a mood to chat.

'What did she say? About whom did she warn you?' Raj's impatient questions brought her back to the present.

'You know, I was upset with my folks that night, and so I didn't talk to her.'

'Did you get a chance later?' Raj's gaze bored into her.

'Actually, that happened just before my departure. I forgot all about the girl since I landed in India.'

'Can you message her? Just in case,' Raj said.

She went to the messenger app on her phone. It showed Dorothy as active four days ago. She typed, 'Hi, I am in Kaziranga,' and sent it. 'If she is alive, she will reply,' she said, sounding not so sure. Raj's eyes were burdened with sorrow. Her look wandered over the chiselled face with a stubble and black wavy hair. Amelia realised how handsome he was; he smelled of a musky cologne that suited him. His eyes were brown and warm. His gaze was soft, but he was perturbed. They did not stay much longer guessing each other's emotions as a violent knocking on the side glass made them disentangle their gazes.

Both turned to see an exasperated Dev wildly gesticulating about what was going on. Raj hurriedly pulled down the windowpane.

'I've been trying to call you so many times!' Dev's tone was accusatory, his head popping inside the car. 'I was anxious about you. The function is tomorrow, and we need to plan many things,' he eyed Amelia.

'I am really sorry.' Raj tapped his mobile. 'It was on silent. I was, in fact, driving her to your resort.'

'Well, why are you guys parked on the side of the road?' The frown made his face so unlike the school-boyish image Amelia was used to. He sounded authoritative. 'I was calling, waving, and then had to bang on the window. You were so engrossed on Facebook, looking at a girl's picture. Who is she?'

Amelia's heart skipped a bit. She hoped Raj would take over.

'Amelia was asking me about a girl she had befriended before coming here. She wants to meet her,' Raj fumbled with his words.

'Why do you want to see any random girl? Come on; this is India. You should not be making friends with people you hardly know. You just had a lucky escape in Kolkata.' Dev's tone was tinged with admonishment. 'Who is she? Can I see the photo?' Dev extended his hand towards Amelia, who had no option but to give him her phone.

He touched the screen to make the picture appear again; his eyes widened, a frown covering his face. 'There are so many girls like her on social media, always messaging and trying to chat.' He handed it back with a shrug.

Soon, Amelia was in Dev's SUV while Raj headed back. Her host's eyes were on the grey stretch of highway, but it seemed his thoughts were somewhere else. Seeing his knuckles, Amelia could guess that he was clenching the steering wheel hard as if suppressing a rage within.

'You look disturbed,' Amelia said. 'I am sorry if it is because of me.'

Dev's face softened. 'I was worried about you. You are my guest. You had a horrific experience after your arrival. I don't want anything to happen to you.'

'I was with Raj all the time. I suppose you know him well. He must be a good friend.' Dev's face had that sheen of a recent shave. Unlike Raj's with stubble, his cheek had a pinkish glow. A surge of relief and happiness arose within her mind. She hid her smile; she had two nice men worrying about her.

'I know Raj very well.' Dev's words jolted her to the present. 'Do you know how I'd put it?' Dev paused, his eyes looking straight. 'Most of the forest department staff is different or could have a different side.'

'What do you mean?'

'All these people stay away from their families. Many of them are married but have not seen their wives for ages. Many, like Raj, are unmarried,' Dev said without looking at her. Amelia got a faint hint of where this was leading. Yes, it had indeed been a group of curious and ogling men. All the eyes had stared at her all the time that she was in Raj's ranger office campus. 'Well, I have nothing against Raj or his men,' Dev continued, his eyes straight on the road. 'But my guest's welfare is my priority. You are my resort's client. I want to see you go safely back to Australia after giving away the raincoats.'

'When do I go for a safari? Jeep or elephant, what do you suggest?' Amelia asked; she wanted to do both.

'Don't worry. I will tell our resort manager to arrange those,' Dev said, continuing to look ahead. Amelia could see a sternness she had not associated with the man.

'I also want to visit some interior patrolling camps where we could give the raincoats,' Amelia said, but Dev pretended he had not heard anything.

By the time Amelia retreated to her room after dinner, it was late. Her head spun. She had drunk too much. Dev had forced her to drink some Indian spirit produced in a place called Nasik, some Sula red wine. They discussed the next day's distribution ceremony. 'We will display a banner with your name,' Dev declared.

'Hey, don't do all those things please,' Amelia said. 'Don't put my name on anything. I just brought the stuff. You guys are doing the actual work.'

Dev gulped down his drink and poured himself another, his face wet and shiny. Keeping the glass on the table with a thud, spilling some spirit, he said, 'Listen, we are just the conduit. It is donors like you who keep the park employees' morale high. They should know who is behind this. Our media should know. Our people should know.' Amelia's head started pounding; she knew the alcohol was to blame, and Dev's theatrics added to that.

'Tomorrow will be a whole day of celebration. A buffet lunch will follow the distribution ceremony. All the guests, including the forest guards, will be fed.' Dev paused; a smile came to his face, his eyes almost closed. 'In the evening, there will be a party here in the resort. We will celebrate your donation the whole night. This charity act of yours means a lot to us. Some of our sponsors are coming in tomorrow.' Dev's droopy eyes twinkled.

It was cold and dark outside. Amelia lay down on the bed after a quick hot shower—it was quite an effort for her to come from the bathroom to the bed. Her groggy head tried to think about her parents as deep and strange fatigue began to set in. She would send them a few photos of the raincoat function. Hopefully, that should soothe their nerves.

It had been a long day, made unnecessarily more

protracted, but then she felt obliged to do it for her host, who had been so helpful so far. She fulfilled it by having dinner with Dev and a few of his business partners. Did the evening seem long because that ranger with curly hair was not there? Amelia reminisced over her lunch more than the dinner as she drifted off to sleep.

Did she hear a slight creaking sound of a door being opened? Was there a shadow against the wall inside her room? She tried to shake off her sleepiness but could not make herself wake up as the shadowy figure crept towards her.

★★★

Chapter 14

Day 3 (Night)

As Raj walked to his SUV, his heart ached. Why did it feel like a separation? He regretted the proximity with the foreign tourist who would be gone in a day or two. He had no business to get involved with her. She was, after all, Dev's guest. He was surprised about the rage building within him, seeing the way Dev had almost dragged her to his car.

Amelia settled down in the passenger seat as Dev brought the car to life. He looked straight at the road as if Raj didn't exist, his jaws clenched. Amelia lowered the side window to wave goodbye as the vehicle swerved from the grassy sideways to the highway's centre and sped away with an acceleration seen in race cars.

The moment the roaring of the exhaust from the angry speeding up car died, a shiver ran down Raj's spine. Why, he didn't know, but he felt he should not have left Amelia with

Dev. He thought of following her to the resort. But then Dev was her host. Raj's breathing quickened.

Raj dialled Arjun's number. 'Can we provide police security to the Australian girl as long as she is here?'

'I already have one of my men as a waiter in that place. I had discussed this with the director,' Arjun said. There was a pause. 'What is in your mind? Did you find anything?'

Dev's taut face, the way he took Amelia away as if he were her guardian in the park, flashed in front of his eyes again.

'Dev knew the murdered girl,' Raj said, exasperated.

'Who told you?'

'The Australian girl, Amelia, told me.'

'How did she know the dead girl?' Arjun almost shouted on the line; the rant hit Raj's ear.

Raj distanced the phone from his head. Once Arjun calmed down, he narrated Amelia's Facebook incident.

'The man I have sent is a young ASI, my best man. I will send one more man as backup.' Raj felt relieved; even Arjun was entirely on board with him.

'Did you talk to the Kolkata police? Any more leads?'

'Yes, as you said, those two men got instructions from the park. Can't link to anyone as they used pre-paid Sims, but the pinging towers are from this area.'

'And that's why they waited with Amelia's name.' A shiver ran down Raj's spine as he hung up.

If only I could get her out of that damn place. Raj vaguely remembered the disappearance of media personnel from Dev's resort around three years ago. He was supposedly kidnapped by wildlife traffickers as he was in hot pursuit of those unscrupulous elements, publishing story after story about them.

Raj knew it would be such an outrageous act to crash into the resort at that time. What would he tell Dev?

I fear for her life, and I want to take her away? And from whom?

'Amelia, it was not a random one-off act. You said they had a placard with your name on it. This means someone who knew you were coming organised the abduction.' Amelia recollected what Raj said. Indescribable fatigue set in as Raj's face faded from her head. She slowly drifted to sleep as the days leading to her departure to India flashed through her mind. The shadowy figure stood a few feet away from her.

'Do you really want to go there?' Dad asked. Mum told her the story about Gavin and Sandra in Delhi: the heat, population, dust and how they fell sick.

'Listen, guys, I am not going there,' Amelia snapped. 'I am going to Assam. It is in the far east, and it is beautiful and clean.'

'It is so on the websites. I have only heard horror stories about India.'

'Believe me! I made some contacts in the place. That whole region is pretty safe now.'

'Now?' There was a frown on dad's face.

'There had been terrorism and stuff like that in that state for decades. But now, it seems normalcy has returned to the state. Well, at least that's what the net says. Come on, guys, it's just for a week. I fly to Singapore, then to Kolkata, and then fly to the capital city of Assam.'

'What's the name of the place you are going to?' Dad asked.

'Dad,' Amelia knew she had to do it. 'It's the place where Kifaru comes from.'

Dad contemplated, worry still writ on his face. Amelia continued, 'I think it's all good.'

'What are you going to do for the rhinos in that remote part of India?' The look on her mum's face was a mix of horror and absolute bewilderment. Thankfully, her geography was good; she knew where the park was.

'Mum, it's all planned, and it is straightforward. All I am doing is taking a flight to India. I will go to the national park. My local contacts are arranging a meeting for me with the director. I will hand over a hundred and fifty raincoats to the forest department and then maybe visit the park and come back. Believe me, that's it.'

'Where are you going to stay?' Mum blurted out. 'Surely you are not staying in Kolkata.'

Mum had a great memory. She remembered the trip eight girls in her school made to Kolkata for voluntary work in a charity organisation. They fell sick due to food poisoning, and one of them had to abort her trip.

'I am not stopping in Kolkata. I'll be there in transit for a few hours and take a flight the next day to Guwahati, the capital city of Assam. From there, I will travel by road to my final destination. I am booked in a resort run by the guys I am talking to. In fact, most of their tourists are westerners. Many Australians stayed there. They wrote excellent reviews on TripAdvisor. Let me show you some pictures.'

As both her parents glanced at the resort photos on her iPad, they looked a bit more convinced. The place was like one of the Balinese spa resorts. Amelia lingered a bit longer on a photo of all foreign tourists having drinks around a bean-shaped pool with sparkling blue water. The cottages shone in the soft glow of moonlight with a tree cradling a hammock. One photo was a close-up of the culinary spread in the open-air dining hall. Another was of a group of tourists—their faces dark under the moonlit sky. They stood watching a local dance performance. One among the group with a boyish face advanced slowly towards Amelia, his hands outstretched and fingers curled.

The shadow halted, its hands drawn towards the chest, palms closed in a fist. The figure's head then turned to look outside, and then it crouched and disappeared into the wall.

Amelia's eyes were wide open. She looked around her room, eyes adjusting to the darkness. Everything was still. She had no strength to shout or even register what was happening. She lay there lifeless; there was a sudden stillness all around her except her head throbbing with a pulsating pain. That red wine was the cause, now worsened by the blinding flash coming from outside. The beam bobbed up and down over her head, passing through the windowpanes. The bamboo bridge creaked under someone's hurried footsteps; a frantic knocking on her front door followed. Amelia used all her strength to sit up. Confusion and irritation soared in her mind, seeing a mosaic of light and shadow on the wall. She was blinded by the glare. The crouching shadow of someone who had undoubtedly entered her room a few moments ago, had vanished. It merged with the partition as silently as it had appeared.

The knocking on the door became more desperate. 'Madam, are you alright?'

Amelia pulled her exhausted body to the door and opened it to see one of the hotel staff waiting outside. He switched off his high-power torchlight. Groggy though she was, she remembered him as one of the young waiters, a taut looking young man with a crew cut who had kept a steady stare on her while Dev was filling her glass, one after another.

'Madam, sorry to disturb you at this hour. Your phone was lying in the bar area. Messages were coming, so I thought...' The man, short but well-built, stood at the door, his eyes scanning her room. Amelia regarded the shadowy features of the man. She was still tipsy, and her head throbbed with pain. In the moonlight, the man's face shone like an angel.

'Madam, I will stay here on the veranda. You may sleep without worrying.'

Amelia thanked him; her sleepy eyes regarded the man standing in front of her. He held a gun at his waist level. A distant roaring of an engine drifted to her. A few shadowy figures ran towards the entrance, and she heard the vehicle zoom away soon after.

★★★

Chapter 15

Day 4

The image of the rain-drenched guard, one that had prompted her to decide in a flash that she would donate raincoats to the park, flashed in front of Amelia's eyes. A smile came to her as she saw a man haul the box to the back of Dev's car. Dev was his effusive best, talking to the organisers on the phone, ordering his men, instructing his resort staff, indulging in small talks with the tourists, all the while looking cool in a pair of brown cargos and a half-moon fishing vest. He appeared exactly as what Amelia saw on Facebook. However, except for a cursory hello and informing her about their departure time, he had been reticent with her. As they drove to the director's office, he was always on the phone on speaker mode while Amelia gazed at the park's roadside fringe area waking out of its slumber.

Amelia sat on the first row, facing a makeshift stage decorated with green and red festoon, the forest department's colours. At the back, the banner said, 'Raincoat Distribution Ceremony by Rhino Warriors—Donor Amelia Brown.' The programme started with a homage to the the forest martyrs, that is what the personnel who laid their lives fighting poachers, or were killed by the wild animals they protected, were called. The figure astounded Amelia. For Kaziranga, the toll was eighty-two in its forty years of existence as a national park. Eighty-two young and brave souls like Raj, she visualised.

As she looked around, she saw among the gathering the director Ajay Mathur for the first time. A man of medium height, in his late thirties or early forties, he oozed dynamism and a positive aura. With short-cropped hair and a well-trimmed moustache, the man was quite different from the other people Amelia had met so far, Dev, Raj, and Arjun, the police inspector. Raj and a few other officers sat in the same row as her. Dev was seated on the stage with the director.

Around this time she noticed a rotund man in his fifties, with bulbous eyes, oiled and combed hair, gesticulating to Raj, who kept on nodding. He wore an ill-fitting, somewhat oversized suit. His face had a disparaging look as he continued blabbering, unmindful of the proceedings happening before him. On the other hand, the director's eyes were glued to the show being presented by the children. After the cultural program, he gave a little speech, thanking Amelia for her generous effort and called her on to the stage to hand out the first few raincoats to the guards. Dev announced that the remaining coats would be distributed by organising similar ceremonies in the other park ranges.

The director walked up to Amelia. 'We are grateful to you.' The aroma of his cologne wafted to her nose. 'If you wish, you may visit one of our interior camps. We don't allow tourists to go to those places, but you are special.' When he smiled, was there a trace of flirtatiousness, or was she overreacting? 'You will be able to see first-hand the conditions our men work in to protect the rhinos; how these men will value the gift you gave them,' he continued. 'Really, it is much appreciated.' There was genuine gratitude in his voice. 'Thank you very much.'

'How long do you intend to stay here?' Dev asked after the director went away. Amelia realised she was at a loss for a proper answer. She was not sure. Dev's eyes probed to understand what her plan was. Now that he had the raincoats, he would be happy to see her go. 'I am not really sure. Maybe in a couple of days,' she ended up saying as she saw a smiling Raj surrounded by the forest guards who seemed as if they had been gifted the most precious thing on the earth.

She thought of the remaining raincoats. Her dad had mentioned charity items being sold off after a token distribution. Dev had only distributed thirty; a hundred and twenty remained to be given.

'I need to talk to Raj about the raincoats,' Amelia said.

'The director wants them to be distributed in the other ranges. That means we are through with Raj. We gave thirty to eastern. There are four other ranges, so they get another one hundred and twenty, and that finishes your one-fifty raincoats,' Dev said, a tinge of annoyance evident in his tone.

'I thought we had earlier discussed giving everything to Raj's range. Thirty were to be given out during the ceremony and the rest by visiting the guards at their interior camps.' Amelia knew it was up to the authorities; she was surprised that she was being so insistent.

'Amelia, you are an inspiration.' Dev forced a smile. 'Raj is just one of the rangers of the park. You should meet the others too. They are daredevil people. Some of them are much more experienced than Raj. They will be moved when they realise that you came all the way from Australia to distribute raincoats in their range.' His chirpiness seemed forced.

'All right, as you wish. I will see you later. I will go and say hello to Raj now,' Amelia said, pointing to Raj. Dev was about to say something, but stopped as the rotund man she saw talking to Raj during the function strode across and held out his hand.

'Hello, madam. I am Roy, the divisional forest officer of the park.'

Amelia reciprocated the greetings; the man with a round face, a broad forehead that displayed a permanent frown, and bulbous eyes, indeed seemed funny.

'All the rangers report to Roy sir. He is the main man

here,' Dev said.

Roy waved his hand dismissively at Dev, and looking at Raj, gestured him to join them. 'I thought you were going to give a speech,' he said to Raj with a chuckle. 'Your friend from Australia has donated so many raincoats.' Roy bared his stained rows of teeth. Raj blushed. The men got embroiled in discussion in the local language as Amelia made a mental note of the park's hierarchy: the director Ajay, his deputy Roy, and then rangers like Raj.

Dev ushered all the guests to a dining area where a sumptuous buffet lunch was laid. 'Want to go for a walk? I will drop you at your resort later.' After they finished eating, Raj's sudden proposal surprised Amelia as she thought he was happy to stay in the role of a gentle giant among his men who were elated with their brand-new raincoats.

As most of the visitors and officers dispersed after the lunch, Raj and Amelia sneaked out to a side track, walking along the tea garden edge. Mile-long cultivated greenery of the shrubs shaded by cassia trees merged with the thick forest of the hills.

'Where does this road lead to?' Amelia asked as they walked away from the highway.

'You know, this path ends at the base of the hill which forms the district's boundary from where Dorothy came.'

Both sat on a stone, their bodies touching. Wind from the river sweeping across the park blew Amelia's hair over Raj's face.

'Did you get any reply from the message you sent to the girl?'

'No, it is not active.' Amelia noticed an immediate shadow of gloom on his face. She went through her old chats with Dorothy, predominantly random sketchy conversations.

The afternoon sun descended upon them. A tea bush hid them from the road, from the curious eyes of the tourists returning from their evening jeep safari back to the lodges. No one noticed them. Her gaze stayed on Raj's face; he reflected some uneasiness, perhaps thinking about the situation's appropriateness, a bachelor forest officer with a young Australian tourist amid the tea bush. A jeep load of loud tourists went past them, leaving a trail of dust and smoke.

'What else had she said in her messages?' Raj's question brought her back to the present. His tender eyes sought some answer.

'She said she worked in the forest department.'

'Are you sure? Did she say which office?'

'Some hill division office. Do you know where it is?'

Raj nodded his head. 'I think so.' Over the tea garden's manicured greenery, the dark blue hills arose. 'Those hills fall under that division.'

'Can we go there?' Amelia wanted a change, and she did not want to go to her next destination; not yet at the least.

Raj gazed at her, wonderstruck. 'When are you going back?'

'I am not sure when I am going,' Amelia said what she

felt. 'Hey, we need to get back to the resort. I want to check something in my room.'

When they reached River View, it was a carnival-like atmosphere in the middle of darkness. Amelia realised how short the days were in that part of India. Many swanky cars were parked outside. Laughter from the groups huddled around the bonfires resonated through the foggy air. Waiters moved around with plates full of sizzling tandoori delicacies.

The exquisitely crafted wooden bar counter was the busiest spot. The bartenders continuously churned out cocktails and drinks of various kinds. All the guests seemed to be affluent people with glasses in their hands, with their curvy wives in beautiful saris by their sides. Many of the men had attended the donation ceremony lunch just a few hours ago.

'Come to my room,' Amelia said to Raj, holding his hand for the first time. Both proceeded to the room through the path lined with hedges and shrubs lit by twinkling fairy lights.

'Your room?' Amelia could sense a tremor in Raj's voice. A white girl almost pulling an Indian man through the crowd raised quite a few eyebrows.

'Something strange happened last night while I was asleep. Someone entered and left my room through the wall.'

'Through the wall?'

Amelia nodded as she unlocked her room and switched on the light. Room service had made her bed and decorated the room with flowers. All her scattered belongings had been tidied.

'Look at this.' She pointed to a door, which was part of the partition; the door didn't have any locks or handles. The white wooden frame almost blended with the light-coloured room divider.

'Someone came through that door to your room?' Raj's voice was hardly audible, his lips trembling.

'Yes, he came and then slipped away quietly. I don't know why he came and then vanished. And then there was another guy; I think he was one of the waiters who watched me through the evening. He appeared strangely at the time I saw the shadow, and knocked at my door.'

'When this waiter came to your room, that shadow disappeared?' Raj's forehead glistened with pearls of sweat. 'You didn't do anything?'

'I was quite groggy. The shadowy figure faded away into the wall, and the door closed.'

'Any idea who stays in the other room?'

'Dev.'

Amelia could sense a slight grimace on Raj's face.

'It's a bit weird if Dev came through that door to my room.' Amelia inched towards Raj. She buried her head into his broad chest.

'Did you ask him if he came into your room?' Raj asked tenderly; she could feel her strands of hair playing with his nostrils.

'No, I didn't get a chance. Now I am telling you, I am coming with you to that hill forest office.'

She pushed her head, digging deep into him. Her hand touched his face; it was hot. His firm hands held her back, a tender, unsure touch. Something that she had never imagined would happen in that trip, acually happened. It possessed her as she drew him even closer. Lost in a tight embrace, they drifted towards the bed, their lips almost touching.

They stopped, and Amelia disengaged herself quickly as the bamboo bridge creaked under the rapid stride of someone heading to the cottage.

★★★

Chapter 16

Day 5 (Morning)

Sunshine streamed through the leaves of the tall trees falling on Raj's tanned face as the SUV's engine laboured its way up the steady slope of the hill. The landscape changed from dusty plains to blue hills. In the distance, a misty waterfall splashed from the sky to a rocky riverbed in the lush green valley below. She did not fail to notice Raj's occasional side glances. The SUV took a turn around a shady corner with a muddy pool near a tall tree hollow. Amelia's head moved out of the car window. 'Look at that spot. Rhinos would love to wallow in that mud puddle.'

'Our animals do come to the hills, but they don't climb up this high. They just take refuge in the northern hill forest during the floods and then go back to the park,' Raj said, concentrating on the sharp turn.

'No, these hills had Javan and Sumatran species also.

Just imagine a two-horned Sumatran rhino wallowing in that mud pit.'

Raj raised his brows. 'I didn't know about other species of rhinos in the hills.' He turned his gaze to the shady spot, which was now below them. 'By the way, two-horned rhinos are not found in this part of the world. You find them in Africa.'

'Yes, I know they are found in Africa.' Amelia suppressed her smile. 'I did the Masai Mara-Amboseli-Serengeti circuit.' She guessed Raj might not have travelled to those places. 'I was talking about the Asiatic two-horned rhinos. They were found in this part of the world. Your region had it all: Indian rhino, Sumatran rhino, Javan rhino. You didn't know about it?' Her brows creased, but she meant it in the right way without being amused or surprised at a wildlife ranger's lack of knowledge.

'Well, I am not much into zoology and wildlife science. I just do my job,' Raj said with a grin.

'And your job is...?' Amelia asked good-humouredly.

'To shoot people who come to harm our rhinos.' There was no smile. His jaws clenched slightly while the SUV grumbled as he changed to a lower gear, pressing the accelerator hard as the slope steepened and the road became more torturous. His eyes concentrated on the tricky turns ahead, his hands firm on the steering wheel.

Amelia hid her smile, her mind reminiscing Dev's arrival at a most inopportune time, the night before. Lost in the embrace, her heart fluttering like a trapped bird, she first thought it was an earthquake. How frantically Dev knocked on the door.

'Amelia, it's me, Dev.'

Disentangling from Raj, Amelia rushed to open the door, and Dev almost fell on them, tottering with a glass in his hand. He had taken a fair share of drinks by that time. His wild eyes took them in, his gaze sweeping rapidly over Raj to Amelia. 'I told you we had the partners visiting us. This party is for celebrating supporters like you. But you are nowhere to be seen.' Wow! How he spoke and how he turned to cast an accusatory look at Raj!

Amelia found her voice. 'Sorry, Dev, I am not at all interested in meeting anyone. I came here to give the raincoats to the forest guards. I have done my job. I think it is...' Amelia stopped short of finishing the sentence.

'Okay, I understand; you may be longing to go back.' Dev came to his senses, and his slurring reduced. 'One of our partners is returning tomorrow morning. He owns a travel agency. If you go with him, he can sort out your tickets, and other things.'

Amelia was not listening. 'Did you come to my room last night through that door?' Amelia pointed to the door. She gave Raj a sideward glance, who eyed Dev to see his reaction.

Dev gulped down the drink. He held up the crystal glass, revealing his fingers, each glistening with different gemstones in gold rings. The look on his face changed from a smirk to amusement. 'You mean did I come to my room last night,' he emphasised the word 'my' quite loudly. 'I couldn't find my phone charger and realised there was a spare connected to that power socket. I sneaked in to collect it. That door, I told you, can be opened from my side. I didn't come by the front door as I didn't want to wake you up. I think it was around twelve-thirty, and my mobile had run out of charge.'

Amelia remembered the waiter with the pistol. Why did he look so perturbed?

'As you see, our resort is fully booked,' Dev continued. 'People book this place months in advance. I think we started talking just a few weeks ago. I had no room left for you to stay. Therefore, I gave you my personal cabin and shifted to my office. I couldn't ask you not to come because we didn't have enough rooms. These raincoats mean a lot to the guards.' His gaze moved from Raj to Amelia. 'Shall I tell the gentleman that you will go with him?'

'Dev, I know it is peak tourist season. I don't want to occupy your resort's room, or for that matter, your private room.' She turned to Raj, 'Can you help me book a room at another place tonight?' Amelia took a quick deep breath and faced Dev again. 'I don't think I am going back tomorrow. I need to meet a Facebook friend. I will go to her place to see if I can trace her.'

'Looking for a Facebook friend? Do you even know her? Where will you go? Who will go with you?' A rage burned in Dev's eyes, his breathing heavy.

'She was quite friendly and lived nearby. Now that I am here, I might as well meet her. She, and you are my only Facebook friends in India.'

'Who is she? Can I see her?' Dev grimaced.

Amelia took out her phone, touched the blue icon and

went to Dorothy's page. She handed it over to Dev, who viewed the photo intently, removing his glasses. He almost spat, disgust scrawled on his face. 'I know her, Dorothy, a crazy girl. Always messaging and trying to chat. I had enough of her and unfriended her. She is no longer on my friend list.'

'You knew Dorothy personally?' Amelia remembered that the other day, when he saw Dorothy's picture, he did not say that he knew her.

'Oh, not really,' Dev said with a shrug. 'I get friend requests from all random people. My friend list is almost five thousand strong,' he explained in that smug tone. 'I am choosy with my contacts. I go through it regularly and cull off annoying or useless friends or even overactive ones who waste my time.'

'Raj is going to her place for some official work. I am joining him. We are leaving tomorrow.' She never imagined that she could come up with something like that so quickly.

Dev shrugged. 'Okay, up to you guys to decide. That stretch is an extremist-infested area.' He gave Raj a grim stare. 'Are you sure she should be going there? What is this thing you have with that forest division?'

Raj held back his reply, perhaps thinking about how to put it. Amelia could see him clenching his jaws.

'Dev, I need to meet someone,' Raj said with conviction.

'Did you tell Ajay sir about your trip?' Dev's face was still wobbly and contorted in disgust.

'I don't report to him.' Raj could not hide his irritation. 'I am just a ranger. I will apply for leave. No official duty and no need to tell anyone.'

'I am worried about Amelia. What would Ajay sir say?'

'She is not Ajay sir's guest,' Raj said. 'I think she is on her own.' He smiled with feigned helplessness. 'Young tourists like her are very independent. I don't know what connection she developed with that girl. She says she wants to meet her.'

She remembered Dev's sullen expression as he melted into the crowd, leaving the two of them alone. By the time they reached the town, the sun was over their head. Raj drove straight to their destination, a colonial wooden house with a tin roof with the forest department's familiar green and red signage. The campus, shrouded in a blanket of sleepiness, had very few signs of activity.

Raj told her that it was an all-pervading sign of the government offices in the state's remote districts where the babus attended office only a few days a month. They preferred spending their time in the larger towns where their families lived. Raj got out and walked towards the entrance, Amelia following a few steps behind.

'Is DFO sahib in today?' He asked the first man he saw.

'No, he is out of the station,' the man replied.

Raj looked relieved. There were many empty desks. Those present either browsed the morning newspaper or cast Raj a glance as he strolled through the maze of cubicles to see who was in the office. Some cabins were assigned to the assistant conservator of forest and ranger officers, where the incumbents were at their desks, but were busy with their mobile phones. A lady in the accounts section was busily redressing issues of the people surrounding her.

'I think if Dorothy really worked in this office, she would not be a frontline staff. She would be in a clerical or accounts department role. It is almost twelve-thirty. Most of these guys will soon break for lunch, and some might just sneak home. So, let's get inside to find someone,' Raj said to Amelia.

When they entered the main hall again, everyone stared at them wide-eyed. Even the busy lady stopped working. They approached an inquisitive-looking man whose eyes were fixated on Amelia while his glasses rested on the tip of his nose. He was picking his teeth with a toothpick.

'Hello, I am Ranger Raj from the eastern range of Kaziranga National Park,' Raj said as the man looked up, startled, snapping his eyes back to Raj, his paunch overflowing his sagging belt. He threw the toothpick and gave Raj a wide grin.

'Sir, please take a seat.' Raj got the required attention. Amelia had learned by that time that a ranger from Kaziranga usually meant it was serious business—a poaching case, rhino depredation, or some terrorist-poachers nexus.

'Sir, our DFO sahib is not here. You can talk to our ACF, Victor sahib.' The man pointed to the room with a floral curtain, the gap through which was revealed a stern-looking bald man glued to his computer screen. He wore a feeble goatee.

'It is not exactly official,' Raj lowered his voice. Amelia noticed that most people pretended to be not looking at them. However, now and then, someone's head would pop up from the cubicles to get a glimpse of the beautiful girl. Raj pulled a chair and gestured Amelia to sit. 'I am looking for an employee of this office. I hope you can be of assistance to us.'

The toothpick man's eyes narrowed, and he smiled as if he was all ready to help. Raj went near the man. 'Do you know a girl named Dorothy?'

The man's demeanour changed as if he had heard something unexpected. 'I need to finish some work before the DFO sahib returns,' he said and walked away from them in haste without even looking back once.

Raj looked at Amelia and shrugged. As they headed outside, Amelia's eyes fleetingly caught a newspaper headline on the man's desk, the one which read, 'Kaziranga ranger nexus with tiger poachers'.

★★★

Chapter 17

Day 5 (Noon)

'Why did Dev enter her room when she slept? What would have happened if Arjun's man had not knocked at the door to wake her up? Is it Dev about whom Dorothy wanted to warn Amelia?' Raj's thoughts wandered, his tender gaze on the girl standing next to the SUV, looking at some chirping birds high up in the canopy. He shook his head, brushing off the thought, no, it couldn't be! It was already 1 pm. The afternoon in the hills turned into evening in a short span. It would be impossible to return before it got dark.

Will we get two rooms in the forest IB at the hill town? What will happen if we are given one room?

A shameless shiver ran down his spine. He glanced around to see if anybody was looking at him or at his object of scrutiny. Amelia, unmindful of his stare, watched the birds through binoculars, her sunglasses resting on her forehead.

Raj dragged his eyes away from her as Amelia started walking towards him, the winter sun caressing her face. The leaves of the conifers swayed to the gentle wintery breeze. He longed to hold her hand and take her into the woods for a long walk. No, this gorgeous girl cannot become another Dorothy. Raj's restlessness soared; he had to protect her.

'Hey!' Amelia's raised eyebrows brought Raj to the present. Her deep blue eyes urged him to look over his back. Raj turned to see a short man in a bucket hat walking briskly towards them. The toothpick man followed him. The tough-looking man had a roundish face with small eyes and a sparse, straggly beard. Raj assumed he was the local officer, the bald man on the computer inside the room with the floral curtain.

'ACF Victor sahib,' the toothpick man said.

There was no warmth on Victor's face as he extended his hand to Raj. 'What brings you here, ranger? Hope everything is fine in the park. The state's most-loved treasure must be safe in your hands.' The sarcasm did not go unnoticed.

Victor did not waste time; he wore an impatient look as he tried to mask his annoyance. 'I understand you are looking for Dorothy. She worked as one of our casual employees. We have not seen her for around two weeks.' He turned to the other man. 'Have you?' Expectedly, the toothpick man shook his head vigorously.

'Why are you after her?' Victor raised his brows, his tone frosty.

'Was she married?' Raj realised it was a strange way to start the conversation.

Victor's eyes opened wide. Was he surprised or amused? If he had found it funny, the smile gave way to a smirk on his face. 'Married? You can say so. Without marriage, she might have dozens of husbands. Be careful if you see her; she could say she is carrying your baby.'

Wow, so many aspersions at one go!

'Does she live here?'

'Yes, she is from this place, from a very humble background. She leads a high-society lifestyle. I don't know where she gets all the money from,' Victor continued his vilification campaign. Raj understood what the man alluded to.

'That girl over there came from Australia. She is Dorothy's Facebook friend and wants to meet her.' Amelia had drifted away from them, trying to photograph a flock of hill mynahs perched noisily atop a roadside tree. Her skirt grazed above her knees, revealing her long, shapely legs, where Victor's eyes got transfixed. Raj cleared his throat to distract the man.

'She is such a nice girl.' He scanned Amelia from top to bottom. 'Why does she want to see Dorothy? She has a bad reputation.' Victor removed his hat, and his bald head glistened in the afternoon sun.

'What do you mean?' Raj asked.

Victor kept a steady stare at Raj as if surprised by his naivety. Amelia continued photographing the birds.

'Well, she is a characterless girl, and we don't have much to do with her.' Victor started jiggling his one foot. 'A bad role model for our society! Our small town is better off without people like her. I don't want to talk about her any further,' the man said with a sense of finality, indicating to Raj that the interview was over. 'I need to go back to work. What is your plan? Are you returning to the park? Or do you intend to stay here tonight?' He asked, looking again towards Amelia.

'I will go back. Well, you know,' Raj fumbled. 'The tourist girl donated one hundred and fifty raincoats to our front-line staff. She wanted to get in touch with the girl, so I could not refuse.'

Victor seemed to hide his smile; a five-hour drive through the hilly terrain, all for a Facebook friend?

'I will leave you guys then. In case you change your mind, do let me know. I can ask the caretaker of our IB to make two rooms ready for you both.'

'Thank you very much, Victor sahib.'

'I think you will be better off keeping a distance from this girl, Dorothy.'

'When is DFO sahib coming back?' Raj changed the topic.

The vein on Victor's forehead throbbed as he clenched his jaws, holding his reply. 'He hardly stays here,' Victor said dismissively. His authoritative demeanour made it amply clear that he was the de facto head of the office. He relaxed a bit; a twinkle came to his eyes, and a naughty smile touched his lips. 'Are you sure you don't want to stay back here?' His brows moved to turn to Amelia, who was returning to the vehicle.

'I need to report for duty tomorrow.' Raj felt relieved that

Amelia was already inside the car.

'It's quite late. The road is terrible,' Victor said. Was it genuine concern, or was the man trying to play him, Raj wondered. 'I can be discreet about it. I will not tell your director,' he whispered the last bit.

That was the final straw. 'Thanks, we will make a move.' Raj shook hands with Victor and proceeded to leave. A few people were already leaving for home, their curiosity still not abating seeing a departmental colleague with a stunningly beautiful memsahib.

Amelia waited inside the car, going through the photos she had captured in her digital camera. She lowered the side window. 'What did you guys talk about for so long? Anything about Dorothy?'

'Yes, I got some information.' He was not sure what to share with her. 'Let's get back.' To stay in this small town's forest lodge with her would set tongues wagging. The men in that office, who had nothing good to say about Dorothy would not spare him either. 'Kaziranga ranger kidnaps Australian girl and rapes her in the hills', he could almost hear the rumour mills running fast and furious.

Raj felt goose bumps all over his body as Amelia said to him, 'Is it not a long drive back? Are we not staying here overnight?'

Heights of innocence! Raj thought, remembering the smell of her hair as she buried her head in his chest. Did her fingers trace patterns on his back? What would have happened if Dev had not knocked like a maniac? Confusion and excitement swamped him at the same time, her simplicity and insistence unnerving him.

'Actually, I need prior permission to stay away from my range. I am so sorry; we will have to leave right now,' he made up an excuse. He hid his smile, thinking of his reluctance to go to the airport to receive her. Yet here he was, tormented by a pair of blue eyes while calls of hill birds floated in the air, hardly expecting to have such a conversation with the girl he had met only three days back.

Raj started the car and moved out of the office campus to the deserted road. On their right was a roadside tea stall with a few benches and tables. The wall of the shanty eatery was covered with posters of film stars. The owner, immersed in a newspaper, was unmindful of his surroundings while the lone waiter, a boy of around fifteen years of age, served the customers.

Some office staff finished their lunches and got ready to go back to work. The flavour of typical *dhaba* curry wafted into Raj's nostrils. He realised they had not eaten anything since the morning. 'Is this place okay for you?' Raj knew food in the roadside restaurant would be fresh and tasty, but then the place was a shanty.

Amelia scanned the eatery. 'It's fine with me. Let's have lunch here.'

Raj parked the car across the road and got out from his vehicle. The boy came running to greet them.

'Please come, sir and memsahib.' There was an exuberance and genuineness about the boy despite the trite routine.

Maybe the unusual combination of a forest officer with a beautiful girl did the trick. The owner lifted his head above the newspaper and ignored them after a cursory glance.

'What would you like to have for lunch, sir? We have chapatti, chicken and dal.'

The return journey would be another five hours. It would get dark by the time they left the town, and hence, speed through the hilly terrain would be slow. It wouldn't be safe to stop for food on the way.

'Get all three items and make it quick,' Raj said.

The owner, a heavyweight man, got up from his seat, yawning and came to them. 'Sir, please make the payment to him. I need to go home.' He tottered away, looking exhausted.

'Babu is going for his afternoon nap.' The little waiter's chubby features puckered into a grin. He had a friendly smile and soulful eyes.

Raj asked Amelia to take out Dorothy's photograph from Facebook.

'Do you know her?' He asked the boy.

'Oh, yes, Dorothy *didi*. She worked in the forest office.' The boy's eyes sparkled, and the face shone.

'Where is she nowadays?'

'I have not seen her for the last few days. She is a nice girl, but many people dislike her.' He pointed to the office. 'ACF Victor sahib detests her the most.'

'Why?'

'That man didn't leave her in peace. He always made unwanted advances towards her. She said she didn't like him, but he would still pester her. Everyone is aware of his mischief, but nobody raises a word against this harassment. She has been in this state since the DFO sahib left.' Despite his age, the boy was fully aware of what was going on in the office.

'I thought he was out for a day or two?'

'No, no, not this one! The previous one, the tall sahib from Delhi. He went away a few months ago. He gave her a job in this office,' the boy said in an all-knowing way.

'You mean to say the previous DFO gave her the job?'

'Yes. Dorothy *didi* worked in the sahib's bungalow looking after memsahib. She used to be sick.'

Raj wondered if he should tell the boy about the girl's fate. 'Dorothy is missing. Any idea what might have happened?'

A blanket of gloom shrouded the boy's face, but he did not look surprised. Munching his roti dipped in the spicy chicken curry, Raj shook his head in sudden realisation. Ajay Mathur, director of Kaziranga National Park, was the DFO of the hill division office before his current posting.

★★★

Chapter 18

Day 5 (Evening)

Raj and Amelia left the town bathed in a hazy mist. The air was filled with the smell of smoke from the patches of forest reclaimed by the cultivators for the age-old slash and burn cultivation. The short wintry day was over. Farmers in makeshift cottages hidden by the canopy of trees, huddled around a fire caressing a mix of warmth and smoke; a long chilly night lay ahead of them.

Raj suppressed a strong urge to make a U-turn and check into a hotel. The drive back was a lengthy one, and his mind was all muddled up, but he flinched at the thought. If he chose to stay back, the consequences would be too many. Even if they slept in separate rooms, the rumour would be scandalous. His breath quickened; he opened the car window to let the crisp mountain air in. A few long, deep breaths made him lightheaded with relief. He was happy to be heading back.

'Other than Dev, who else knew about your trip to India?' He consciously shifted his focus to the dark moment of her abduction in Kolkata.

'My parents, Dev and Dorothy,' Amelia said, engrossed in the sight of the lazy descent of the sun in the faraway plains in the west.

'What will Dev gain by getting you abducted?' Raj spoke his thoughts aloud. 'Or, for that matter, Ajay sir, if he came to know of the dates from Dev?'

Amelia did not say anything; the rays of the setting sun caressed her pink cheeks. The fast falling dusk burnished the woods with gold; the fragrance of the forest overwhelmed them as the SUV cruised leisurely on the curvy hill road. It was just the two of them, their little vehicle piercing through a continuous green veil rumbling past the trunks of majestic trees, the aroma of the jungle captivating their senses.

Amelia remained in some deep thought, gazing into the dark, mottled trees blurring in front of their eyes. 'What is she thinking about?' Raj wondered.

Raj's phone rang. 'Are you guys back?' It was Dev.

'Yes, we are on our way back. I have arranged Amelia's accommodation in the government tourist lodge. Tonight onwards she can stay there.'

'We just had a vacancy in the evening. Amelia can come back to my place. No need to take her anywhere.'

Raj took the call on speaker mode, gesturing to Amelia to seek her reaction. What should be his reply? Amelia shook her head with an emphatic no. She would not go back to that spooky place with the door in the wall.

'Actually, the room is already booked. The caretakers are expecting her.'

There was protestation from Dev's side. Then, he mentioned something about today's paper.

'What is in the newspaper?'

Raj could not hear what Dev said; the network played up again. Raj hung up.

'Oh, thank God! I really wanted a change from that place,' she sounded relieved.

Raj thought of his quarter warm and spacious, with the double bed, cosy and comfortable. He felt heady. He knew the car interior was saturated with the slight aroma of her perfume, or her natural smell was to blame. He took a deep breath as chilly air gushed in through the window of the speeding car.

By the time they reached the plains, the place was drowned in tarry darkness, the yellow fog light of the SUV getting lost in the swirling mist descending from the hills. He enjoyed the river breeze sweeping across the valley, increasing in strength as it wound through the highlands near the park's approach.

'Mind if we drop at the police station for some time?' Raj asked, wanting to stop at a restaurant but was unsure. A stopover at Arjun's place would not be considered a delaying tactic.

'Why did you go there?' Arjun sounded brusque and business-like. It was late, but he was going through a file, which he closed as Raj and Amelia settled on chairs facing him.

'The dead girl lived there. We went to check if we could get any leads,' Raj said.

Arjun craned his neck to see if others were near the office door. He looked at Amelia and nodded a greeting; at least, there was a smile. And then he turned to Raj. 'How did you know she was from that place?' His voice was even.

Raj again narrated how they deduced she was from the hill town by going through her messages with Amelia. Arjun listened in attention, his face blank.

'Now that we know she was an employee of the forest department, can we launch an investigation?'

'Somebody should lodge a complaint that she is missing. Moreover, it would be in the jurisdiction of her home police station,' Arjun said, shuffling some papers on his desk.

'But her body was found here, in the camp where I stayed.'

'Officially, no dead body has been found here.' Arjun's tired eyes gleamed in the dim interior of the office; his voice reeked with slight irritation. 'They conducted the post-mortem on an unidentified and unclaimed body, and the body has been disposed of. How will we prove that the girl's body is from the hills? Anyway, let's... .' Arjun was about to say something, but then he softened his look.

'It was a long trip.' He turned to Amelia. 'Did you like the hill drive? It is much cooler and serene there. Wait, let's have a cup of tea.' He rang the bell. A constable came in. 'Send three chais.'

'You know when the girl worked in the hill division

office, Ajay sir was the DFO there,' Raj said. Arjun did not say anything; instead, he took a long sip of the milk tea infused with ginger. 'Aren't you going back to your quarters?' Raj asked.

Arjun smiled a faint, tired smile. 'I am on something. I will be here for a few more hours.' He moved the paperweight to pick up a newspaper. 'There is coverage on today's paper about the tiger poaching in your range.' He sounded sombre. Raj's heart started pumping. How did the news get out of his ranger campus? He didn't feel like reading the news. He held the chair's handles and pushed himself up, feeling weak as he walked out of Arjun's room.

'Raj,' Arjun called out. 'Where is she staying tonight?' His forehead creased in thought.

'In the tourist department lodge.'

Arjun nodded, looking relieved. 'You guys go ahead. I will send two of my men there. After what happened in Kolkata, we can't take any risk. Orders from the top.' Arjun dismissed them with a wave as he picked up his phone to dial a number.

Raj's chest felt heavy as they neared the tourist lodge.

'Thank you very much for the trip. I am thinking, tomorrow...', A tractor rumbled past, appearing from nowhere, drowning what she said.

Raj's heart skipped a beat. 'Are you planning to leave?'

'No, I was wondering if I could visit some interior camps in your range. I wanted to hand out as many raincoats as I could before I departed.'

Raj's lips flickered; he restrained his smile. 'Okay,

tomorrow we will go to Khaspur. It is the most remote camp in a savannah strip surrounded by a deep evergreen forest on all sides except the north, where you can see the river Brahmaputra. There is an abundance of all kinds of animals. Our biggest bull rhino, we call him Sultan, grazes in that patch of grassland. We will also give the raincoats to the camps on our way to that place.'

Reaching his quarters, Raj did not feel any lighter or wiser; it was all muddled up. He wanted a respite, a quick warm bath, and some hot food; his stomach growled. No sooner did Raj lock the door of his room to jump into the cushiony comfort of his bed, than someone knocked on his door. It was a slightly tentative knock, but he could hear some people talking in a hushed, excited tone.

What is it? Is it about the coverage on the paper? He wondered. A dozen of his men stood with sullen expressions. Vijay was in the front, his face puckered, brimming with something terrible.

'Just before you arrived, we found another carcass. It is a juvenile, I think it is the sibling of the one they killed the other day.'

'What?' Raj wanted to grab something in reflex and hurl it at the bearer of bad news.

'Same place. Just a hundred metres away from our gate. I stumbled upon it when I went for a smoke,' Vijay said with such stoicism; it sounded like practised rhetoric for what had become a daily event.

Raj regarded his men. He loved them to death. Most

of the faces were worn out and exhausted. Some had been working as forest guards in that hostile terrain for decades, their khaki uniforms were torn and crumpled, boots soiled and sodden. In their fifties, many of them persevered with their arthritic knees and their aching backs. The young ones, the lot who were still not sure what they had signed up for by joining the park as frontline staff, fared no better. Some of them had just returned from three days of continuous patrolling in the riverbank areas where every step taken in the silvery sinking sand was a laboured exercise. They stood resolute, and upright despite the strain of the long day.

'Relax,' Raj said, his eyes scanning them in the dark. No, they had not failed him. They were not at fault. Raj found himself clenching his jaws. It was not about the animals; it was a battle to finish him. Why? Was it because of his crackdown on the poaching network? However, he was not alone in this? Other rangers were also doing the same. He would not lose to an invisible enemy, one who had killed an innocent beauty and one who almost hurt the most beautiful soul he had ever met. He accepted the gauntlet thrown at him by the adversary. Soon this news too, would get out; the ranger tours the hill station with an Australian tourist while poachers kill yet another tiger and throw the body at the gate of the ranger's office.

★★★

Chapter 19

Day 6 (Evening)

The mood in the campus was as gloomy as the wet, overcast day. Half the day was gone while Raj reported the incident to his seniors, a post-mortem was carried out, and the remains were burnt. Raj walked towards his office, thinking of the files piling up on his desk. With the plethora of issues waiting to be attended—salary disbursal, annual leave, anti-poaching patrolling roster changes, compensation demands, tender reviews—the girl, her yellow raincoats, and the proposed trip to Khaspur would have to wait.

He was unsure why he had this warm, fuzzy excitement after spending time with someone who would depart in a day or two. Would it be plain and straightforward pain once she departed? Raj smiled at himself; it would be a first. His heart skipped a beat whenever he looked at her or even thought about her. It was such an unreal and new sensation. For her, it would be another one of the exotic lands she had visited, with its list of interesting characters that she had interacted with before returning home. She would soon be on the lookout for her next charitable act, somewhere in Indonesia, Vietnam, or even a country of which he had never heard. How he wished he could shake off the thoughts of the girl as he tried to immerse himself in the bureaucratic maze of his office paperwork. The day passed quickly, and the weather cleared, but it was not enough to lift his mood. Two tigers in three days were too much.

He thought of Amelia. He owed her an apology; he called the tourist lodge manager.

'What? She went to the Rhino Warriors Resort?' Raj almost jumped off his seat. 'When did she go? Why did you send her?' He almost growled at the man.

'Who are we to stop our guests? Dev sir himself came to collect her in the morning. An important function is happening there,' the manager said.

Soon, Raj was on the national highway, cruising past the trucks and an inordinate number of official cars, some of them belonged to the police, some to the district administration and some were of his office colleagues. He found himself in a traffic jam as he turned to take the side road to the River View Resort. Another big bash at the Wildlife Warrior's place? He wondered wearily.

White-coloured official cars with red beacon lights and black-tinted SUVs with police escorts lined the resort's entrance. A temporary gateway with a welcome sign on it heralded him to a carnival-like atmosphere with trees festooned with balloons. The place was full of his colleagues. The clouds had cleared, and there was no trace of precipitation, but the guards wore yellow-coloured raincoats. At a distance, daredevil Rahman inspected his waterproof gift with childlike happiness, a smile brimming under his handlebar moustache. On a makeshift stage on the far end of the sprawling lawn, a stocky, dark man with a thickset neck, wearing a raincoat, spoke on the microphone. It did not take Raj long to understand what this entire hullabaloo was about.

The forest minister, known as 'Buffalo', was on a resort trip. Raj noticed the others seated on the dais. They were Ajay sir, the district collector, and Amelia, who also was in a raincoat. As he spoke, Buffalo repeatedly pointed towards Amelia, addressing her as the girl in a yellow raincoat. So, it was a ceremony to distribute raincoats and thank Amelia for her generous donation by none other than the minister!

'I called you a few times,' Dev accosted Raj. 'Amelia has been trying to contact you since morning,' He added, eyes boring through his Harry Potter glasses.

'Dev, it has been a crazy day. I forgot to charge my mobile.' Raj remembered the tiger's skinned carcass. While Buffalo kept acting like a circus joker in yellow, Raj was wondering why none of his departmental seniors asked him to attend the meeting.

'I thought you had a busy day yesterday. A long drive to the hill station?' Dev's eyes twinkled with a sharp gleam.

'How did he land at your place?' Raj ignored the jibe.

'He made a sudden stop to check the park's patrolling preparedness. He saw the news items regarding the raincoat distribution ceremony. I thought we could organise another function so that he can thank Amelia. Now she realises how much her gifts mean to the department.'

Dev then cast a glance at the stage, where the top officials sat with Buffalo. 'I think he also came to discuss the spurt in tiger poaching. The newspaper coverage is quite one-sided. I think you should give a rebuttal.' Dev paused, his eyes scanning for Raj's reaction. 'Should I arrange one for you? All the television channels are here.'

Raj was not listening. His eyes were on Amelia, sitting with Buffalo and others. The dais was surrounded by camerapersons and journalists with their long microphones displaying their channel's gaudy logos.

'Sir, you look good in the raincoat,' said one of the TV news people who looked more like a roadside ruffian than a journalist.

'It is not about me looking good. It is about feeling good. I feel great!' Buffalo paused, took a deep breath, and closed his eyes for a moment. 'This lovely girl flew from Australia to bring raincoats for our guards. This means our Kaziranga National Park is well-known even in her country. That must be due to our government's excellent work to protect the rhino. We have zero tolerance towards poaching,' Buffalo went on.

'But what about the tiger killing three days ago? The

carcass was found in front of the ranger's office,' a thin woman with her glasses resting on the tip of her pointy nose, asked in a shrill voice.

'We are looking into the incident.' The minister sounded sombre. Ajay sir fidgeted on his seat.

'We heard from reliable sources that another carcass was found yesterday. Two tigers within three days. Don't you think the forest department failed in its duties? Is the ranger responsible for all this?' The woman carried on with her tirade.

'Don't pay heed to them.' Dev put a hand on Raj's shoulder. 'Anyway, it's good that you came. You stay now. We have arranged a dinner in honour of the minister and the visiting dignitaries.' Dev was sweating, and his face flushed red. A tense host and copious amount of alcohol, Raj guessed.

After some time, Buffalo finished his charade and came down from the stage, followed by his minions and the guards. The babus' swell drifted towards the bean-shaped pool, where a makeshift bar, christened 'Water Hole', became operational, with the bartender lining up expensive whiskies and other drinks for the guests to choose from.

Raj's eyes met Ajay sir's for the first time; he was busy talking to his colleagues who had come from other places. It was a cold, uneasy glance, and Ajay sir turned away quickly. Two tigers in three days; somebody in the department had to be made the scapegoat to placate the media and public. Seniors would like to show some action to their higher ups, to the minister. He was running out of time; Ajay sir's awkward stare and avoidance confounded his fear.

'Let's grab a drink.' Somebody lightly tapped Raj's shoulder. It was Arjun in civil clothes, hanging on to an empty glass, looking relaxed, maybe because of the drinks. 'Today, our warrior is opening up his vast collection of spirits. Let's go for the best.' He gave Raj a wink and smiled.

The residual strands of dusk disappeared, drowning the resort in an intoxicating evening. Waiters moved around with plates of delicacies and trays laden with glasses filled with various drinks. The foreign tourists added beauty to the festivity, standing out among the Indian guests and the officials. By that time, Buffalo had changed into casual jeans and a t-shirt. He resembled a mafia don with a gold chain around his short, thick neck. The golden dusk had long turned dark, but he still wore his small, roundish Ray-Ban sunglasses, head bobbing from one tourist to another as he mingled with the resort guests.

The crowd broke into diverse groups. Buffalo was surrounded by his cronies and the local political leaders; the district officials gathered around the collector, Ajay sir conversed with other senior IFS officers, and the park rangers formed another group. A group of foresters huddled around DFO Roy, who was already intoxicated. He kept on mouthing profanities, sitting in a lax position on a chair. There was amused suppressed laughter as a few of the men tried to calm him down, urging him to lower his voice so that he would not be heard.

'They are saying the minister came to check our

patrolling. What is he doing here staring at the foreign tourists?' Roy slurred.

'Sir, please have this *nimbu pani.*' Someone came up to him with a glass of lemonade.

'Bloody, I don't want *nimbu pani.*' Roy pushed the man away, knocking the glass out of his hand. 'Do you think I am drunk?'

The circle of curious onlookers around Roy grew bigger. Members of the other groups craned their necks to see what was going on.

'Sir, I need to report something,' Raj whispered in Roy's ears. It had the desired impact, Roy's face turned grave, and his mood sombre.

'What is it?'

Raj helped his senior up and wrapped his arm around his shoulder as they slowly walked away towards his car.

'Yes, what is it?' Roy demanded.

'Sir, let us get into my car. Your driver can bring your car later.'

After Roy settled himself in the back seat of the car, he could not contain his curiosity. 'Now tell me. I hope you didn't want to trick me. I don't want to miss all the fun. Where do you get so much of single malt for free?'

'Sir, forget about the drinks. Something more serious is happening, this tiger thing.'

Roy leaned forward to grab the backrest of the front seat. He almost shouted into Raj's ears. 'Is it out in the media? The second one? Was that nasty woman in green asking about yesterday's killing? We all will be in a soup, partying while tigers are killed one after another.'

'Sir, does the minister know the details?'

'Yes, of course. The director briefed him. They had a huddle before the meeting in the resort. But does he care? He does not love the forest or wildlife. I see him as a minister for environmental clearance and commissions. However, what is it with our director? Two tigers dead in a tiger reserve in three days, and that clueless man is applauding that gorilla's dance on the stage with the Australian girl.' Roy gave an amused look as if he enjoyed the situation.

'Sir, I think it is just one group doing all these things. They want me out,' Raj said, his eyes straight on the road.

'Is it somebody from village number eight?' Roy's tone from the back was meditative. He paused and then asked, 'How did your interaction with them go? Do you see them moving out anytime soon?' Raj mulled over the frustrating negotiation with the villagers. The astronomical sum offered to them to move out of the plot surprised even the settlers. It was much more than the market price of their prickly holdings. Pulled by some unseen strings, they shook their heads, 'No, they would not relocate.'

Who is instigating them to stay put?

'Sir, the compensation being offered, you know the details better than me, is too good to be refused. They are adamant; they won't budge. I want to make sure that we get that area. That's a key animal corridor. Let's have a discussion with the director.'

Roy let out a heavy sigh. 'Don't bother; he will not do anything. There is a lucrative deputation job waiting for him to while away his time; our director will soon return to Delhi. He will go there and get his wife treated in a renowned hospital. Does he have any clue? Does he care?' Roy's rant hit Raj's ears, hurting him. 'Let's discuss this tomorrow. Can you take me to my quarters? I don't feel very well. I might throw up.'

Please don't do it in my car; Raj prayed silently.

'You had better go back to the resort after dropping me. Go and save that girl. The minister made this sudden stop to seduce your Australian friend. Ever since he saw her on TV, he has been behaving like a man possessed. Also, who knows, Ajay Mathur may also join him. He is a deprived man.' Roy laughed, baring all his rows of stained teeth.

'She is a very decent girl,' Raj made a feeble protest.

'The girl is good, but our director is a spineless bastard. He is not without his weaknesses. Do you know where he goes to release his tension?' Roy's eyes were half-open, and an all-knowing smile touched his lips.

Raj shook his head.

'Dimapur, Nagaland. I maintain a full diary of his trips to that place using our official car. What has he got to do in Dimapur every fortnight? Huh?'

As Roy tottered to his quarter, Raj made a U-turn. The vision of a grunting Buffalo trying to lure Amelia made him floor the accelerator, and dread uncoiled in the pit of his stomach.

★★★

Chapter 20

Day 6 (Night)

A sigh of relief escaped Raj, seeing Amelia in conversation with a dapper-looking Arjun, who seemed to be enjoying the chitchat. What were they talking about, he wondered? Her golden-brown hair was done in a small, messy bun. The long floral frock she wore accentuated her lovely curves. His heart raced as heat swept across his cheeks.

'Hey Raj!' Arjun's address brought him back to the present. Pushing aside what had crept into his mind, he was surprised at the kinds of thoughts he had started having. He forced a smile to Arjun and then apologised to Amelia for failing to turn up for the Khaspur trip.

A group of girls from the nearby village performed an enchanting folk dance in the distance under a makeshift gazebo. They danced rhythmically to the sound of drums being played by the men. Raj's fleeting glances were on

Amelia. After the scare Roy gave him, he was not afraid of being caught staring at her, but she did not notice.

In the gleaming moonlight, her face reflected the joy of the nubile girls dancing in gay abandon, eyes sparkling with warmth, giving her a girl next door kind of beauty.

'Where did you vanish?' Dev appeared in a jolly mood; his hands shook a bit, spilling some spirit from his glass.

'I went to Roy sir's place,' Raj said. Dev was not listening; he walked towards Amelia, his gait unsteady.

'Amelia!' Dev raised his hand, holding the glass to get Amelia's attention, but she was busy taking photos of the dancers. 'Please take our photo. One with my favourite ranger and one with our dashing police inspector.'

Dev put his hand around Raj's shoulder and posed for a few clicks. He pulled a glum-faced Arjun into a hug with his arms outstretched, forcing him to pose.

'Thanks, Arjun. I know you are doing your bit to take care of our guest from Australia. I see two new waiters in my resort whom I never appointed.' Dev chuckled. 'Great stuff, isn't it?' He pointed to Arjun's glass, gave a cheeky smile, and tottered away.

Once Dev was lost among the crowd, Arjun came near Raj. 'Be ready tomorrow. We will go to that girl's hometown. Hey, by the way, what's your deputy doing here?' Arjun trailed off as Vijay came towards them. Raj looked at Vijay, surprised to see him at the party. Vijay did not have a glass in his hand, but from the happy glow on his face, Raj could make out that he might have had his fair share of liquor from behind the bar. He stood in attention, gave a salute to Raj, and moved away, but not before giving a fleeting stare to Arjun. He turned from there to vanish in the darkness. Raj could see the disapproving glare in Arjun's eyes.

The guests gathered around with their drinks, enjoying the sudden bonanza. Fairy lights bathed the resort in rainbow colours—an artificial, ephemeral paradise while the real heaven called Kaziranga remained clouded in the darkness beyond the resort's edge. Vast expanses of grassland that eventually merged with the deep, dark green forest that started right across the boundary wall. Raj strained his ears to listen above the light instrumental music playing in the background; he could hear an explosion of a night bird's song erupting from the wilderness beyond. His trained ears picked up the call—the low bark that marred the evenings of Kaziranga, the alarm calls of a hog deer. He shivered with a sense of excitement. A tiger lurking just a few hundred metres away from this wine-sipping crowd? As a tarry blackness engulfed the park, the last of the telephoto lens-wielding tourists left in jeeps, leaving behind a trail of dust; that's when the big cats came out to reclaim the territory. Their stealthy movement was announced to the world by the panicky deer. They came all the way to the edges of the forest, to their old terrain. When he joined as a ranger, he had heard about a nefarious nexus of Rhino Warriors with the forest and the revenue department personnel to record the land as non-forest and add to the NGO's ever-expanding landholding around the park.

A light touch on his shoulder brought him to the present. He turned back, startled to see Amelia dazzling under the moonlight.

'So, had fun with our minister?' Raj smiled at Amelia.

Amelia shook her head and broke into a smile. 'He is a funny man.'

'Why did he address you as the girl in a yellow raincoat?'

'You people should know. He is your minister.' There was a teasing gleam in her eyes.

'What were you talking about with them? I mean with the minister and then with Arjun.' Raj was curious, and he cursed Roy for unnecessarily giving him the tense moments.

'The minister asked me about Australia. He wanted to know about the beaches there and asked me if I regularly visit the beach.'

'Pervert,' Raj grumbled.

'He said he is going to another national park tomorrow. He asked me to accompany him out of politeness.'

Raj's heart skipped a beat, and his breath quickened.

'He respects Dev a lot,' Amelia said with a smile.

'The man knows that Dev can make him resign. Dev and his NGO can create mass hysteria about poaching, and the people of this state are very emotional about rhino killing. The minister and our senior officers have no choice other than to keep him in good humour. By the way, what was Arjun saying?'

Amelia mused, 'He asked me about our trip to the hills. He was quite curious, actually.'

'Listen, tomorrow I am going to the place with Arjun.' Raj's heart hoped she would insist on joining them.

'Again?' Her face lit up with an astonished glee. But she stopped at that. The suspense made a dreaded feeling pass through Raj's body, will she ask or won't she? 'Can I come along?' Amelia's eyes almost pleaded.

'Aren't you going back?' Raj tried not to betray his elation as both headed towards the food counter.

Dev appeared from nowhere. 'Hey, have you guys eaten or not?' He asked; his shirt was drenched in sweat. He had excessive drinks and excitement while doling out endless hospitality. 'Tomorrow, I am going with the minister to inspect a patch of land for potential rhino translocation. IUCN rhino specialist group had identified the site.' He then looked at Amelia. 'Are you interested in coming?'

Raj waited for Amelia's reply with bated breath. She was his guest, and she had every right to accept his invitation. Raj wanted to kick himself because he had not shared his suspicion with Amelia yet.

'Thanks, Dev, for the invite. I will just move around. I don't want to get into your official dealings.'

What a polite refusal! Raj let out a sigh. Dev's usual charming demeanour hid the disappointment as he picked up a chicken skewer, smiled and went away.

'What is the plan for tonight? No need to stay here. I can drop you at the tourist lodge,' Raj said.

'Dev is insisting that I stay here.' Amelia gave a faint smile. 'He was not happy that I stayed in the government tourist lodge yesterday. He made me bring back my luggage.' Only one door separated them. A sigh came to Raj as nervousness swept through his body. 'What are you thinking?' Amelia held a spoonful of pilaf rice. 'Nice food. Don't you drink? Most of your department people are drinking.'

'I don't feel like drinking today. I'm not much of a drinker.' Raj never felt more intoxicated. Her bun had loosened, and the strands of hair flew in the breeze. 'I am driving.' He shook his head; why could he not get her out of his head?

Raj's eyes fell on an officer's wife. She tipsily swirled a glass of red wine, her diamond choker glittered. A smile hovered around his mouth as he remembered the many times Dev had invited him to stay back in the resort for the night after a party. He had always refused; he found the place too elitist for him, and he did not want his friendship with the NGO chief to cross certain limits. However, that night he did not want to leave Amelia alone. The lady with the wine glass gyrated, balancing on her stilettos.

An exhausted Dev hurried through a group of resort workers, barking out instructions. He stopped and came towards them; beads of sweat lined his brows, it was ten in the wintry night. He kept a hand on Raj's shoulder. 'Why don't you stay back today? I know it is quite stressful at your campus, with two tiger deaths in three days. You can sleep in my room, next to her.' His head moved to eye both together.

'It's all right. I can go. I did not drink.' Raj hid his embarrassment, but sensed that would get Dev started.

'You will stay.' Dev stomped his foot like a child

demanding something from his parents. Amelia suppressed a smile; Raj knew there was no point arguing with the thoroughly drunk man.

'I don't like to dislodge you, Dev.' His heart was pounding with excitement and relief, if she stayed in the resort, he had to guard her.

'I'm not going to get much sleep anyway. I need to discuss many things with my staff as I will be away for a couple of days. The minister is an early riser, so we will be leaving after a few hours. He has a lot of programmes lined up on the way. So, don't worry, you can stay in my room. I will send the key to you after I take away my belongings.'

'Amelia, I will take leave of you,' Dev said, looking at Amelia. 'Thank you for everything, in case I don't see you in the morning.'

'Oh Dev,' She hugged him. 'You have been such a kind host.'

'Don't worry about the other raincoats. We will organise more distribution ceremonies. Please do keep in touch through Facebook.' Dev then addressed Raj. '*Dada*, you have to take care of her. If she leaves before my return, make sure that she safely reaches the airport. Last time, those idiots messed it up big time.' He brought himself near Raj's ear. 'Enjoy your stay. Listen, don't open the connecting door.'

A naughty smile beamed on Dev's face, or was it a sneer of sheer malevolence?

★★★

Chapter 21

Day 7 (Morning)

The morning sun shone brightly from an open sky, a few streaks of white wisp in the sea of blue. Raj was all attention only to the glow of Amelia's pale skin; he tried hard to act normal, hiding the elation of sitting next to her in the rear while Arjun sat in the front with the driver, Thapa. Did they reach the sleepy town way too soon? They stopped by the roadside restaurant, that tin-roofed shanty with those long tables and benches. Flies buzzed over the food remains on the table of the empty eatery. A sad-looking old man stood near a door that perhaps led to the kitchen with a curtain whose original pattern would be difficult to guess. He peered expectantly at them—prospective patrons. The nonchalant owner, sitting in his usual place behind the wooden cash box, had buried his head in the spread of a newspaper.

'Hello!' Raj shouted. 'Where is the boy?'

The man raised his head from the paper, his irritated demeanour quickly changing when he saw the query posed from a police vehicle. He lifted his plump body from the mattress, pulled and tidied his long-flowing shirt, and crossed over to them. A smile beamed on his face as he recognised Raj. It was a superficial one that stayed fixed on his lips.

'He didn't come to work today,' the owner said in a matter-of-fact way. 'Sir, masala tea?' He asked, seeing Arjun eyeing him intently.

'Who can tell us about that girl, Dorothy?' Arjun said, ignoring the offer.

The man took a gulp, his head moving side to side. 'Why don't you ask the servants and the cooks in the DFO sahib's quarters? Sahib and his family are out of town. They are idling their time.'

'How do they know about her?' Arjun asked.

'She often visited that bungalow when Ajay sir worked here. The cook Bhola cooked for many DFOs. He will have all your answers.' Clearly, the owner, with nervous perspiration appearing on the forehead of his round face with a bulbous nose as he kept looking towards the forest office, wanted to get rid of them as quickly as possible.

'This is my number. When the boy comes back, if he remembers something about Dorothy, ask him to call me.' Raj handed the man a chit of paper, thoroughly convinced that it would be binned as soon as they left.

The short drive to the DFO's bungalow led them to a sprawling tin-roofed house under a large shady tree, shrouded in a mosaic of light and shadows. The dappled sunlight through the foliage hardly reached the ground. Thapa honked the horn a few times. A man working on a vegetable patch in the front yard came running.

'DFO sahib is not here,' the gardener answered as he opened the iron gate, pushing it over the rail.

'Call everyone here.' Arjun headed to the courtyard and made himself comfortable on a cane chair on the airy veranda with numerous potted plants. Raj and Amelia also joined him, and soon, they had a group of half a dozen caretakers standing in front of them. Their eyes almost fell out at the sight of a fair memsahib with a policeman and a forest officer.

'Who has worked in this place the longest?' Raj asked.

All the heads turned towards a squint-eyed, wrinkly old man.

'Are you Bhola?'

The smallish man with a slight limp, in an ill-fitting departmental cook's uniform nodded with a bored expression. He was not as nervous as the others; he seemed tired.

'Who else worked for the previous DFO Ajay sahib?'

Another grey-haired man, wearing thick glasses, raised his hand. 'I was his driver.'

'What are you doing here? You didn't drive today?' Arjun asked.

Raj stole a glance at Amelia. She could not follow much of the conversation, but she showed interest.

'We are trying to find out who worked here for the longest so that we can ask about the girl,' Raj whispered to her.

She smiled. The same beguiling smile conveying that he need not worry about her. Biting her lips, she scanned the two men. Raj realised that she was taking the visit far more seriously than.

'I don't drive nowadays. Eye problem,' the old driver said.

Raj gestured to the duo. 'You two stay back. Others can go back to work.' He knew that they had just been sitting idly as they had nothing much to do with the sahib and memsahib away. The old cook's eyes almost drooped shut, revealing his veined eyelids. The driver's glasses had not been cleaned for a while. Hope he could see through all the smudges, Raj thought.

As if on cue, Amelia handed him her phone. 'Show them.'

Raj showed Dorothy's picture to them. Sunlight dimmed the screen's brightness. They inspected the photo from different angles, and then, looking at each other, they said together, 'Dorothy.'

'Yes,' Raj said. 'Listen, it has got nothing to do with you or your present boss. We are interested in some information about the girl when Ajay sahib worked here.''You guys don't worry. We just need to check some old facts,' Arjun echoed Raj.

The men relaxed. 'We will tell you everything,' Bhola said, and the driver nodded.

'How do you know her?' Raj asked.

'She came here to take care of memsahib.'

'Why?' Raj feigned ignorance.

'She used to be sad and unwell. Sahib arranged for

Dorothy to look after her.'

'Did she stay here?'

'No sir, she used to come here after sahib left for the office. She finished her duties once he came home.'

'What was her relationship with sahib?' Raj knew he had to ask this.

The question didn't surprise the men, as if they expected it.

'He treated her just like any of us,' Bhola said.

'Did she stay back after he came home?' Arjun jumped in.

'No, no, she used to leave as soon as he came home. The only time she used to stay overnight was to take care of memsahib when he went on tour.'

'Did you drive him when he went on trips?'

'Yes sir, most of the time.'

'Where did he go?'

'Sir, he mostly went to Dimapur. Sometimes to Delhi.'

'Dimapur?' Raj remembered what Roy had told him about the director's recreational trips to the place just the day before. 'What did he do in Dimapur?'

'I have no idea, sir. I used to drop him in a hotel and then come back later to pick him up.'

'You go all the way to drop him and then come back?'

'Yes sir. It's not that far; it just takes two hours.'

'Did you go to bring him back the same day?'

'No, no.' The driver shook his head. 'He stayed at that place for at least one night.' He bent his head, looking over his glasses. 'Sometimes for two nights too.'

'Did Dorothy ever go with him?'

'No, never,' the men said in unison, resolute and confident.

'Are you sure?' Arjun asked. 'Tell the truth! It is not about your old sahib; it is about the girl.'

Both the men became indignant. The old cook's left eyelid started twitching; he shook his head as if he had heard something sacrilegious. Arjun turned to Raj and raised his brows, querying if he had anything more to ask. Raj narrated the conversation to Amelia.

'You said Dorothy sometimes stayed here when the director went on tour. Just ask them one thing. When he went to Dimapur, did she always stay here with his wife? Or were there exceptions?' Amelia said.

'One last question,' Raj said. 'During your sahib's Dimapur trips, did the girl stay with memsahib?'

Again, the men got immersed deep in thought. 'She stayed here when sahib used to go to Delhi or Guwahati. But when he went to Dimapur, she never stayed here. Dimapur is nearby; sahib could easily come home if we called him if memsahib became unwell.' Both nodded at each other to confirm.

When Raj told Amelia what the men said, her eyes were lost in thoughts. 'Your director had an affair with Dorothy. Ask them where they dropped him.'

'Where did you drop him in Dimapur?' Raj asked the driver.

'Hotel Osprey, sir.'

Raj had made up his mind where they would go next as all three got into the jeep. 'Thapa, where is the taxi stand?'

Arjun turned back, surprised. 'Why do we need a taxi?'

'We need to round up the drivers and ask them if one of them ferried the girl to Dimapur. I think they travelled separately. Otherwise, why would Ajay sir stay in a goddamn hotel in Dimapur, which is two hours away from his home? They spent their nights together. The cook and the driver confirmed that Dorothy stayed with the director's wife only when he went on long official tours.'

The taxi stand across the street was an orderly parking area of a dozen black and yellow-painted cabs with a one-room ramshackle house next to it, which housed the booking office. They crossed the road to approach a group of drivers waiting for passengers at the premises' veranda. The men broke their huddle on seeing the trio come as the air buzzed with murmurs of excitement among them; a foreigner girl meant a tourist needing transportation. However, a police officer and ranger accompanying her confused them.

'How is business?' Raj asked.

'Well, we've been sitting here since the morning, as you can see,' one of the drivers said, pointing to the line of cars—Maruti Altos, Wagon R, Innova, and a Toyota Etios.

'Whose is that Toyota Etios?' Raj thought the girl alone would not go by a big car. Ajay sir would not want her to travel in a basic car like Altos. A shorthaired, thin guy with beetle nut-stained red teeth came forward, smiling expectantly. He wore skinny jeans and a tight T-shirt which had a skull wearing earrings.

'Is it for the madam?' He eyed Amelia.

'No, can you come to the side? We need to ask you something.' Raj put an arm around the driver and took him under the shade of a banyan tree next to the office. Arjun and Amelia followed.

Raj asked Amelia to bring up Dorothy's photo on her mobile. 'How many times did you drive this girl to Dimapur?' Raj showed him the picture. The man stared at it. Raj repeated, 'How many times? She works in my department. The police is with us.' Raj pointed to Arjun. 'In fact, she told me that she takes your Etios from here.'

The thin driver was flummoxed, but he regained his composure quickly, a smirk appearing. 'She is our regular customer.' He smiled and shouted to his mates, who stared at them, wondering what was going on. 'Sahibs are asking about the Dimapur one.'

All the drivers broke into laughter as if they shared an open joke.

***

Chapter 22

Day 7 (Afternoon)

'Sir, what is our fault? We just carry passengers. We don't judge,' the taxi driver said.

Arjun waved his hand to stop him. 'It's okay. Tell us where exactly did you drop the girl in Dimapur?'

'Hotel Osprey, it was the usual place for the last two and a half years,' he said in a matter-of-fact way. 'When was the last time...?' He creased his brows, thinking. 'Hey, who took our beauty queen to Dimapur last week?' He moved his head, eyeing the other drivers. 'I had another booking when she came last time. Raju drove her that day. He is not in today.' He turned to Raj, his eyes curious. 'Why are you asking all these questions, sahib? Is madam all right? She is a nice girl. What she does in that place is none of our business.'

'What do you think she did in the hotel?' Raj asked.

'Sir, she earns a paltry amount from her job. She is not like forest officers who work for the timber mafia.' He regarded Raj for a moment. 'No, I am not saying all department people are like him. But the people in this office, that Victor and his cronies, are bastards, very corrupt.' The driver spat out in disgust.

Raj reflected upon the driver's contorted face. He could have been swayed to join one of the rebel outfits of the hill district. He had a lot of vent-up frustrations, but luckily, he chose a decent occupation.

'I am not asking you about the other staff in that office. Tell me about the girl. What did she do in Dimapur?'

The taxi driver took a deep breath. 'Sir, everyone needs money. She indulges in that business.' He raised one of his brows, conveying, 'You know what I mean.'

'Did you see her with her customers? Who did she meet in the hotel? Was it just one man?' Raj asked.

'No sir, we didn't see her with any men. We take her, she pays us, and we come back,' he said with a sigh.

Arjun, glued to his phone, asked, 'What's next?' His face reflected his impatience.

'A quick visit to the forest office for some dates,' Raj said.

'What are you after now?' Arjun sounded piqued.

By the time they reached the place, most of the staff had left. The toothpick man had disappeared. Victor's office was also empty. As expected, the hard-working woman in the accounts section was still bent over her files. Raj gestured to Arjun that he would do it alone.

It did not take much persuasion from Raj's side to obtain the girl's leave dates. He lied, pointing to Arjun standing outside that the police was investigating a taxi driver on the charges of ferrying members of a terrorist gang. The man said that he drove a girl from the forest office on those days. Hence, the dates were needed to corroborate the truth. The sincere lady wrote Dorothy's days of absence on a piece of paper and handed it over to Raj.

Thanking the woman, Raj stepped outside and dialled a number. 'Sir, I need your help.'

'Why? What is it now?' Roy didn't sound enthusiastic. Maybe the hangover was not entirely gone.

'Sir, the matter is a bit confidential. Can we talk now?'

'Yes, go on.' Raj could sense a flicker of excitement.

'You said you maintain a log of Ajay sir's visits to Dimapur. Can you share that with me?'

'Hey, young man, what are you up to?' Roy sounded sceptical, but Raj knew what it would take to make him forthcoming.

'Sir, I am checking on some of our usual suspects. I want to know about our director's dates, the days he comes here for rest and recreation. I want to check if there is any match. One can never be sure who could be hand in glove with him.'

That did the trick.

'I will send you a WhatsApp message. Give me a few minutes.' The phone disconnected.

Raj went back to the car. Amelia fiddled with her mobile

phone while Arjun paced around the vehicle, tapping his fingers. A yawning Thapa waited for the next order.

'Can we go to Dimapur? I want to go and check the hotel,' Raj said.

'Your director and the girl had an affair. Why do we need to go to the room where they slept?' Arjun gave a weary sigh.

'It's only two hours from here. Let's go there and close the loop,' Raj said, while Arjun's expression said he had other plans.

'I will go to the local police station. Need to check with them if anybody lodged any missing report,' Arjun said, checking the messages on his phone. 'Let's drop the Dimapur plan. You won't find anything new.'

Raj regarded his friend's sceptical eyes. Amelia was out of earshot. 'Ajay sir slept with the dead girl.'

'So what?' Arjun hid his irritation. 'We are losing precious time.' He shook his head and signalled Thapa to start the jeep. 'I will drop you at the taxi stand. You take the same car she took to Dimapur—the Toyota Etios!' Arjun forced a smile.

Soon, the Toyota Etios slid downhill, rattling over the pothole-ridden road. The driver swayed his head in sync to some Rihanna hits, blaring out of the audio system. Everything must be so alien to Amelia, Raj thought. What had she got herself embroiled into? He stole a glance at Amelia who was lost in deep thought, the shafts of afternoon light coming through the window painting an orange halo on her face.

'What would have those thugs done if the police had failed to spot the car?' Raj was brought to the present, least expecting the silence to be broken with such a question.

He paused for a while, wondering how to put it. 'Somebody from the park didn't want you to come here.'

'Why? I just came to hand over the raincoats,' Amelia said.

'Maybe in the process, you picked up some information that you should not have.'

'You mean something from Dorothy? But she didn't say anything. We didn't talk.' Her voice broke as if she sensed a betrayal.

'Well, that someone does not know that she didn't share those secrets with you.'

'Who do you think is that someone?' Amelia asked with some trepidation.

A sigh escaped Raj; Dev's face floated in front of his eyes. Dorothy was one of his thousand-plus Facebook friends. What secret would she know about him? Or could it be a case of unrequited love? Ajay sir's face, his hand clasping his chin, came to his mind this time.

'Perhaps, the girl loved Ajay sir, but he was not willing to accept her. Maybe she felt he was exploiting her. Or maybe he stumbled on the knowledge that you knew her, and that she might have divulged his extramarital affair to you. If you came forth and shared this with Dev, it could have disastrous consequences for the director. So maybe he didn't want you to come here.'

'What would Dev do with that information?'

'He is politically connected. Didn't you see how he had our stupid minister under his spell? All our department people are afraid of him, especially the IFS officers from outside the state.'

'Your director didn't seem that perturbed seeing me.'

'He is a calm and composed man. These guys are selected for the forest service through India's toughest exam. He is a post-graduate from one of the top colleges in Delhi. They are brilliant people. They can hide their emotions well. He is so efficient at work that you would hardly believe that he has an invalid wife to take care of. How well he has hidden his affair with Dorothy!'

A stench filled the inside of the car as they entered a dusty, crowded town area with people milling around the narrow roads. It was a sudden change from the quiet and serene hilly terrain.

'Sir, Hotel Osprey,' the driver said as they stopped in front of a gaudy, multi-storied building with a manicured lawn and a poorly crafted fountain. Bird droppings on its surface indicated that it had not seen water for some time. The place seemed to be one of the high-end accommodations in the small town, which revealed itself as a haphazard mosaic of dilapidated buildings, small roadside stalls, and a few new building constructions underway.

Both walked into the lobby's reception along the tiled path lined by garden lamps. A gaunt man sat behind a counter made of varnished bamboo, looking bored. A shelf behind the man displayed brochures of a tourism festival, featuring local girls in red and black and some travel magazines. His disinterested demeanour changed into a hospitable one on seeing a foreign tourist with an Indian man.

Before Raj could say anything, the manager said, 'Only one deluxe AC room left. You are lucky, sir.'

'Well, we are not looking for a room. We wanted to ask you some questions about one of your guests.'

'We don't give away information about our visitors.' He busied himself to read some papers.

'I am from the forest department. Your state police asked me to come and talk to you.' Another lie!

The man raised his head up, his gaze softened. 'Yes, what do you want to know?'

Raj first showed him Dorothy's picture from Amelia's phone, then the director's photo from his. The manager did not make any utterances, biting his lips as his eyes almost closed, but Raj guessed that he recognised both the faces.

'The man is a forest officer from Delhi. The girl is a local girl. We are investigating the involvement of officials in wildlife product smuggling. Have you seen them in your hotel?'

'I can go off the record and say that the man has been a regular guest for the last two and a half years. Don't ask me his name. You should know about the breach of confidentiality. The girl comes here after the man arrives and then stays with him the entire day or night. She leaves after giving her services, and then he goes after clearing his room bill. Should we be bothered about them?' He asked Raj.

'No, of course not! As far as you are concerned, he is a guest, and she is his visitor.'

'A deluxe room for you?' The man smiled.

'No, no, we are going back. Can you tell me one last thing? Were they in your hotel on the seventh of January?'

The manager grimaced. 'I told you whatever I could without looking at my register. That should be good enough. Take my card; you may need it to book a room for your next visit.' He forced a smile, eyeing them together as lost business and wasted time.

Raj scribbled his number on a piece of paper and handed it over to the manager. 'If you remember anything about them, please send me a message or call me.' Raj regarded the elderly man with taut features, a proud Naga man doing his job sincerely. 'Next time I come to Dimapur, I will stay at your place.' Raj smiled at the man.

'Wait, there is one more thing.' The man's face contorted in recollection. 'That girl, I think, accompanied other men also. I think she is...' The manager left unsaid what he had in mind, but the grimace on his face said it.

Soon, the Etios meandered its way out of the congested town.

Amelia took a deep sigh. 'It complicates the matter, doesn't it?'

'No, it does not,' Raj said to himself. His breathing quickened, and the feeling of relief that it was not Ajay sir, was short-lived. Arjun's frustration rang in his ears, 'We are losing precious time'.

Raj shivered, knowing that the warrior would strike any time now, and he didn't have any proof to pin him down. He would fight it alone. Amelia was not safe if she hung around. He took a deep breath to suppress the soaring restlessness. She will stay at my place as long as she is here.

★★★

Chapter 23

Day 7 (Night)

A shroud of darkness with specks of millions of twinkling fireflies buried the place when they arrived. 'You can stay at my house tonight,' Raj said, not daring to look at her. He could not see her reaction, but he sensed a hot flush on his face. Before she could reply, he continued, 'We will visit Arjun's place first, we need to brief our friend.' His breathing quickened. He wanted to take a detour before taking her to his quarters if she was okay with it.

'Can't we do that tomorrow?' Amelia said, her voice heavy with sleep.

This means she is fine with staying at my place. Raj's heart skipped multiple beats.

'No, it is important we see him now.' Raj kept the waver of excitement out of his voice. 'I want to see if he got any other leads.' Despite being in the car for the entire day, he found a new freshness.

Lost in thoughts, Raj did not realise when they reached the police station. A bored-looking sentry manning the guard post reinforced with sandbags gave them a cursory glance as Raj went past. Arjun was talking to someone on the phone, his expression glum. He raised his palm to ask Raj to wait outside. His voice was barely audible, and he hung up after some time.

'Come inside. Want to have some tea?' Arjun asked. He did not show any signs of irritation at the arrival of the unbidden guests. He shouted to the office boy to bring three teas without waiting for the answer.

'Sorry, I had to abandon you guys.' Arjun switched to English, acknowledging Amelia's presence. He then turned to Raj, his hand resting on his chin. 'The girl has a brother who lodged a report about his sister missing for a week. Don't quote me on this, but your boss, Ajay Mathur's name, is on the list. It's obvious. His name had to come up; I am not surprised. He also named a few more people—a forest officer called Victor,' Arjun said. 'The man thinks many people pursued Dorothy. He said one of her admirers gave her a Scooty.'

Raj kept staring at Arjun.

'No, he did not mention our friend,' Arjun said. 'No, not yet.' He let out a sigh. 'What did you guys find?'

'We showed the manager the photos of the director and the girl. He confirmed both to be regular guests at the place,' Raj said. 'He also said that she used to go to the hotel with other men too.'

Arjun's tired eyes gleamed with interest. 'I'm sure she had a string of men she was involved with. One of her lovers might have made her pregnant, and that person wanted her out of his way. Or maybe she came to know some secrets of one of her boyfriends, and the disgruntled person may have turned against her. The post-mortem revealed her pregnancy.'

'How did she die?'

'The body was in the water for many hours. The report is inconclusive.' Arjun bit his lower lip, lost in checking some messages.

Raj regarded Arjun as he fiddled with his phone. Having known the policeman for long, Raj knew that his unemotional mannerism was a charade to hide what went on in his mind. The cold stare of the policeman's eyes said that he was much more involved in the case than he showed.

Raj took a deep breath. 'Did Ajay sir make the girl pregnant?' He asked, eyeing Arjun for his reaction. 'He is a family man. His wife comes from an army background. They must have many connections with bureaucrats in Delhi. He couldn't afford the girl wrecking his marriage. Just imagine the scandal. A North Indian IFS officer having an extramarital affair with a local tribal girl.'

Arjun moved his head forward over the table. His eyes seemed carefree as if urging Raj to continue.

'This is where I got stuck. Will Ajay sir go all the way to kill her to hide the affair? Would he jeopardise his entire life and career?'

'So, is it someone other than your Ajay sir who had a

relationship with that girl, a relationship that had gone sour?' Arjun probed, creases on his forehead reflecting his thoughts, his eyes gleaming in anger.

A pair of bright, sparkling eyes behind the rimless glasses flashed in front of Raj. Amelia was outside the cabin, freshening up in the washroom. 'It's him, isn't it?' Raj let out a huge sigh. 'Bastard!'

Arjun kept on staring at him as if challenging him to utter the D-word.

Raj hit the table with his fist. 'He could have eliminated the girl in her hometown. Why bring her here and kill her in the camp where I stayed? Why drag me in?' Raj's voice rose.

'It is easy to put the blame on you. Of the four range officers of the park, you are the only bachelor—handsome and debonair. And maybe you are giving him some grief.' Arjun smiled, or was it a smirk. 'The murderer had instigated the villagers so that they would find you with the dead girl.' Arjun took a long sip of the masala tea.

'So, what now?' Raj took a deep breath. It was a weird feeling of conviction as well as helplessness. Dev killed Dorothy. Dev went after Amelia. Yet, what could they do about it? They did not have any proof against the living legend.

'Do you remember that *Times of India* journalist case?' Arjun asked.

Raj remembered the curious incident of disappearance without a trace of a media person a couple of years ago. The man wrote stories exposing pangolin trafficking. He stayed in Dev's resort, and one night, he just vanished into thin air.

The police and the authorities blamed the shadowy network of wildlife traffickers, and they stopped the investigation after some time. Pangolin smugglers did not evoke the same intense emotion as the rhino poachers.

'Yes, it was a strange case. Nobody asked anything about it even though he came from a reputed media house.' Raj shivered, thinking about the intrusion into Amelia's room. 'So, you believe that night he was after Amelia?'

'Yes.' It was an emphatic nod from Arjun. 'My man saw a few people leaving the resort in a van just after the incident. I think Dev had placed them there so that they could ferry her, or her body away and make her disappear without a trace. He will try again. Very soon.' Arjun moved his head forward, and his eyes bored into Raj. 'We are running out of time.' Arjun paused, bringing his chin to his clasped hands. 'It's too late now. He is going to strike at any time. And then I have no idea how your Ajay sir will take this; after all you are probing into his affair. He does not know that the girl is dead.'

'He would have come to know that I enquired about Dorothy,' Raj said, taking a sip of the hot tea. 'The ACF of the hill forest division used to work with him.'

'Dev also would somehow make sure that your director comes to know about your probing into his affair.' Arjun shook his head, eyes lost in thought. 'And then these two back-to-back tiger cases.' He leaned back on his chair, taking a deep breath. 'I don't have a good feeling about the poaching incidents and the minister's visit. The minister will want to show some action on the ground.'Arjun's eyes said, 'He has got you, man; your end is near'.

Raj did not say anything. The faces of his old mother and unmarried sister flashed in front of him. How they had cried in happiness when he landed the forest department job without paying any politicians or middlemen. 'Now that Raj has got into government service, that too in such a lucrative branch, all your worries will vanish.' Some relatives alluded to the family's windfall; landing a ranger's post in the state was a road to instant prosperity through socially accepted unscrupulous means.

Amelia joined them. Raj turned to her. 'You must leave tomorrow.'

Amelia's brows creased.

'Amelia,' Raj almost pleaded, 'this place is not safe for you. Once in Kolkata, and the second time in your room, someone wants to kill you. We are up against...,' he choked with the emotions overwhelming him, that of her imminent departure and the circumstances of it.

Arjun lifted his bulky frame and glanced at Amelia and Raj. 'No, tomorrow it will not be possible. The Farmers Union has called for a state-wide strike. All the student associations and opposition parties are supporting it.'

Amelia looked puzzled. Raj shook his head in despair. What will happen to this place with all these strikes, bandhs! 'A protest is planned tomorrow. The protesters will not allow vehicles to ply on the roads,' Raj explained, his breathing heavy. 'Can we arrange to take her to the airport under police escort?'

'No, my men will be busy handling the sensitive spots.

For non-essential travel, we won't get permission. One extra day won't hurt; I hope it is all right with you,' Arjun said, his clasped hands against his chin. 'You people better get going. It has been a long day for you all. Go and grab some sleep.'

As Raj and Amelia left Arjun's office, Arjun called out to Raj. 'She is staying at your place.'

Raj expected to see a naughty smile in Arjun when he turned back. No, instead, there was a never seen before sternness on the tired police officer's face.

Soon, they were in the Etios driving to Raj's quarter. The inside of the car was cold. Raj inched towards Amelia, unconsciously. Amelia moved slightly closer till their bodies touched. Raj gasped as their hands met. He gave her hand a soft squeeze; he loved the warmth and softness of her hand. She leaned back and closed her eyes.

Amelia took a long breath on reaching Raj's place, stretching her arms. In a white and blue floral kurta and churidar with a stole around her neck, she dazzled like a star in the dark campus of the range office. She displayed no trace of exhaustion. Once inside, Raj took Amelia to the guestroom. 'I am not going anywhere tomorrow,' she said, cupping a yawn with her hands.

Raj's heart sang as he smiled. His quarter felt like home, warm, cosy, and complete. 'I hope you are happy with your room.'

'It's beautiful. I quite like it. I wish I had stayed here at your place. Dev's place was creepy, especially with the door on the partitioning wall.' She made a face in mock horror.

Raj wondered how he would sleep that night, knowing she was in the next room. What would be her reaction if he crept into her room to snuggle up beside her? He shivered as shameless excitement ran through his entire body. And then he visualised the media scoundrels with their microphones shouting at the top of their voices, 'Breaking news, the Kaziranga ranger molests Australian tourist in his official residence,' with all the lurid concocted tales of how the corrupt officer lured the innocent girl to his quarter. He shuddered at the thought.

'Amelia, you've had a tiring day. I think you should retire,' Raj said hastily. 'Goodnight.'

'Goodnight,' Amelia said.

Raj sensed a tinge of disappointment in her voice, or did he just imagine it as he retreated to his room. His mind reminisced the events of the day, and his heart longed for the girl in the guest room as he headed to the bathroom to have a warm bath. Raj realised they had been together for more than sixteen hours and, most of the time, inside a car.

After a long shower, he slid his exhausted body under the warmth of a blanket, hoping for a blissful snooze. A distant booming sound floated to the room. A realisation dawned that he would have to forego sleep for the night.

★★★

Chapter 24

Day 8 (Morning)

Stars paled out with the dawning of the sun. Amelia stood in the veranda, hugging her arms across her chest to stave off the early morning chill. Her lustrous hair covered half her back. The dawn chorus of the birds of the surrounding forests drowned the fog-shrouded sleepy campus.

'It's so peaceful here. I love listening to the beautiful birdsong in the morning.'

'Yes, we are at the edge of the park. We always hear birdsong as there are many bird species around this place,' Raj said. 'There is one sound we commonly hear which we don't like, though.'

Amelia regarded him with her sleepy blue eyes, confused.

'Gunshots.'

Raj shuddered, thinking about the sensational journalism that would soon unfold: a massive bull shot dead within a few hundred metres of a clueless ranger's office, the same ranger who seemed to be in league with the tiger poachers. All in just one week. Two tigers and a rhino broke all previous records, especially for a park that was in perennial war with the killers. During his childhood, he had heard of the famous story of the entire rhino population of a nearby sanctuary decimated in one year. But that was a different time; this was 2023. He had everything at his disposal—upgraded weaponry of semi-automatic weapons, active network of informers, supportive seniors, proactive police support—all except what he needed most: luck.

Raj and his guards reached the spot in fifteen minutes of hearing the gunshot; the perpetrators had fled, leaving the horn intact. While his men mobilised the logistics, the only question Raj kept on asking was why did they kill the rhino in such close vicinity of the range office, knowing that armed guards would reach them within minutes, giving them no time to hack off their prize.

It was obvious that the killer did not want the rhino's horn. The tigers were also not poisoned for their skins. He smiled grimly at himself. Was it the end of his career? The new director, who was just beginning to trust him, would he be able to shield him? Or would he now really want to protect him, given the way he had been poking his nose in his boss's affairs?

'Gunshots, when?' Amelia asked.

Amelia's question brought him to the present. 'Just after midnight. We lost one more rhino last night, the first one in my range after six months.'

'You mean to say you were out in the forest while I slept?'

'A routine part of a ranger's job is not moving around in a Toyota with a beautiful girl,' he said with a smile, thinking of the massive bull lying lifeless a few hundred metres from where they were. After finishing the formalities with the poached rhino, Raj and Amelia headed towards Roy's place. Roy, who was the director-in-charge in Ajay Mathur's absence, fanned himself with a newspaper. 'I had to do a TV interview. The bastards kept asking me the same thing, how had the poachers managed to make a kill so near the range office.' He moved his brows to point to Amelia, waiting outside. 'When is she going back?' A sudden pang of defensiveness rushed through Raj. Was he alluding that she was partly responsible for the poaching as the ranger was too occupied in showing her around?

'Actually, she was supposed to go today. She is stuck here because of the strike. I think she will go in a day or two.'

'In a day or two? Send her back as soon as possible, man. Can you imagine the headlines? The forest officer is busy frolicking with a lady tourist while a rhino is shot dead near his office. Does it sound like good publicity to you?'

'Sir, what can I do if she doesn't want to go? We can't force her to leave. She donated a hundred fifty raincoats to the department.'

'So? Does it mean that she gets a departmental ranger as her escort 24/7?' Roy's frown was fiercer than his mood. He paused, shook his head as if to ward off what they had just discussed and a mischievous smile seeped through his lips. He came near Raj and almost whispered, 'Why did you want the director's travel details?' He moved his brows in rapid succession, looking into Raj's eyes for any reactions. 'Recreation?' A sly smile came. 'Tell me why you were after the dates.'

'Sir, I've found whom he meets at Dimapur. The girl works in the hill division office. He used to meet her regularly in a hotel. After he shifted to Kaziranga, the practice continued even though it entailed a four-hour drive. The girl, his girlfriend, is still in that town,' Raj said hesitantly.

Should I say that I found the girl's dead body in the camp? No, not yet.

'Why are you doing all this sleuthing, going from one place to another? Just go where it matters!' Roy said with an all-knowing attitude.

'Where, sir?'

'Go to the director's residence now,' he snapped.

'But he is not in!' Raj was confused.

'That's more the reason you go to the wife now. She is a nervous wreck and will tell you everything.'

Meeting the wife while the director is away? Is he joking? What is on his mind?

Soon afterwards, they walked towards the veranda of the forlorn-looking two-storied house. Never in his wildest dream had Raj thought that he would be going to the director's bungalow to ask his wife about her husband's extramarital affairs. 'You will take the lead,' Raj said to Amelia, who smiled, looking into his eyes as he rang the bell. A servant came out to open the door. His expression could be described as if he had seen a ghost in broad daylight.

Is he the Nepali cook Daju told me about? Now, have I seen this guy before?

'Is madam home? Tell her that someone from Australia wants to meet her,' Raj said. The short man with darting eyes reluctantly ushered them in and urged them to take a seat. The lounge room with a fireplace had the walls covered with souvenirs and memorabilia that Ajay sir had collected from various places of his postings—cane works, pictures on bamboo mats, tribal shawls and spears. A framed photo of the director and his newlywed bride posing in front of the Taj Mahal adorned the wall. Amelia gazed wonderstruck around the place; it seemed like a museum to her.

'Hi, I am Asha.' A melodious voice rang through the hall, making them turn towards the door. The director's wife stood there with a smile on her face, hands folded in greeting. In her late thirties or early forties, she had long black hair, a red bindi on her chiselled face; she had hazel eyes—a rarity among Indians.

'Hello, you are from Australia? Ajay told me about you. He said you had donated raincoats for our guards.'

Raj, awestruck by the woman's sweet and thoughtful articulation, her convent-educated English accent, and her stunning looks, wondered what a contrasting vision he had of the woman being a sick and bed-ridden person!

'Sorry, I didn't get your name. I have seen you around.'

'I am Raj, madam,' he said, fumbling with his introduction. 'I am the ranger, I'm the officer for the eastern range.'

'It is where we had the poaching incident last night.' Raj nodded sheepishly. 'So, what brings you all here? You know Ajay is not in town. By the way, Ajay speaks quite highly of you.'

Raj wanted to kick himself for listening to Roy.

'I am going back to Australia soon. I am aware your husband is not here but I want to convey my gratitude to him through you for his hospitality.' Amelia came to his rescue. 'Also, if it is alright with you, for my blog, I would like to interview you as the partner of a forest officer who spent his working years in such remote locations to protect wildlife.'

'Would you two have lunch with me?' the wife asked. Before Raj could refuse or come up with an excuse, she said, 'Please, I feel lonely during the day. Ajay is hardly home.' Her eyes pleaded with them.

Amelia seemed fine with the request. 'Okay, madam.' Raj agreed.

Asha went inside to give instructions to the cooks and servants. How can someone with such a beautiful and gracious partner, cheat? Raj thought.

'Are you going to interview her?'

'I will have to. You looked shit scared in front of your boss's wife.'

'Hush! I didn't expect her to be so elegant,' Raj said, thinking about the shriek that night.

'Ajay called. He is not sure if he can come today as the

strike is total in Upper Assam. I didn't tell him that you both are here.' Asha came out from the inner room, smiling. 'It's okay, isn't it?'

Smart lady! Raj felt like a fool. She sat on a chair facing Raj and Amelia. 'Fire on, what did you want to ask?'

Amelia stared at her with a blank face. 'The interview!' She said like an excited schoolgirl. Her pearl-white teeth dazzled as she flashed a broad smile. 'Your husband worked in so many remote locations. Have you been with him throughout? What did you do in those places? You are someone from the city,' Amelia said.

'Yes, I was a city-bred girl, a hard-core Delhiite. Then I met him.' She stopped for a while before continuing, 'Fell in love.' She looked lost.

'Was director sahib your classmate?' Raj joined in to break the awkward silence.

'Wow, you are interviewing me too! How sweet!' She broke into a giggle.

'What the hell?' Raj cursed himself.

'What happened then? Did you both marry before he started working in this department?' Amelia took over.

'Oh, no. I cleared the civil services and got into central services group A; he didn't. He passed the Indian Forest Service instead. He got into the Assam cadre, and I sacrificed my career to be with him because we married just after his results came out.'

Raj wanted to ask about the director's posting locations; he refrained, fearing another jibe, another giggle.

'And then?' Amelia asked, keeping her phone on, recording the conversation; it seemed like an actual interview.

'Five places in the last seventeen years—each wilder and more desolate than the other. I don't like it here though. This place is Ajay's most prestigious posting. But I feel lonely.' She stopped; a sudden veil of sorrow descended on her beautiful face. 'This bungalow is too big for the two of us. However, Ajay likes it here.'

Raj hoped that would provide Amelia with a segue to ask the 'question'.

'Which place did you like the most?'

'The hill division posting! It was a small town no doubt, but the friends you make there, make the place special.'

Before she could say anything more, the Nepali cook came to inform them that lunch had been served. 'Madam, sahib called to remind you about your medicine time,' the man said, his voice caring towards her but eyes untrusting the visitors. He didn't have a kind face like Daju. There was something different about how he regarded them, a steely hard look.

'I will join you both after I take my medicine.' She smiled and gestured for them to proceed to the dining room.

The servant seated Raj and Amelia in their places while his madam went upstairs. After a few minutes of awkward silence, while they sat waiting at the table with various mouth-watering dishes in front of them, her laboured footsteps echoed along the long, narrow stairs as she came down. Her charming self was lost; a fatigued woman with an irritated demeanour stood before them.

Raj felt a lurch in his stomach as he realised that she must be coming down from her bedroom, the same room from where the shriek had emanated that night.

Asha madam started eating, ignoring the presence of her guests. Raj and Amelia had no option but to eat that sumptuous spread awkwardly. They finished eating without talking until Amelia broke the tense silence by thanking her host for a beautiful lunch, but was met with a silent, cold stare.

As they walked on the paved pathway through the lawn towards the gate, Asha madam called them from behind, 'Excuse me, can you both come back for a moment?' She stood near the wire mesh door on the veranda, holding a piece of paper.

When they reached her, she showed them a photograph of a group of people having fun in a stream. Some people were wading in the water; some sat on rocks spread among the foamy river.

'This is a photo of the forest staff picnic while Ajay worked in the hill division.' She placed her finger on a few faces. 'Can you see him? He had lots of hair one year ago. I am in the water. Wow, it was freezing cold!' Suddenly, she seemed to have come back to the same woman who had greeted them. 'Do you see this girl?'

Raj and Amelia's eyes hovered over Dorothy's smiling face.

★★★

Chapter 25

Day 8 (Afternoon)

The coolness of the January afternoon notwithstanding, when Raj came out of the director's bungalow campus, tiny beads of sweat had formed on his forehead. Asha madam's unexpected query kept ringing in his head.

'She was my good friend in that place. One of the nicest souls I have ever met. Did you want to ask about her?'

'What do you think of her?' Raj asked Amelia as they both got into Raj's SUV.

'Obviously, she has got mental health issues. However, she is a smart woman.'

Asha madam's teary eyes burning with some anguish, or was it hatred or jealousy, flashed in Raj's mind. 'She is beautiful, isn't she?' Her face was all contorted like an angry child when she said, 'I used to like Dorothy a lot. But not anymore.' Raj shivered, thinking of the look she gave as she slammed shut the door. Was it nasty or that of sheer despondency? He let out a long sigh, a frown creasing his forehead as he floored the accelerator, his heart hammering in his chest.

'Where are we going now?' Amelia asked.

'We are going to Roy sir's place. I want to update him on our visit.' 'Bastard!' Raj murmured under his breath. 'He never let it be known that Asha madam is such a smart lady. If you had not come up with that interview idea, we would have been fully exposed.'

Amelia smiled. 'Well, I run a blog site where I put the interviews of the partners of the individuals who make their mark in society. Players, professionals, bankers, firefighters, and health workers—I have done it all. This is the first time I met a forester's wife.' She paused, her dreamy eyes lost in some thought. 'They do lead difficult lives, the foresters. It takes a toll on the family members.' Then she broke into a smile; her beguiling, oyster-white teeth lit up the space between them. Asha madam's anguished face vanished from his mind as he felt a jolt of electric current. 'Sorry, I won't be able to feature you though. You don't have a partner.'

Raj was at a loss of words, what could he say! After giving her a vague smile in return, he turned his attention on the road, wanting to just drive on with her as his companion. But he slammed the brakes and got down from the car as they reached Roy's place, a stone's throw from the bungalow.

Roy sat on his cushioned chair, browsing through some papers. 'Come on in,' he said as he saw the duo standing near the door. 'The minister called. He must have lambasted the director, too. I am sure he will force him to do something. I don't feel good about this,' he said with a sombre face. However, a bright smile spread on his face as he asked, 'So, what did you manage to fish out from our director's wife?' Before Raj could say anything. 'She is beautiful, isn't she?' He cast a furtive glance towards Amelia, hoping she would not understand a word.

Language is not a barrier to figure out rascals like you, Raj felt like saying. 'Sir, you should have warned us. I expected a sickly woman. You had always referred to her as a vegetable.'

Roy burst into laughter. 'You have remained a bachelor too long. You don't realise what our director sahib has been going through all these years.'

'I was extremely nervous meeting Asha madam. She asked me about last night's poaching incident.' Raj wanted to change the topic.

'Bah, so you picked her name also.' The look on Roy's face was of sarcasm or amusement; Raj was not sure. Roy beamed a broad smile, his hands folded behind his neck. 'Well, I didn't tell you in advance because I wanted you to be surprised. Despite having such a beautiful and intelligent wife, he is sneakily having these dirty liaisons.'

The smile changed to a sneer. He waited for some time, shaking his head slowly, a grin appearing again. 'Do you want to know more? There are still some pieces of the jigsaw missing. They may fall in place if you talk to her sister.'

'Asha madam's sister?'

'Yes, her sister,' Roy said, thumping his desk. 'Do you guys want some tea or snacks? No? You might have had a heavy lunch.' He then turned to Amelia, a smile plastering his lips. 'Would you please come to my place for a simple dinner tonight? It won't be as grand an affair as the director bungalow's lunch.'

Raj was not sure whether he was sarcastic or serious; the smile seemed fake though he had seen the man grin like that before. He hoped Amelia would turn down the invitation; instead, she gazed at Raj for guidance.

'Both my children are at home. They will be delighted to host you. My daughter wants to go to Australia for higher studies.' Roy smiled again. 'I take that as a yes.' He turned to Raj. 'You too must come, and please be on time. Sharp seven, okay? We can have a drink or two.'

'Sir, what of Asha madam's sister?' Raj did not consider dinner with Roy an attractive proposition.

Roy again pushed himself back and gazed at the ceiling as he philosophised, 'Our director's relatives are in the right places all over India. He is a lucky man—his wife's elder sister is married to a manager in a nearby tea garden. So, when he goes to meet his girlfriend, he takes your Asha madam with him.'

Both Amelia and Raj stared at Roy in bewilderment.

'Till the midway! Yes, he drops his wife at his sister's place, and then he proceeds to Dimapur for some rest and recreation.'

'How do you know all this, sir?' Raj asked.

'He is my boss. I need to arrange for his driver when he goes on those pleasure trips.' Roy made an innocent face.

No way am I going to see the sister. I don't have any business to poke my nose into the messy personal life of my senior.

He remembered Roy's rant a few months ago when the director took charge. 'What will this guy do in the wildlife division? He made a fortune spending his entire lifetime in territorial divisions. I think he gave millions to the minister. Now, he is getting a plum posting to get some publicity, and after that, it will be on deputation in Delhi.

'He has become head of our park because he is an IFS officer. He does not have an iota of interest in wildlife protection. This role is to earn the goodwill of the people and his political bosses. People of the state are oblivious. A rhino is poached, and they remove a good director. After some hue and cry, they bring these people from nowhere. The public is happy. The park gets a new man. Do they bother to check if the new man is suitable for the job?'

'They have issues between them. I don't want to get involved,' Raj wanted to say to Amelia, but he said it to himself.

Amelia's eyes narrowed, but they gleamed with interest. 'They don't like each other, do they?' Raj shook his head; departmental politics, egos, professional rivalries, the list would go on as his mind drifted to that night. Was there a small bump beneath her T-shirt? A new young life within that beautiful body?

'Do you think we will get any leads talking to Asha

madam's sister?' Raj's breathing quickened as he settled on the driver's seat, his hand about to turn on the ignition, mulling over the words of Roy, who seemed hell-bent on ruining the director's reputation. He wanted to be sure that Ajay sir was not behind the girl's murder; at least they had some common agenda.

Amelia's brows were creased. 'If you went to the sister, why would she entertain you? That too if you ask personal stuff about her brother-in-law?'

Raj was not sure. 'So, you suggest we should not get into this business.'

Amelia bit her lips. Raj turned away; the wetness of the strawberry redness was too much of a hindrance for the rational thinking needed at that time.

'Let's go there. However, let's take Arjun,' Amelia said. 'See, the brother named your Ajay sir as one of the suspects. Arjun has the right to do some investigation. He is in the police, and you are in the forest department.'

Raj regarded Amelia; he shook his head incredulously. How quickly she had grasped the departments' dynamics in the country's bureaucratic mess! Raj got down from his car and headed again to Roy's place. Roy scribbled something on a piece of paper and handed it to Raj. 'This is the sister's address, an hour's drive from here. You have a couple of hours in your hands. You can visit the sister now itself, and who knows what crucial details you may uncover.'

'Thank you, sir. It all depends on whether Arjun is free or willing to go. We can't force him,' Raj said.

'Good that you are taking Arjun with you.' Roy came near Raj, touching his shoulder. 'You should involve him. I think he will go. For this mission, he would be useful. Nevertheless, for God's sake, don't bring him along when you come to my place.'

Raj nodded, convinced that Arjun's presence would make things easy; he headed towards his SUV to join Amelia. The car smelled of the sweet fragrance of the girl. Raj opened his window, debating about going to the police station or giving Arjun a call.

'Arjun,' Raj called his friend. 'Where are you? Are you available this afternoon for a bit of investigation?'

'Well, I am here in town.'

It was a relief that he was nearby; it saved a precious hour at the least. Raj told him about their visit to Asha madam's place and their plan to go to the sister's place.

'What else would you learn from the sister? We already know that they were in a relationship?' Arjun sounded peeved.

'No, he is not coming,' he whispered to Amelia, who eyed him with interest.

'Has Roy suggested that you go there?' Arjun thundered from the other side. 'I honestly have no clue what he has got against your director. I am surprised that you could even agree to his suggestion. What he does in his personal life is none of your business.'

'Arjun, I think a visit will help us in building a fool-proof case against...'

After talking to Arjun for a while, Raj disconnected the line.

'Is he coming?' Amelia's hair glinted in the afternoon sun.

Raj nodded, but his head reeled under confusion. 'Yes, but he will not be with us for long as he has got his transfer order. He is leaving this place in three days. His replacement takes over next week.'

Raj suddenly realised that he had never felt so helpless before. He closed his eyelids, forcing back the tears that had welled up.

***

Chapter 26

Day 8 (Evening)

They entered an expanse of greenery that was manmade yet tranquil, taking a side turn off the highway. The canopy openings of the shade trees threw open visages of the brilliant blue dotted with many circling swifts. They passed alternately through gardens and settlements with shanty dwellings, dilapidated community buildings, and smiling children.

The villagers herded back cattle home, lush greenery hiding the squalor of the labour lines. Working women in a riot of colours dotted the bushes interspersed with trees with their trunks painted white. They had wicker baskets on their back held by a band across their forehead. Their faces reflected the strain of the long day spent in the bush. Their heads turned towards the vehicle; a police jeep in the garden aroused curiosity.

On entering the bungalow's sprawling campus, Raj felt

apprehensive. He was unsure whether Roy was being helpful or had his personal agenda in the matter. Thapa drove through the manicured garden to the portico of the house. Raj wondered if Asha madam's sister would be as smart and intelligent as her. How would the woman react once she knew why they had come to visit?

He rang the bell, and after some time, a bespectacled, heavily built woman with a slight limp, probably due to arthritis, opened the door. Yawning and seeming visibly annoyed at the intrusion, perhaps because it was time for her late afternoon siesta. She asked them in Hindi, 'Whom do you want to meet? Manager sahib isn't at home.'

'We want to talk to you.' Raj realised that the woman would be none other than the wife, her fluent Hindi confirmed the fact.

'Hello, madam, we have come from the police station. We just want to ask you a few questions,' Arjun intervened.

She stared at the three of them: a uniformed officer, a tall foreigner, and the third one dressed as a civilian—they made an odd combination.

'Come inside,' she said at last. 'Could this not have waited till manager sahib returned?' A strong smell of butter and ghee emanated from the woman. Either she had come straight from the kitchen overseeing the evening meal preparation for her husband, or the odour was ingrained in the folds of her flabby body.

'Actually, it involves your sister, so we thought it would be appropriate to talk directly with you,' Arjun said.

'What has happened to Asha? Is she all right?' She said, her face creased with doubt.

Raj took over. 'Don't you worry, madam, she is all right. It does not concern her.'

'Wait,' the sister said and pointed to Amelia. 'Who is she?'

'She is a student from Australia. She is here to study how the forest department, I mean the police, works in India.' Raj had no other option.

The sister looked convinced. 'Does she understand what we are saying?'

'No, she does not know Hindi. Don't worry about her; we will brief her later,' Arjun said.

'No, it does not work that way. It would be rude. We should speak in English.' Raj's trepidation increased; he hoped that the woman would not turn out to be as bright as her younger sister was.

'Now tell me what happened to Asha. What do you want to know from me? Or should I say what do you want to tell me?' The woman said, her head bobbed sideways, eyeing all three of them.

Raj thought it would be better to be upfront right in the beginning. 'Madam, the matter is slightly sensitive. Your brother-in-law's name cropped up in the disappearance of a local tribal girl.' He knew that highlighting that the girl was a tribal would be helpful. 'So, it is all about you cooperating with us so that we can clear his name.' Raj took a gulp of air, feeling strange as he knew he was acting as an investigator while did not have any authority to do so.

'I will surely cooperate if it helps you find the poor girl. I will help you even if my brother-in-law is involved,' the sister said with conviction. She had the same hazel eyes as her younger sibling, the same long hair with a few grey strands appearing, and the convincing tone of an army man's daughter. The sedentary lifestyle of a manager's wife had taken its toll, and unhealthy layers of fat had robbed her of beauty and poise.

'Madam, how would you describe the relationship between your sister and brother-in-law? Are they happy in their marriage?' Arjun asked.

The woman shook her head as she tried to think about where to start. 'As you might know, Asha is not keeping well. She has mental health issues. So obviously, there is not much happiness in that house. It is just the two of them and Asha's mood swings. So you can well imagine the atmosphere in the house?'

'When did all this begin? Surely, she wasn't like this during the early days of marriage?' Raj asked.

The woman blew heavily through her nose into a handkerchief. 'You should have seen her when she was in college. She was film star material.'

Raj reminisced the morning encounter; he could not agree more.

'Ajay was pretty average.' Snide, in her voice, was evident. 'He came from a conservative *Baniya* family. We are open-minded Punjabis with an army background. His forest service job and posting in remote places ruined their life.'

The woman took off her glasses to reveal her moist eyes.

'She delivered a stillborn baby in a basic hospital. She didn't get proper prenatal advice because of untrained doctors. After this traumatic turn of events, Asha went into depression. For two years since the childbirth, they didn't consult any doctor.' She sounded flustered. 'Ajay immersed himself in work. You couldn't blame him, too. He was patient with her. He did everything possible to make her happy. However, he didn't realise that she needed to see a psychiatrist. We forced them to go to the All India Institute of Medical Sciences in Delhi. That changed everything.' The woman took a deep breath and wiped her eyes with her dupatta.

'What happened in Delhi?' Arjun took a sip of his tea.

'They prescribed her some strong medicines. Either the dosage was wrong, or my sister didn't take them as instructed. Her personality underwent a change. Earlier, she was a docile, withdrawn person. After coming from Delhi, she became schizophrenic. She would be normal and bubbly during the daytime, and by afternoon, her mood would swing. She would become unfriendly, rude, and sometimes dangerous.'

'Dangerous?' Raj said.

'I mean, she could hit you if she didn't like your presence.'

Raj took a deep breath, thankful for his narrow escape.

'She physically assaulted Ajay several times. How much can a man take? Things improved when they shifted to the hill division. She befriended a local girl. Her name was Dorothy, a lovely girl.' The woman stopped, her eyes wide open. 'Wait, are you guys saying that girl is missing?'

Both Arjun and Raj nodded.

'I am not surprised Ajay's name came up. We went to their place a couple of times. We saw that Ajay was enamoured of her.' She paused for a while. 'The girl was stunning, smart and friendly. Ajay created a position for her in his office. On some days, she would be at their residence looking after my sister. I think that is when it began.'

'Their affair?' Arjun added.

'Yes. It had to happen. Sometimes, Asha didn't allow the poor man to even enter his bedroom. She just didn't want him near her. It has been going on for fifteen years now. Ajay started going to Dimapur to be with that girl. Asha was aware of it. He would be out every weekend. It is continuing even now, with Asha accepting the arrangement. They come here, she stays with us, and he goes ahead to Dimapur. Then the girl meets him there. We don't ask. In the last three or four months that they have been posted here, I think he must have made six or seven trips.'

Raj raised his brows, looking at Arjun; he was unsure what else to ask the woman.

'What else could he do? He, too, has his needs.' She eyed Raj, who baulked at her openness. 'He is extremely caring of Asha. Even from Dimapur, he would be checking with us to make sure she took her medication on time.'

'Do you think your brother-in-law would take an extreme step like killing her to prevent these embarrassing details from coming out?' Arjun asked.

'Ajay killing that girl? No way!' The sister was aghast.

'Anyway, what has he got to hide? His relationship with Dorothy is an open secret.'

'What if the girl is pregnant with his child, and she wants some legitimacy?' Arjun raised his brows.

The woman again blew her nose. She shook her head. 'I don't think Ajay would do that.' She paused, taking a deep breath. 'People change. He changed a lot during his posting in that hill district.'

'Madam, one night, I heard a loud shriek from the bungalow. It had to be her as only Ajay sir and your sister were there in the house. Does your brother-in-law get violent towards her?' Raj asked.

The woman shook her head; her eyes were moist. 'It could be my sister's mind playing up. She sees herself in all sorts of situations at night. She shouts, screams, or kicks if Ajay is around.' The woman paused. 'It is a bizarre situation. In this liaison with Dorothy, though Asha accepts the arrangement, a part of her still cries out at her husband's infidelities. And Ajay...' The sister shook her head.

'Yes, do go on , what of Ajay sir?' Raj asked.

A smile seeped through the sister's lips. 'You know, Ajay loves Asha to death; still, he goes to meet the other girl.' The shaking of the head continued at the incredulity of the situation. 'I don't think he will accept that hill girl even if she is pregnant with his child. But he still mourns the death of his only child. He would never harm a pregnant woman. He loves children.'

They cruised back to Roy's place through the tea gardens.

Though the strike was over, the otherwise busy highway did not have a lot of traffic. Raj sat in the back seat with Amelia, who looked lost in deep thought.

The words of Asha madam's sister rang in Raj's mind, 'He would never harm a pregnant woman. He loves children.' His thoughts were shattered by a crashing sound. Arjun hit his fist heavily on the dashboard as a nervous Thapa pushed hard on the accelerator. Arjun turned his head, his face like an angry volcano, eyes bloodshot red.

★★★

Chapter 27

Day 8 (Night)

The long wisp of fog over the highway disseminated a sense of foreboding that failed to lift the spirit of the evening. Raj and Roy huddled around a fireplace in the backyard while servants kept them supplied with various starters and nibbles to go with the drinks. Raj felt as clueless as he did when his grade twelve results came out: What next? His restlessness soared with Roy's blabbering, who poured another drink into Raj's glass against his protestations.

'So, all clear now?' Roy swirled his fifth or sixth peg of whiskey while his corpulent wife glared at him in annoyance from the corner of the house's back door.

Raj wanted to go inside where Amelia was. It was cold outside despite the brazier's smouldering charcoal, and the smooth single-malt whiskey. Amelia seemed to be enjoying her time with the children, both bright and handsome teenagers, so unlike their father. The occasional opening of the door revealed her with the kids, chatting, while a Bollywood movie played on the television.

Roy leaned back on his chair and merrily hummed a tune, an expression of contentment on his face for no apparent reason except the alcohol, the dark shadows of the night accentuating the wrinkles on his face. He slowly shook his head, closing his eyes.

Should I tell him about Dorothy? What would be his reaction? A few drinks make a man loquacious, they act like truth serum.

'Sir, I have a confession to make,' Raj started. 'It is a huge secret—a life and death situation for me.'

'Carry on, what have you got in your mind? Spit it out, man!' Roy said with a slur without opening his eyes.

Raj narrated the dead body incident and ended by saying, 'Please don't utter a word about it to anyone. I will be ruined.'

By the time Raj finished his story, Roy's wide-open eyes were gawking at him. He gulped down the remaining drink in his glass. 'I heard about the mob marching to your camp looking for a missing girl.' He raised his brows. 'I didn't know you found a girl's body. I mean to say the director's girlfriend's body.' He craned his neck; his wife was busy in the kitchen, and Amelia was glued to the movie with the children. 'So, nobody except Arjun knows?'

'No, sir,' Raj nodded.

'And the director?' Roy wanted to be sure.

'Arjun told me not to tell anyone,' Raj said. 'Sir, now

Arjun is being transferred.' He could not keep the waver out of his voice.

'You are fortunate. A bachelor forest officer is surrounded by hostile villagers, and a dead girl is found in his bedroom! What audacity! Do you think I would've believed you to be innocent? To top it all, it happened in that place, village number eight, I don't like that area. Something fishy is going on there.' Roy's voice rose in the excitement. He came near Raj, his face resembled that of a confused child. 'But who killed the girl? And this sudden removal of your police friend?'

'Papa, is everything all right? You promised not to drink more than two pegs.' The daughter popped her head out of the door.

Roy's eyes smouldered red like the burning charcoal, and both his palms spread around the fire. 'Raj.' His eyes gleamed with what seemed like genuine concern. 'You are targeted in a big way. The girl, two tigers, rhino, Arjun's transfer; they are all linked.' He took a noisy gulp from his glass. 'But I am not sure how the Australian girl comes into the picture. Who tried to kidnap her? Why?'

Roy's breathing grew rapid. 'You are on the wrong track, going after the director's extramarital affairs.'

'Go on, sir,' Raj murmured. 'You had nothing to do with it by sending me to all those places?'

'Someone with a lot of connections, who knows this place like the back of his hand is behind all these,' Roy concluded, his breathing heavy.

A profound feeling of disquiet swept through Raj's head.

Again, that face flashed in front of his eyes. He couldn't hold it any longer. 'Sir, is it Dev?'

Roy let go a long sigh as he regarded Raj with a guarded stoicism. Even with an alcohol-fuelled brain, he held back his response. Nobody would easily dare to raise a finger at the region's most vocal NGO chief. Not even this maverick man. Raj thought of his association with Dev. He had known the activist for the last four years, yet he remained an enigma. The man was passionate about rhino conservation. Kaziranga National Park stayed in his mind day in and out. Some, like Roy and Arjun, always pointed out that the modest tin-roofed house of Rhino Warriors acted as a façade while the upmarket resort continued to be his primary workplace and home. He came from one of the wealthiest tea planter families in the region, whereas his recruits for campaigns were the farmers and the villagers.

Raj wondered about the blatant partisanship he saw when all hell would break loose if a rhino were poached, but there would be sheer nonchalance towards other wildlife offences. He remembered the pangolin haul incident. The forest department apprehended a man with a dozen live pangolins. Raj informed Dev about the seizure; he did not even bother to bat an eyelid. Leopards had been killed, bears had been snared, but those things never interested the warrior.

Two recent tiger poaching incidents took place and the carcasses were thrown at the ranger's doorstep, however, the region's most passionate wildlife conservationist did not ask for a single detail.

'If it is him, you, I mean, we are up against the...' Roy stopped with a snort, bringing Raj back to the present.

'Sir, this latest killing of the bull rhino, I think it is his doing. A poached rhino gives him all the licence to shake the earth.'

'He killed it near your place not for the rhino's horn, but for your head,' Roy said, biting his lower lip, his eyes bloodshot red.

Raj wanted to go home. 'Sir, I think I will skip dinner. You should go and eat. I think your children are hungry. It must be quite late for them. Madam is also tired after all the cooking.'

Roy sneered, but refrained from passing comment. Instead, he bent towards Raj and touched him on the shoulder, 'Are you sure you don't have any plan with her tonight? Is that why you are so keen to go back? I am advising you; don't be adventurous. The timing is not right. She is a nice girl, though.' His characteristic wink followed.

'Come on, sir, how can you say such things?' Raj looked at his watch. It was ten, so much for the early dinner.

They reached the quarters quite late, and both went to their respective rooms. Raj, drunk and exhausted, but unable to sleep, tossed and turned on his bed. A loud knock on the door irritated him. He rushed before the person knocked again, lest it disturbed his guest.

'What is it?' His annoyance unnerved the visitor, Vijay stood with an apologetic face.

'Sorry to bother you, sir. Director sahib asked me to give you this.'

'Is he back?'

'Yes, he arrived this evening.'

This means that when we interrogated his sister-in-law, he was back in town despite the strike.

He took the letter, wondering about the urgency, that it couldn't wait until tomorrow. It said urgent and confidential. However much he wanted to flick it on the dining table to open the next morning, he could not do it. He opened the envelope, his fingers trembling. The heading read suspension order.

'Suspended with immediate effect for dereliction of duty.'

Raj read and reread the letter, his mind fogged up, devoid of any emotions. Ajay Mathur had signed the letter. He slumped on the sofa and fanned himself with the envelope despite the cold. The guest room door cracked open. Amelia walked in, wearing a white nighty.

'You are still awake?' Raj quickly looked away. It was too transparent, too short.

'I heard a loud knocking on the door. Who was it?' Her soft voice sounded so pure and sweet.

'My deputy came to deliver my suspension letter.' Raj said as a never felt numbness descended upon him.

'Suspension letter? What does it say?' Amelia asked, confused.

'That I am suspended with immediate effect.' He felt thankful that his father was dead. It would have killed him to read about his son's suspension in the newspaper. The news would have devastated the honest schoolteacher; the word suspension was taboo. It happened to bad, corrupt government officials. A suspended forest officer meant he made money by conniving with timber smugglers; that is what most people would think.

A sigh escaped him as Amelia sat on the sofa close to him. 'Are you all right?' She ran her hand through his curly hair, and an electric shock passed through his body. The feeling of numbness was replaced by a sudden desire as their bodies met, her body soft and smooth as satin. 'Did you expect it?' The tender gaze from her blue eyes pierced through his heart.

Arjun's warning rang in his ears. 'He will act fast.' Yes, he did—one girl, two tigers, and one rhino–all dead, Arjun's transfer and now his suspension letter. The departmental proceeding would start at lightning speed to convert the suspension into dismissal. What would be the reason? Negligence of duty, roaming around with a woman tourist when the animals were getting killed, criminal conduct, and allowing poachers to kill tigers under the very nose of his ranger guards.

He heaved a heavy sigh. 'I have been here for four years, but it seems I don't know anything about this place. I don't know what to expect and what I shall get. It is a vicious group; they just don't want me here. They will create a condition where my seniors will have no option but to take such steps.'

'Who are they? Dev?' She inched closer, and her knees touched his. Raj could feel the excitement building up within him. Her hair tickled him.

'Is this real?' He murmured as he tried to make sense of the situation, Amelia's tender eyes glued to him.

His mind blanked out as Amelia clasped his arm tighter,

pulling him towards her. Entwined in a tight embrace, his arms were around her and then all over her. He removed strands of hair from her face and lowered his head to discover her incredible lips; she let out a soft cry.

He lay along with her on the sofa, their mouths melted into one, and their limbs were in a frenzy to explore each other's bodies. It did not take much of an effort to get the tiny white satin out of their way. Her body, devoid of any clothing, surrendered itself to Raj's wild exploration. Within no time, he was inside her, rocking her in frenzied passion on the cushiony comfort of the sofa.

As he gasped for breath, still mounted on top of her, that face mocked him with a snide smile. Raj could hold it no longer. 'It is Dev. That bastard killed the girl, and he wanted to have you kidnapped. And on that night before the ceremony, I think he almost got you if Arjun's man had not intervened. After that, he became cautious. He knew Arjun was after him. He used his connections to transfer him. He wanted to eliminate me with that mob's help; I survived. But now this suspension letter.'

Headlines would read: Foreign tourist dies of alcohol and drug overdose in Resort or an Australian girl disappears while going for an evening run. Yes, it would have been big news, but nobody would have suspected anything when a teary eyed Dev read out the eulogies to the TV folks.

Dev would hold the raincoat ceremony, saying that this was the last wish of the donor.

★★★

Chapter 28

Day 9 (Morning)

They lay on the sofa; Raj smelt Amelia's head buried in his chest while her fingers traced patterns on his body. As she touched the curls of his hair, running her hand down his high chin and feeling his stubble, a realisation hit him. The girl with half-pursed lips after giving him everything he yearned for, gradually drifting to sleep, would be gone in a day or two. He would be left alone to deal with what he faced; a shiver ran through his spine.

If only it was as easy as what BBC had dubbed Kaziranga to be: a park that shoots to protect rhinos. This time, there were no intruders, no poachers. An intelligent, ruthless enemy challenged him at his doorstep, trying to ensnare him from all sides. The sense of restlessness was suffocating, so strong that the bliss of being together with the most beautiful girl he had ever seen evaporated fast. He got up from his sofa without disturbing Amelia and tiptoed to the veranda.

He saw some movement near the gate. A group of forest guards departed for night patrolling. A sudden pang of guilt flooded him, seeing the poorly equipped, shivering-in-the-cold party vanish in the darkness to do the thankless job of protecting Kaziranga. Only those who toiled in the savannah of Kaziranga could know how thankless it was. The men vanished in the night, sacrificing their sleep. Raj shook his head as the dark forest swallowed his men. The park was built on sacrifices. Guards had sacrificed their comfort and lives; women had given up their desires; and men had been stripped of the memories of their children growing up. Rangers had left warm, cosy postings and decided to station themselves in a terrain infested by mosquitoes and leeches.

Would you know of a hospital where the doctors get beaten, kicked, and killed by the very patients they tried to save? Welcome to Kaziranga where caring forest guards who endangered their lives fighting with poachers day in and out died, got trampled to death because the elephant did not like their smell, or were gored to death as they could not get off the path of a charging rhino in time. It was the same beast, the guard had hand-reared and fed after rescuing as a tiny cub from being swept away in the fury of floodwater decades ago. There could not be any other job more thankless than this, but he would not give it away for his life. Raj loved Kaziranga and loved being its ranger—suspended or otherwise.

'Dev,' Raj mused. 'Why does he call me *dada*?'

Arjun once told him. 'He would be at least ten-fifteen

years older than you.'

A smile dawned on his face as Raj recollected how he had become a fan of the young nature lover. When there was no satellite TV or mobile phones, the local papers always carried stories of a young crusader, Dev Pratap Bhatt, the scion of the region's wealthiest planter family. In his early years as an activist, he led an agitation against rail track alignment through a Ramsar site. His NGO campaigned to the government to create the first community sanctuary in the state. He almost singlehandedly forced the authorities to declare a timber-rich reserved forest as the region's first rainforest national park. He urged the locals to take up afforestation in degraded sandbanks to generate an artificial forest to check erosion. As an expert bird watcher, he had spotted rare birds like the masked finfoot and the white-winged wood duck in the state's wetlands. Yes, as far as Raj remembered, Dev had acted as the catalyst for nature conservation movements in a state otherwise plagued with various student and ethnic agitations. By the time he joined the forest department, Raj had become an ardent fan of the man who had distanced himself from the family-owned tea garden business to become a full-time conservationist and wildlife activist. Soon after, the three Rs followed Dev. He became famous as the Rhino Warrior due to his high-profile activism around rhino poaching. He chose the heart of the rhino country, Kaziranga, as the home turf for his NGO and showed his business acumen by opening one of the first exotic resorts near the park—River View Resort. And the third R was the rumour that began to surface that he was forming syndicates, siphoning money from foreign donors, taking cash from forest officers to facilitate favourable postings, and holding durbars in plush hotels where the babus queued to get his audience.

Yes, Raj had heard it all. But in his last four years, he had seen only one side of the man, the enigmatic warrior with his dogged stance when it came to the loss of a rhino in the park. With his thousands of followers on social media, he remained a darling of the emotional public, a trusted advisor for every forest minister of the state and an activist of choice of the state's popular chief minister. A sigh escaped Raj as he brushed his hair back from his forehead. He was nothing but a fly compared to the powerful NGO chief, that is what Dev must be thinking.

Raj shook his head as a smile seeped through his lips; the warrior had chosen the wrong man to mess with. He opened the door, inhaled the cold, damp air, and walked towards the communal kitchen. Dawn had not broken yet, but Daju was already there, stoking the fire, preparing tea for the returning night patrol party.

'You told me that the Nepali cook at the director's bungalow had worked at a resort?'

Daju raised his head from his crouched position. He had no sleepiness in his eyes, but appeared irritated. 'Sir, you have met him so many times. He used to be the main cook at Dev sahib's resort.' Daju kept looking at Raj, his hand holding the hollow bamboo tube with which he blew at the fire. Daju was not done.

'Sir, he is Dev sahib's trusted man. When the new director came, Dev sahib got him a job in the department and put him in the bungalow. He keeps going to the resort almost daily for reporting.'

Raj walked back to his quarters, birds chirping, heralding imminent dawn. He regarded his surroundings. Amelia was still blissfully asleep, her mouth slightly open, hair dishevelled. He let her sleep and came out again to the veranda. Daju came running to him with a flask of hot tea.

Raj pushed the door closed, lest his cook's sifting eyes fell on Amelia sleeping on the sofa with a Naga shawl covering her naked body, and her nighty on the floor. He sat down on the cane chair, took a sip, and wondered whether he had the entitlement to sit or remain in his official quarters. He thought of his plan to take his mother for a medical check-up in Mumbai. The suspension meant his salary would be reduced to half. He would not be able to go anywhere; he would be required to represent his side of the case in front of the Investigation Committee. What would be his defence with two tigers and a rhino killed in his range within a week? He then shuddered thinking if the dead girl was also linked to him, then it would mean living in jail as an under-trial prisoner forever, whether he was guilty or not. He drifted to sleep, sitting on the chair till daylight broke around him.

'Morning,' Amelia's greeting from behind startled him. He didn't hear her wake up. She was dressed in denim jeans, a t-shirt, and a leather jacket. 'I feel like going to see some wildlife today.' She smiled.

'Of course! Do you want to go on an elephant safari now? Or in the evening, you could go for the jeep trips.' Raj realised that with everything happening, Amelia had missed out on what most tourists came for to Kaziranga.

'No, I was just joking. Not really in the mood,' Amelia said as creases showed on her forehead. 'How are you going to deal with this suspension order?'

Raj did not have any idea. But Amelia's concern gave him hope for everything except what happened in the night, that was so toxic and confusing.

'Raj, I think you should not worry about the dead girl. I mean Dorothy. They tried to pin the blame on you and failed. However, now they can't do anything,' Amelia said.

'How?'

'The villagers who came to attack you are your alibi. They came for the girl from the village and not for Dorothy. It's a different thing that the thugs among them wanted to find you with Dorothy's body.'

A soft whistle blew through his lips as he went inside his quarters to freshen up. Once the mid-morning sun brightened the whole campus, Raj rang Arjun's number.

'Good morning, Raj,' Arjun said from the other side. 'Came to know of your suspension. Things become bad to worse very quickly here in the park.' There was a pause followed by a sigh. 'I am also cleaning my desk and writing my handover note.' Raj didn't say anything. 'Hello, Raj, are you there?'

'I wanted to ask you about the girl of village eight.'

'Yes.'

'Has she returned?'

'The kidnapped girl?' Arjun paused for some time. 'Yes, she has come back. My men were told so. I couldn't get to meet her. Her parents said that she has left the village.'

'Are you going to talk to her?' Raj asked.

'I don't think so. I already know what I need to know. There is something funny going on in that household.' Arjun sounded hesitant.

'The missing girl?'

'Her father too.'

'What is he up to?'

'He sold his plot to some businessperson in Delhi and is urging others to do the same. This is going to make your department's relocation project difficult. The girl worked in Dev's resort for a few months. I am trying to find some more information about this whole thing, and I will let you know. But then what will you do with all this information. I will not be here from Monday.' Arjun hung up.

That's when the face of the Nepali cook at the director's bungalow, and his suspecting eyes, came to his mind. Yes, Daju was right; he remembered seeing him at the resort. The girl and the cook both worked in Dev's resort. Now, what about the third man he had in mind?

Is he also working for Dev?

★★★

Chapter 29

Day 9 (Noon)

The skinny driver leaned against his car, perhaps wondering when he would be able to go back to his hill town. Raj chuckled; it was quite an effort to persuade him to stay back.

'I will pay you daily whatever you earn. Just for a few days till this Australian madam is here,' Raj said.

The skinny driver grinned. 'Okay, sir, I will stay with you.'

Soon after, Raj and Amelia were in the Toyota car as he cast a glance at Amelia looking exquisite in blue denim jeans and white t-shirt, the jacket on her lap. They passed the campus gate; Vijay stood near the boom end with perplexity or was it some amount of anxiety painted on his face. Raj was happy not using his official SUV, not before he could get to the bottom of the quagmire.

Has the news of his suspension already made it to the TV channels?

The highway had the usual rush of jeeps returning from their morning safaris.

'Sir, is it true what they are saying?' the skinny driver asked.

'What are they saying?'

'Sir, everyone knows that they suspended you for your crackdown on the poaching network. This rhino killing near your office was just an excuse to generate a public outcry so that they could suspend you. We may be poor people, but we all know how these politicians work. The forest minister is useless.' He shook his head, changing channels from Bollywood to English songs.

Raj did not answer. He found himself humming to the song.

As the vehicle navigated the uneven, bumpy road through the thatched hamlets of village eight, curious onlookers gathered around the path. They reached the end of the settlement, near the edge of the forest, where the girl's cottage was located. The villagers got alerted after seeing an unfamiliar car. They were as wary and nervous as Raj was feeling while entering the place. Unlike the other surrounding areas living happily with the park, reaping the benefits of eco-tourism, this settlement acted differently. It was as if some outsiders had poisoned the villagers' innate innocence for their selfish gain. Raj could figure out who it was, but he had no clue about the reason. As Raj came out of the car, the restive crowd surrounding them relaxed considerably. But a pair of eyes, a short boy, spied on him, hiding behind the trunk of a tree.

'Oh, our ranger babu!' A sense of relief erupted among the group. Some looked apologetic; some were part of the original mob that had attacked the camp.

'Hello sir, so happy to see you and memsahib,' the girl's father said with a weary smile. 'Those rascals freed my daughter. She has gone back to town. It's good for her.'

Raj regarded the short, bare-chest man with squinty eyes who did not look savvy enough to start the village's land-selling spree. He did not appear any happier, given that his daughter had returned, than he seemed the other day.

'Now the boy, where did I see him before this', Raj wondered. He eyed them standing behind the last thatched cottage of the village at the bank of the rivulet beyond which the vast expanse of the park started. It was a bright sunny day, but the chilly nip persisted in the air. The crowd had dispersed. The little boy was nowhere in sight. A few boys ran around at a distance, throwing a ball at each other. The same group played around his stationary vehicle when he was in the village. At that moment Raj realised that one among them, the one who eyed him from a distance, worked in the car workshop in the town, and his eyes gleamed with a guarded curiosity instead of childlike innocence.

Did someone ask him to tinker with my car the other day?

Soon after, he was in the Toyota with Amelia as the driver navigated the vehicle out of the haphazard cluster of thatched dwellings. A bitter wind swept the village, and the ground was slick with muddy water. The villagers stood in line, their gaze fixed on the car and its occupants. The general nervousness on being visited by the forest or government department was missing. The settlers—a motley group of a diverse community that occupied the prime land during the state's disturbed period, stared at them, their faces emanating relief as the car moved away from them. A sign of newfound courage and defiance replaced the meekness of the villagers he had interacted with a few days ago. It had become apparent that they were not interested in relocation. Their confident demeanour said that they did not fear forced eviction because legally, they were not encroachers. The village retreated into the backdrop as the car hit the narrow track that Raj had taken on that fateful afternoon.

The tall grasses swayed languidly to the morning breeze while the bright sun burned down from a clear winter sky. A girl he didn't know even existed a week ago was on a mission to save him from the invisible enemy. Their eyes met, or she caught him eyeing her like an awestruck man. 'Was she kidnapped? Or was she made to disappear?' Amelia said when Raj composed himself. Raj realised what Amelia was hinting at. They had removed the girl from her parent's place or she was hidden, to make it appear like an abduction by Raj, who was camping in the nearby camp. The thugs then instigated the villagers to go there to discover another dead girl. That discovery would have sealed Raj's fate there and then, and this girl would have quietly returned home.

Taking a deep breath, Raj remembered reading in the newspaper that despite his preoccupation with the conservation movement, the young activist, Dev Bhatt had topped the state's school-leaving examination.

Brilliant he was then; brilliant he is now.

'Sir, what is that place?' The skinny driver's question brought him back to the present. The hillock of Vulture Hill came into view.

'Let's stop here for a while and check on the guards,' Raj said as they reached the base of the cliff. The forlorn cottage stood on the top; the silk-cotton tree's dark shadow swept the ground in broad daylight. Raj and Amelia walked up to the camp. No one responded when they knocked at the door.

'Sir, we are here.' A shout came from the wetland. There were three boats with some guards and a few men were swimming in the water. A flock of waterfowl milled above, disturbed by the congregation. Raj realised the spectacle did not have anything to do with fishing. He urged Amelia to follow him, and they descended the hillock to rush to where the action was taking place.

'What is going on?' Raj asked, his boots sinking into the mud.

Ronald, the boatman, shouted back, 'Sir, we found something heavy and metallic under the water. Rahman dived and touched it. He says it may be a scooter.'

Rahman, wet like a cat, crouched on a boat. While fishing, Ronald must have stumbled upon something and had called everyone to help him retrieve it.

'Go, get a long rope,' Raj instructed as Rahman disembarked. He returned with a thick rope, the one used for tying elephants.

'Good, now tie one end to the handle of the scooter or whatever it is under the water and the other end...' Raj inspected the Toyota's bumper—would it be able to do the job?

After some cajoling, the driver agreed to tow the thing out of the water. Within half an hour, a red Scooty, covered with muck and weeds, was pulled from the water body's depth.

Amelia's forehead creased in thought. 'This is Dorothy's scooter!' She whipped out her phone, opened her Facebook to go to Dorothy's page, and then clicked on the photos. Wearing a bright smile, dressed in blue denim, the girl posed on her shiny new vehicle. The photo caption said, 'My new baby. A gift from my...'; three red hearts followed.

The sleek new machine's glove compartment was closed. Raj wondered whether it had become a police job or could he do what he wanted. He called Arjun's number, but as expected, he received a busy tone. Raj asked the guards from the nearby camp to go back. Only Ronald and Rahman remained.

'Check if the compartment is locked.' Raj wiped the sweat from his forehead.

'Can't open it,' Rahman said.

'Let me see.' Ronald knelt and pushed Rahman away. He picked up a rock and broke the compartment's plastic cover with one blow. The inside was dry. He removed a lady's purse and handed it over to Raj.

Raj unzipped the bag and searched its contents, hoping he would find something useful. He found what he had hoped for. It was Dorothy's mobile phone, a new Samsung

S23. A new scooty, a costly mobile phone—somebody had been showering her with expensive gifts!

'Yours is a Samsung phone, right? Got the charger with you?' Raj asked Amelia as they walked to the camp.

'Listen! You don't mention anything about the mobile and the broken glove compartment. Understand?' The pair nodded, looking uncertain. Had they come to know about his suspension?

Dorothy's phone powered to life as it crossed the zero per cent charge mark. Raj hoped it did not have any password; it did not.

'Can we check the last call she made or received?'

Amelia went to the recent calls. 'There is an unidentified missed call. And before that, at 7 pm on 18 January, there was another missed call. The caller ID is Sir.'

'Could it be the director's number?' Raj wondered. 'What is the number for Sir?'

'985429966.'

Raj opened his contact book. 'Yes, this is his number.'

'There are also many calls from an unnamed number,' Amelia said with a frown. 'And the last call she received is different from the unknown number. That's on the 20th of January.'

'What is the number? The last one,' Raj said.

'98540326. Whose number is it?' Amelia asked.

Raj hoped Amelia would not hear the pounding of his heart. 'Let's get going,' he said to Amelia. 'You two, don't mention this scooty to anyone. I will report it to the police.'

He turned to Rahman, who was in his wet uniform. Ronald, whistling merrily, had changed to dry clothing, oblivious of a lady visitor's presence in the camp.

On reaching the foothill as Amelia sat in the car, Raj said, 'Can I check her phone? I want to see if there is any signal.' He headed to the edge of the water body, away from the prying eyes of the guards and the driver. He stood in front of a patch of wetland with giant water lilies, jacanas played on the leaves, and read the messages he had exchanged with Dorothy.

She was the informer who was supposed to meet him, and the warrior eliminated her before she could talk.

★★★

Chapter 30

Day 9 (Noon)

The rickety wooden bridge over the aquamarine river creaked as the Toyota passed over it, leaving behind the swaying expanse of elephant grass to hit the highway. The skinny driver pressed hard on the accelerator, a welcome change for him from the treacherous hill roads he plied his vehicle on. The sky darkened from bright, cloudless white to a bleak grey. People moved around in the town with umbrellas, aware that a relentless downpour was on its way. The street vendors wound up their spread, whereas the auto-rickshaw drivers continued chatting, gazing at the dark clouds' movement.

'Can you stop?' Raj's head reeled; they had reached the town's centre. A sizeable, motley crowd had gathered on the road, all craning their necks towards the bungalow. A sudden blackness engulfed Raj's thoughts. The shadows of the roadside trees became now twice as long as themselves.

The damp and chilly air smelled faintly of incense and burning coconut husk. Raj inhaled deeply; he liked the smell as it reminded him of the temples and festivities, but he sensed that the timing was not right. A policeman waved at the traffic to slow down and drive carefully, skirting the swelling crowd. There were quite a number of police cars besides Arjun's jeep. White official vehicles with red beacons lined the road; several district senior officials had arrived.

'What is this?' Raj wondered as he got down from the car. He made his way through the people to the bungalow, with Amelia following close behind. The gate was wide open; an ambulance was parked on the driveway. Men and women clogged the otherwise forlorn compound. It was definitely not a happy gathering.

All eyes were set on the spectacle unfolding at the entrance of the bungalow. A woman's body resplendent in a red Banarasi sari covered with yellow and white flowers was placed on a mat. Over the crowd's murmurs rose the howling cries of a distraught woman. Raj recognised the woman sitting next to the body to be the tea garden manager's wife, the elder sister.

Where is Asha madam then?

The corpse in the colourful sari with a vermillion mark on the forehead with the nostrils blocked by white cotton couldn't be Asha madam, or was it her? Yes, Asha madam was draped in bridal finery, as was the custom when a married woman predeceased her husband. A man stood near the body; his head hung low, eyes teary, face stoic—Ajay sir, an epitome of melancholy like he had never seen before.

The director had been bereaved, and the entire forest department was present. However, nobody had bothered to inform the suspended ranger. Quite a few heads turned, seeing him closely following Amelia.

'Is she the director's wife?' Amelia's lips trembled. A pale shade of horror clouded her beautiful face. Raj had never seen her like that before; he immersed himself in her deep blue eyes. Is this why she had come to India, all the way from Australia? A heart full of noble intentions was entangled in a maze of deceit, kidnapping, and murder.

Amelia grasped Raj's arm and pushed him aside. 'Raj,' she whispered, 'we can prove whether the director is involved in Dorothy's murder or not.'

She was distraught and terrified, but her mind was still alert, determined to uncover the person behind Dorothy's death. Now, a new mystery had unfolded: Who killed Asha madam? The insensitive crowd murmured, 'She had swallowed four hundred sleeping pills. She was dead even when she was living. Who knows the truth, her husband might have killed her? How much can a man take? The people working in the bungalow say that she used to throw things at him.'

'How?' Raj asked, retreating behind a bush, Amelia still clinging to him.

'I will call him from Dorothy's phone. Let's listen to what he says.'

Raj sighed despondently. She was doing all this to help

uncover who was hell-bent on destroying him. Nine days ago, somebody strangled a beautiful girl in his camp at about this same time. Now, the lovely woman he met just yesterday, lay dead at the doorway; it was the same door where she stood holding Dorothy's photo. Two girls in nine days; whoever he is, the bastard is in a real hurry to cover his tracks. In the last few nights, he had dreamt of Dorothy, her arms outstretched in a heavenly drift. Those haunting eyes were despondent, as if asking him, why her? They implored him to avenge her death. Her full lips quivered, her cheeks flushed pink, and her nose ring glistened. Raj gasped, returning to the present.

He craned his neck above the swelling crowd to regard the director, suave and sophisticated but looking bereaved. Would this be the right time to ambush him with a call from Dorothy's mobile? What if he was innocent? The vermillion-covered forehead of the body on the ground did not look like the same Asha madam who had stood near the doorway, clutching Dorothy's photo. Did Ajay sir make Dorothy pregnant? He may have refused to acknowledge being the baby's father or may have forced her to go for an abortion. Maybe she disagreed and threatened to go to the press, leaving him with no choice.

He knew the media well, it would have been scandalous. The dirty story that would have been dished out would be about the beautiful innocent tribal girl from the hills and the suave urban babu from Delhi tied in a loveless marriage. Possibly, Asha madam might have asked him about Dorothy, or charged him with the murder, which could have been her undoing.

'Dial the number,' as Raj instructed Amelia, his voice wavered.

Both retreated to the hedge near the compound's end, where they could still see Ajay sir. A few curious onlookers stared at them; otherwise, most people were busy watching the scene before them—a dead woman, a hysterical sister, and a stoic husband.

Amelia dialled the director's number, keeping a steady stare on the man. The director groped his pocket to take out the phone. He looked at the screen for a moment before disconnecting.

'He didn't take it,' Amelia whispered. A beep sounded; a notification showed a new message.

'Raj, your director, sent something.'

'What does it say?'

Amelia read it out, "Hi Dorothy, can we talk later?"

Amelia's eyes were on the mobile phone, Dorothy's new mobile phone, but her mind was elsewhere.

'He does not know about the girl's fate,' she said.

Before Raj could say something, a hand touched his shoulder.

'What are you two doing here?' Arjun's eyes teased them or were they mocking them on their togetherness, given the occasion.

'I don't feel like going near the body. I can't bear to see madam in this state,' Raj said. 'I tried calling you; your phone was engaged.'

'Well, I was busy with all the formalities,' Arjun said

and paused for a moment. 'And all the extra paperwork for handover. This is my last week. From Monday, the new man will be on my seat.' Arjun's eyes burnt with the anguish of unfinished business.

'When did it happen? Suspicious death or suicide?' Raj asked. 'Where is Dev?' Asha madam's distraught face with Dorothy's picture held close to her bosom, flashed before his eyes.

Chants arose from the crowd surrounding the body in the driveway. The director broke into sobs as people lifted his wife's body on to the funeral vehicle. The elder sister, bawling her eyes out, was held in a hug by a moustached man—presumably, her husband, the tea garden manager.

'Dev is still in Upper Assam.' Arjun bit his lips, shaking his head. Dark anger clouded his face, two balls of foamy spit formed on the sides of his mouth. 'My replacement is his choice, hand-picked by him.' His jaws clenched, his mood as ominous as the day or whatever remained of it as the late afternoon sun hid behind the thick grey clouds.

The procession left the bungalow, leaving a scent of burnt coconut husk and incense sticks. It was too much of an explosion of pain in Raj's chest as the face of the beautiful woman who had hosted him just the day before floated in his head. So many hues, so many shades—he remembered her smile, her giggle, and then her sombre, sullen face when she came down from her room. A sigh escaped him as he crumpled to his knees and sat down on the lawn, burdened by the memories.

Arjun's eyes bore into Raj. 'We got her number from her brother. Tried to track all the calls. There were many calls from the director. There were quite a few calls to and from an untraced number. There was also a call from your mobile the day after she was killed. You didn't tell me you knew her?'

★★★

Chapter 31

Day 9 (Evening)

'She was the informer I was supposed to meet that day.' Generally, most of such information ended up yielding nothing. The informer did not want to come to Raj's office. Raj thought it was a man. As usual, Raj confided in his man, Vijay, who suggested Vulture Hill; but why did Vijay send the guards away? 'I never knew that girl. She contacted me saying she had something to share about a poaching racket. Vijay arranged our meeting at the venue. I thought I was talking to a man.'

Arjun nodded. 'That untraced number, as per the network provider, based on the last tower it pinged, belonged to this area. She had your number and the director's numbers saved. The third person called from one of many pre-paid sims. But he also stays here.' Arjun took a deep breath as if trying to put the many things going on, in the right order in his mind. 'That number is the same as what the Kolkata police got from the kidnappers.'

So, it was Dev for both the girls, Raj sighed as he kept a steady stare on Arjun; he was not done yet. 'The girl's brother said that someone had gifted a scooty to her. He had no idea who it was. I asked for the registration. It turned out to be a Nagaland number. I checked with the Dimapur dealer.'

'Did you find Dev's name?'

'No, it was registered under the name–Victor Hanse, ACF hill division.'

'Did you ask him?'

'I asked the brother. He said that couldn't be true as his sister didn't have any relationship with that man. I got stuck there. I then requested the local police to check with Victor about the scooty. He told them that he had bought one for himself for moving around easily through the small lanes of the town, but somebody stole it.' A long sigh escaped Arjun. 'The hill town police station won't do anything more.'

'We found the scooty near Vulture Hill and retrieved her phone.' Raj sounded hesitant, fearing an outburst from Arjun.

'Where is the phone?' Arjun almost shouted.

Raj dug his hand into his pocket and said, 'I kept it in my office.' He was unsure why he was not ready yet to part with it.

Arjun's eyes opened wide as he removed his cap and shook his head rapidly. 'You made things easy for me. I want the phone. When did you find these things?' His tone was troubled. 'Anyway, these things are not going to help. The bastard who is taking my place will hardly do anything.'

'We found it this morning. We tried to contact you, but your phone was engaged. We have not told anyone; thought we should let you know first.'

Arjun eyed Raj with a slight frown, peeved at being left out of the discovery process.

The crowd had dispersed as the funeral van made its way to the cremation ground. The director was in the front in a white kurta; the stark whiteness magnified the melancholy of his face and the emptiness of his heart. Someone he cared for and tended to for the last twenty years as one would a child, was no more. A few attendants and guards, left in the compound that was drowned in smoky fumes, sobbed quietly while the bungalow's garden bed was bereft of its flowers, all adorning the hearse of the memsahib who called the bungalow home. Raj saw the window on the top floor, the one from which Asha madam might have admired the flowerbeds, and noted the wrought iron grills, which she must have felt pressing against her bosom.

'I think you will have to interrogate all the servants, especially that Nepali cook. Not just about what happened, but about what goes on in the bungalow?' Raj shuddered at the memory. 'Has police done a post-mortem on the body?'

Arjun did not reply as his forehead creased in a frown, his old sternness returning. 'Listen, we don't have much time. I should have posted my man in the bungalow.' He stopped, shaking his head. 'Director sahib would have said it was not necessary. He does not know anything. Once I am gone, be assured the new man will make all these leads disappear. Dev will have a free run with his own man here.' He kept a hand on Raj's shoulder; a tired smile seeped through his lips. 'Don't blame the director for your suspension.'

Raj nodded his head.

'Dev instigated the forest minister to pressurise your department to suspend you. Everyone is a winner. The minister can claim he punished the offending officer, and public memory is short. People will quickly forget all the excellent work you did in the past. Dev is happy as his activism is paying off. And you are out of the scene,' Arjun said.

Raj listened on.

'I need to go now. Send me the mobile phone as soon as possible. Don't let our guest stay at any other place. Keep her at your quarters.' Arjun dashed off to join the policemen waiting for him, while Raj and Amelia were left alone in the sprawling campus of the director's bungalow. Raj found himself looking again towards the window on the top floor, the one where he had seen the shadowy silhouette of the woman. Had it been Asha madam or a ghost? The garden swing hung still. If Ajay sir had a typical, normal family, Asha madam would have been pushing a gleeful toddler on the swing set, her white dupatta flying in the breeze.

'I will tell the driver to take you to my place. You should get some rest.' Raj regarded Amelia; yes, she was overwhelmed by the turn of events. 'I will go and join the funeral.' It was strange the way Arjun asked Amelia to stay with him. He didn't mind it, though.

When Raj reached his quarters after the crematorium rituals were over, a blanket of tarry darkness shrouded the campus. It was well past nine. He wondered what Amelia was doing. Wrapping himself in a shawl, the stooping figure of Daju stood on the veranda. 'I forced memsahib to have dinner. She wanted to wait for you. I told her that nobody knows what time you would get back.' In the dim light of the lone bulb mounted atop the door, he brimmed like a proud guardian.

Raj nodded absentmindedly; the pyre was still burning. Ajay sir, other rangers, Roy sir, and many others were there when he surreptitiously sneaked out. 'Okay, you lay my table,' Raj said and quietly went inside to his bedroom. After a warm bath and a hot meal, he slumped on the sofa. The door to Amelia's room was closed.

He took a deep breath to distract himself from his carnal thoughts. Let her sleep, you bastard. She had not slept the night before. He switched on the TV, muting the sound, and surfed through the channels that would do the most harm. As expected, the various news headlines on the local news channels were ruthless.

Along with his suspension, they mentioned an Australian girl. He felt lucky to be free. If somehow the story of the dead girl's discovery leaked, he would be behind bars, guilty or not. He shuddered, switching off the TV. He picked up the mobile and took a deep breath. The call to his curious and ever-prodding sister would be the most difficult one. Raj was sure that more than the suspension, the main discussion topic would be the Australian girl. He retreated to his bedroom.

The sister's parting shot was, '*Dada*, is she beautiful? Please send me her picture.' Raj smiled, shaking his head. As he disconnected the line, his phone rang again. It was an unknown number; a childlike voice blabbered on the other side. The connection played up, and Raj hung up.

There was a slight creak of the guest bedroom's door. Amelia stood near the door, her eyes sleepy. 'When did you come? Sorry, I had to eat without you as your man said you might not turn up.' Her sweet smile revealed those maddening dimples as his thirsty eyes drank her beauty. He had to distract himself quickly. Luckily for him, Amelia did the needful.

'I thought about what the hotel manager said to us and what Dorothy's brother said to Arjun. She went there with other men too. Her brother also said that she had relationships with quite a few men. The person, other than your Ajay sir, going to the hotel can't be Victor.' She settled on the chair in front of him. 'What about Dev?' Amelia's face lighted up. 'He was on her Facebook friend list.'

Raj nodded distractedly.

'Can we give the manager a call and ask him if he can help. We can send him Dev's photo.'

Raj called the manager and coaxed him to agree to send a thumbs up on WhatsApp if the picture he sent matched the person who had accompanied Dorothy to the hotel. It would be thumbs down if the persons did not match up. The man categorically said he would not take any more calls on this matter.

'Amelia, you clicked Dev's pictures at the party. Can you send me one now?'

Amelia sent him a photo she had of Dev and Raj together. Raj sent the photo to the manager, waited for the double ticks to turn blue, and then got a thumbs up within moments. He showed the thumbs up from the manager to Amelia.

The bastard not only knew Dorothy; he used to meet her at Hotel Osprey.

★★★

Chapter 32

Day 10 (Morning)

Raj did not want to get up from the sofa in the living room. He was immersed in a feeling of bliss and laziness from the long night of togetherness, as Amelia's head rested inches away from his, her breath warm against his face. She slowly opened her eyes. He gazed tenderly into her deep blue eyes; they looked even more alluring when sleepy.

She touched Raj's cheek; the brittle stubble of his growing beard rasped under her fingers. He realised that she had to leave soon. The other day, she had talked to someone from the resort in Gorumara, her next destination. She had to give them a final arrival date.

Two beautiful souls were killed in a week. What if this girl lying along with him on the narrow sofa was their next victim? He shuddered, gazing at the ceiling. It did not help when Amelia ran her hand through his curls.

The rising sun pierced softly through a gap in the curtains to fall on her face, but she didn't look as if she had noticed it; she simply kept trying to put the pieces of the puzzle together, her fingers still playing with his curls. The smell of her body overwhelmed him, but he restrained himself by gently pulling away from her and tottering out to draw the curtains entirely to one side, allowing the morning sunlight to flood in. The compound did not show any signs of activity, as if the dappled light filtering through the tall trees had cast a soporific effect on the whole township.

'Are you going to ask Dev about his visit to Hotel Osprey?' Amelia sat on a chair facing him. She covered herself with the Naga shawl, her nighty still on the floor. Raj looked up to meet her gaze, his palms resting on his chin. Her long legs, as she crossed and uncrossed them, sent a pleasurable shiver down his spine. He resisted the urge to reach up and pull the cover away as he felt his cheeks heat.

Dev's face was a much-needed distraction at that moment. 'I hope Dev is back,' Raj paused as there was a mild knocking on the door. He got up from the sofa and dressed to answer the knock; Amelia retreated to her room, picking up her clothes.

Daju came with his tray of morning tea. Raj sipped the hot milk tea with ginger when his phone rang. A child blabbered something incoherently on the other side. As the phone connectivity played up, Raj walked into the veranda. But the connection broke. Irritated, he disconnected the call. It rang again. As it was an unknown number, Raj cut off the call again; he was not in the mood for any prank calls.

Raj waited for Amelia in the dining room. When she joined him a little later, he said, 'We will go for a jeep safari; is that alright?' Raj realised that Amelia had not visited the interior of the park. He was surprised; it was almost ten days since she had arrived, and she had not even seen one wild rhino so far.

She will go on a safari this evening and then leave the place tomorrow.

Soon after, Raj and Amelia stood at the back of a jeep, standing and holding the rods for balance as the vehicle traversed the bumpy road towards the park boundary. Her hair flew around wildly in the wind as the children from the nearby field waved at them—a never-ending ritual for them when they saw attractive foreign tourists.

Indian rollers perched on the roadside electric poles stared them down till the last moment, when the jeep rumbled past, to fly, flashing their brilliant blue. Raj, standing beside Amelia, felt like a tourist. It was a first for him, entering his own park like that with a foreign tourist. The guard at the entry checkpoint saluted him and hurriedly lifted the boom gate, much to the driver's delight.

'Sir, they are surprised seeing you in my jeep,' the driver smiled. 'Hey, hurry up,' he shouted in jest at the guard who took a fraction of a second to lift the boom gate. The guard returned a stare—watch out for me after you drop off sir!

With just a few jeeps that afternoon, wildlife was bountiful. Amelia clicked, focusing her long telephoto-camera on the usual targets: rhino, water buffalo, hog deer, and swamp deer. She repeatedly alternated her camera for her binoculars. Her excitement soared when a waterside spectacle unfolded, an otter feeding itself with a silvery gleaming fish while a stork peered down upon its catch.

They did not talk. After a while, the silence between them felt awkward. 'What is your plan after Gorumara?' His stomach cramped at the thought that this girl standing inches away from him, as they left behind the grasses bathed in orange, would be gone in a day. Why did he feel that he had a chance only if she was with him? It would not take much to dismiss a suspended ranger. An irresponsible ranger allowed the killing of two tigers and a bull rhino, all within a week. How could he expect people to support the shameless guy who openly moved around with a foreign tourist after being suspended?

'After Gorumara, I am... I will go to Dudhwa,' Amelia answered him while she focused her lens on the silhouette of a pelican perched atop a tree.

'Dudhwa... Dudhwa, where is that?' Raj grimaced. 'Why do you want to go there? Do you want to see tigers? The Kaziranga tiger population is much more than Dudhwa.'

Why doesn't she go back to Australia?

The red grass glistened in the setting sun. Beyond the wetland to their right emanated the alarm calls of the hog deer. The hair on the back of his neck prickled—perhaps a big cat had come out to the water body. He told the driver to go slowly. How badly he wanted a tiger to appear before them so that she could see it and drop her Dudhwa plan, and then she would take a flight to her place in Australia.

Amelia turned towards Raj. Dressed in her wide-brimmed hat and khakis, she resembled a Hollywood film star. He recalled the name of the film he had seen in his childhood, 'Out of Africa'. 'I am not going to Dudhwa to see tigers. I am going to see rhinos there.'

Raj hid his surprise as the vehicle jumped up and down on a pothole-riddled stretch. Rhinos in Dudhwa, how come he had never heard of it?

'Well, your state donated a few rhinos to that place decades ago. I want to see the descendants of those translocated rhinos.' She smiled as a flock of pratincoles flew over them, shrouding them in a veil.

Raj realised the girl was crazy about rhinos. So, it was not just Kaziranga. He felt a pang of pain—she would indeed be gone. He mechanically pointed to a black-necked stork with a gaudy red beak as they stopped near a water body. As she eyed the bird through the viewfinder of her camera, Raj blinked and summoned a smile. 'I have asked my office people to book your flight ticket to Kolkata for tomorrow.' His heart froze, waiting for her answer.

'I am not going anytime soon. I have not confirmed my Kolkata-Sydney booking. What will I do in Kolkata?' She said, her face dead serious.

Despite the soup he was in, Raj concealed his glee. If the safari driver had not been there, Raj would have grabbed her and kissed her there and then. But then a little voice in Raj's head asked if he was doing the right thing by wanting her to stay in the park when all these things were going on. He was not as much worried about his safety; poachers, terrorists, and encroachers, he had faced them all. However, should he not fear for this innocent girl fiddling with her camera while the evening breeze swept her hair, a few strands tickling his senses.

He took deep breaths in and tried to calm himself. 'Dev is too powerful, too connected. The proofs we have are not enough to pin him down legally. It is going to get nasty real soon.' The stars hid behind the black cloud haze that stretched in the sky. An impending storm obliterated the lingering light of the rapidly falling night. By the time they arrived at the sleepy ranger office headquarter, a smoky mist had shrouded the place.

A nameless dread, a strange feeling of alienation filled Raj as swallows looped and dived frantically, heralding imminent dusk. With that soaring sense of restlessness over his suspension, Dorothy's phone, Asha madam's death, Dev in the hotel with Dorothy, the dangerous plan he hatched with Roy, and Arjun's impending transfer—he stood at the veranda and looked at the huddle of shadows around a smouldering fireplace. The warmth of the fire hardly removed the dread—the nameless dread that anything could happen anytime for foresters on a night like this. The occasional hoot of a hidden owl was the only sound to permeate the silence until Raj's phone rang. Roy's number blinked. 'Can you see me now? Need to discuss your proposal. You are suspended.' Roy paused for a moment. 'I hope you are not trying to have me dismissed,' he said and hung up.

★★★

Chapter 33

Day 10 (Evening)

'Is your dad at home?' Raj asked Roy's teenage daughter as she opened the door. Looking unsure at first, she erupted into a bright smile on seeing Amelia.

'Hi, you are still around?' She said to Amelia, rushing to hug her. Turning to Raj, she said, 'Sorry, uncle, Papa is home, but he is not in a good mood. He has been drinking continuously since morning. In fact, he started yesterday itself, after coming from the funeral.'

Raj shook his head. It was so difficult to understand this man. Raj could hear Roy shouting on the phone. As they entered, the man sat on a sofa in an inclined position, his rough, calloused feet on the coffee table and a glass of whiskey in one hand. His other hand had a mobile phone; he looked at it, barely stopping himself from hurling the choicest abuses on whoever was on the other side.

'Sir,' Raj said gently.

Roy stopped swearing, opened his eyes, and gestured to them to come in. 'Please don't stand near the door. Come inside and have a seat. You seem to have become a local now as if you belong to our park,' Roy said, smiling at Amelia. He turned to Raj, 'Isn't it true?'

'Madam is not here' Raj changed the topic.

'Madam?' A smirk appeared on his face. 'She left just now. We had a fight, thanks to you. After I mentioned your plan, she became upset and fought with me. Take the girl to your room,' he said to his daughter as if Amelia was a child and should not be present when he conversed with Raj.

'What happened, sir?' Raj knew that he should not be too inquisitive.

'My lovely wife insisted that since I have only a few years of service left, I should ignore all the evil things going on and should just do my duty quietly. And she said I should not get instigated by others. She said, I would be ruined. The children are not yet settled. Therefore, I should meekly watch all these things happening.' He took a large gulp of whisky from his glass. 'I told her to shut up. She got angry and left. Is this the way to behave with your husband?' His tone changed to imply that he was the victim of domestic violence.

'What is the timing, sir?' Raj had no idea that his maverick senior would be able to pull strings so soon.

'Now, it is a bit confidential. Timing is not under my control.' Roy became avuncular. 'I wish I could divulge more, but now it is in the hands of um...' He struggled to find the words he wanted to say. 'Executioners or unwanted visitors!' He leaned forward, his tone conspiratorial. 'I passed on his name. They will do the needful. I am sure they will unearth many secrets. But if I am wrong—'

Raj didn't say anything. Roy resembled an oversized kid in his supine pose, resting a glass on his round belly.

'If I get this wrong,' Roy shook his head, eyes hiding despair. 'I will be ruined indeed. He is not going to leave me. My condition will be far worse than yours. You are only suspended; you can enjoy this free time with that girl. What is her name? Amelia. I will be dismissed, no two ways about it. It will be a straight dismissal. My family will be homeless. I had this massive argument with my wife, and she left!'

'Did you share your plans with Ajay sir?'

'No. He does not need to know. It is not a Kaziranga-related issue. It is much bigger. I am not an organiser.' He stopped for a moment; his face lit up with impish glee. 'I am the catalyst. Now, you also shouldn't mention it anywhere.' He tottered towards Raj and kept a hand on Raj's shoulder, and slurred, 'Please, I can't say anything more. Listen, have dinner with us tonight. This could be the last meal at my house. I might be on the streets tomorrow. I am not joking. Or it may be you. Or both of us.' He gave a sad grin.

Raj waited with trepidation for him to divulge more.

'I hear PCCF and others are coming. They are fast-tracking the departmental proceeding against you. I think he is putting pressure on everyone to start the process to dismiss you now,' Roy said, his face sombre and eyes not meeting Raj's eyes.

His suspension would soon turn into dismissal, and his police friend would be gone in a day—a long sigh escaped Raj. He knew about Dev's power and influence, but he had always thought they were fighting the same battle. Never in his wildest dream did he imagine that he would be at the receiving end of the mastermind's machinations. 'It's okay sir, we will wait and see what happens. But tell me about Asha madam's death. Don't you think it is suspicious?'

'Well, the director called me yesterday morning to discuss the translocation process—they are planning to send four rhinos to the new site. This Nepali cook came running to the lounge room and said memsahib was lying on the floor. We rushed upstairs, but she was dead by then.

'I called the doctor from the dispensary; he confirmed an overdose of sleeping tablets. The cook said she had asked him to bring lukewarm water for her, and she swallowed a handful of tablets. She then dismissed him. When he went to check on her after some time, she was on the floor.'

'Why did he not stop her?' Raj asked.

'This is what I asked the moron. He said he never intervened with whatever madam did.'

'Has the police interrogated him?'

'The director trusts him completely. He didn't suspect anything.' Roy gave a sad smile.

'What happened after that?'

'What happens in such a situation? The media people with their cameras—the usual drama. I think the director pulled some strings to ensure there was no post-mortem. The poor man probably couldn't bear to see his beautiful wife all shredded and dissected.' Roy shook his head as if regretting something. 'I could not come up with anything to make a post-mortem happen.'

There was a frown on his face. 'It is all because of that obnoxious sister of hers! She created such a scene with her loud wailing and chest-beating that there was no other option but to rush with the funeral.' Roy let out a sigh, slowly getting up from his seat. He was about to say something when his phone rang. He started pacing the room as he listened to the person on the other end, vigorously shaking his head. Raj gazed into Roy's eyes, confusion soaring in his head. His stoic face gave nothing away. Casting a vacant gaze, he came near Raj and suddenly shook him by his shoulder. 'Dinner tonight? Or do you have some other plans with your friend?' He raised his brows.

'Okay sir, dinner is fine with me.' Raj knew he had no other choice.

Roy picked up the whiskey bottle from the floor, poured some of the content into his glass, and then emptied the rest into another glass that he handed to Raj. He settled down again on the sofa. 'Yesterday, when we were busy with the funeral preparation, what were you three doing under the hedge in the director's garden? It was quite a curious sight.' He chuckled.

'Sir, we found the dead girl's scooty at Vulture Hill,' Raj narrated the incident about the discovery along with Arjun's input that Victor Hanse had bought the scooty.

'Victor?' Roy's eyes became big like saucers. 'So, Victor, from the Hill Division Office, gave it to her. But you said she avoided the man.' Roy was about to start his deduction.

'Sir, do you know this man, Victor?' Raj interrupted him.

'I know that bastard. Listen, he is helping us with the list.' Roy leaned towards Raj with a chuckle.

'Sir, is this man reliable? The people in the hill town didn't have much good to say about him.' Raj felt his heart rate going up.

'He is one of the most corrupt officials of the hill district,' Roy said in a matter-of-fact way. 'However, he is not into what wildlife crime control bureau people are looking for. He comes clean and knows people who could be involved. That's why I included him in the team.'

Roy took a long breath. 'Look, they were friends for a long time—I mean your Asha madam and Dorothy. Maybe Dorothy had confided in her that she feared someone might hurt her. That's why she looked so scared when she showed you Dorothy's photo. You guys should have questioned her further, but instead, you panicked and fled.' An exasperated Roy's nostrils flared up.

Both Raj and Amelia fell silent. Roy's eyes were bloodshot. 'Listen, all this fear of the affair becoming public knowledge, a love child, etc. are bullshit. Our director didn't conceal anything from his wife. She tacitly approved of his affairs; it kept him away from her physically. Why would he be afraid of his illicit relationship coming out of the closet?'

'Sir, then what is the motive? Why was she murdered?' Raj asked.

'Dorothy stumbled upon something she should not have seen. Those dark secrets scared her.' Roy shuddered in an exaggerated way to underline his revulsion. 'That girl fearing for her life might have confided to Asha madam. Your Asha madam loved her good friend from the hills a lot, as she was the one who relieved her from all the physical nuisance of marital life. 'That's why she was concerned, and she was worried about her friend. Her friend's life was in danger.' Roy paused; his face contorted to reflect the vague clouds of uneasiness forming in his head due to excessive alcohol. 'Can we unearth what she saw? That is the million-dollar question,' he thundered.

***

Chapter 34

Day 10 (Night)

A thunderous explosion boomed in the sky above. The room's air became heavy with moisture—rain was imminent. With the moon hiding behind the clouds, the sleepy town was covered in a shroud of misty darkness when they left Roy's quarter. Raj dialled Arjun's number.

'Yes, he has arrived. He is not in the resort. He is in the town.' Arjun hung up.

As Raj and Amelia settled in the car, Raj instructed the skinny driver to go to the Rhino Warrior's office. The driver turned towards them with glee. 'I met up with some old friends of mine. Sir, most of them were poachers. They surrendered and joined the Rhino Warriors.' He chuckled; it seemed he had been having a party of his own with his old buddies. Amelia, who had been leaning on Raj's shoulder, sleepy and tired, suddenly straightened up, disengaging from

Raj. 'Are we going to meet Dev?' She moved away slightly as Raj nodded, his heart pounding.

A single yellow bulb dimly lit the veranda of the Rhino Warriors office. The SUV was parked in the front yard. Three of his armed guards stood outside, smoking and chatting. *What is he doing at this hour?*

The unpretentious premise was a façade to give the public a humble NGO office-like image; the resort was too upmarket. When protest rallies and sloganeering were planned, this place was the perfect stage for all the drama. The venue of choice for prestigious events, such as hosting foreign sponsors and symposiums on rhino poaching, was the resort.

'Still in office?' Raj peeked into the room from the door, tired and a bit tipsy, as he pushed the door open.

'Hello, *dada*, what a surprise! Amelia too?' Dev looked up from his laptop; his eyes were curious. His face was dark with concern, generally not associated with the man.

'How come you are here at this hour?' Raj made himself comfortable on a chair. 'Dorothy, Amelia's friend, is missing.' He let loose a smile, waiting to see Dev's reaction.

'Is it the same girl whose Facebook profile you and Amelia checked out,' Dev said, typing fast.

'You know her, don't you?' Raj confronted him softly.

Dev shut his laptop. 'Why are you intruding into my private life?' He cried out in anguish. After taking a moment to compose himself, he continued, 'You two have been inseparable for the last few days, but have I questioned you?

Initially, I was concerned about her as she was my guest. Then I realised she could take care of herself, at least when you are around, and I backed off. I don't understand why you are trying to question my connection to that girl?'

'She is no longer missing. She is dead.'

'She is dead?' Dev repeated.

'Really?' Dev said.

'Why don't you look surprised? Was it something you expected?' Raj knew he was being insensitive.

'I am not because I knew she was in a kind of a mess,' Dev's voice choked.

'Will you tell us what you know of her? I gathered from my sources that you used to meet her in Dimapur hotel.'

'Well, who is doing the investigation here? The forest department or the police?'

Raj felt a hot flush appearing on his face; his nostrils flared up. He moved to the other side of the desk and placed his bare hands on Dev's shoulder. Standing, Raj loomed large over the bespectacled NGO chief crouched on his comfortable chair. Resisting his urge to get hold of the slender neck in his arm and strangle the man, he said, 'Dev, don't bother about that. I need to clarify certain facts.' With alcohol high in his head, he might lose his patience despite the presence of those henchmen outside.

'What is it?' Dev asked, his voice wobbly.

'An innocent girl was killed, and there was an attempt to pin the blame on me.' Raj stated the Vulture Hill incident, 'And she was the person who I was supposed to meet at the camp. She had said that she had some vital information to share with me.'

'You didn't tell me about it?' Dev's tone was accusatory.

'Why should I tell you?' Raj shook with rage. 'You say you hardly knew the girl. On the other hand, you used to link up with her in a hotel.' His eyes bore through a visibly shaken Dev.

Dev took a deep breath. He sank on his chair like a deflated balloon, removed his rimless glasses, his gaze at the ceiling. 'What do you want to know from me about that girl?'

'Everything,' Raj thundered as he came back to face him from the other side of the desk.

'I met Dorothy when she came with some of her friends for a safari to the park. I invited them to stay at my resort, and that's when it began,' Dev started. 'A beautiful innocent girl, she caught my eyes. We became friendly. She suggested a hotel in Dimapur where we could meet. I would go to her place, pick her up and then we would spend a couple of nights in that place. I always had business in Dimapur, talking to the informers about poachers and, in exchange, keeping them happy.'

'So, the girl you claimed you hardly knew was your lover.' Raj shook his head; the smile just seeped out. 'Did it continue till the day she was killed?'

'No, no, *dada*,' Dev's voice rose, 'nothing like that. Within months, I found out that she was involved with the director. Then I started distancing myself from her.'

'Did you love her? Or were you merely...?' Raj could not

slow his breathing.

'*Dada*, I will be honest with you. She loved your Ajay sir and believed that they would eventually marry. I was infatuated with her.' Dev let out a long sigh. 'I know I should not have done it, but I slowly distanced myself from her. It was difficult. She was lovely, and she had a beautiful heart.' Tears rolled down his eyes.

'When did you see her last?' Raj deliberately sounded acerbic.

'We had not met for at least six months. But a few days ago, I received a call from her. She was here to meet the director.'

'Why did she call you?' Raj's teeth gritted.

Dev paused; he took a deep breath as if trying to remember every bit of the conversation. 'On her birthday, I think in the middle of last year, I gifted her a scooty. After we broke off, Dorothy kept pestering me to take it back. I was not bothered as I wanted her to keep it. So, when she came here, she rode it down here to return it to me. She told me that the director wanted to marry her.

'I think she found it hard to believe that he would marry her. She sounded unsure and very apprehensive. She asked me what she should do about the director's proposal. She thought it was a trap, that the man actually didn't want to do it. And then she said something quite unexpected.'

'What did she say?' Raj asked in trepidation.

'She said even if the director was ready for the marriage, she was not sure. She had seen certain things at his place in the hill town, which scared her.'

'Did you ask her what she saw?' Amelia sounded shaky.

'Of course, that got me interested.' Dev repositioned himself on his chair, leaning towards his audience. 'I asked her what it was. She said I wouldn't believe it, and then she stopped, saying she needed to hang up as a police jeep was coming to her, and she hung up.'

Raj looked at Amelia—now what? A streak of lightning lit up the sky, followed by a thunderous boom seconds later. The unreliable power supply was gone, engulfing the room in ominous darkness while the unfinished story muddled up their heads.

'Did you call her again, Dev?' Raj asked after some time, sitting next to Amelia as his eyes adjusted to the dark interior.

'I called her immediately, not once but many times, but she neither received nor returned my calls,' the shadowy storyteller from the opposite side of the desk said.

Raj remembered Amelia showing Dorothy's call records: one outgoing call to an unknown number and quite a few missed calls from the same number.

'I thought of checking on her the next day. But then I got busy—the old rhino death incident, the kidnapping news, the raincoat distribution ceremony; all came one after the other, and I completely forgot about Dorothy.' Dev sank onto his chair, clasping both his hands and bringing them to his chin. The power supply had not yet been restored, and rain began to fall from the tar-black sky. The downpour was immense, and the heavens thundered once again.

'Did you say a police vehicle came to pick Dorothy? The only police vehicle would be from Arjun's police station, wouldn't it?' Raj waited to see Dev's reaction.

Dev shrugged. 'That's what she said.'

'Did the village girl who was kidnapped, work in River View?' Raj changed the track.

'*Dada*, honestly speaking, I don't know. My resort gives employment to so many people.' Another shrug followed. Raj stopped short of asking him about the cook in the director's bungalow, needing a whiff of fresh air to clear his mind. As Raj walked out of the room, Dev's eyes were glued to his mobile, frantically typing something. A cold gust hit his face; the sky was getting cleared of the rain clouds. Moonlight shone on the puddles of rainwater.

'What do you think of what Dev told us?' Amelia asked.

'Dev was lying—they were all concocted tales. If he gave Dorothy the scooty, how could it be in Victor's name?' Raj's heart started pounding.

They are together. This means the bastard is aware of the plan he hatched with Roy. A shiver went down his spine as, standing near the door, he took one last look at Dev, who was reading something on his laptop. In the dim light of the monitor's glare, his eyes gleamed with the cold stare of death.

★★★

Chapter 35

Day 10 (Late Night)

Stepping out of Dev's office, Raj called Roy's number, who received calls 24/7.

'What's up?' The man sounded chirpy. Perhaps he had opened another bottle after the guests departed.

'Dev and Victor are together.' Raj was almost out of his breath. 'We should not go ahead with our plan.'

'It's too late now. It is not in my hand,' Roy almost growled.

'Sir, please do whatever you can to stop them.' Raj knew the limits with his temperamental boss. Yet, he said, 'Sir, are you drinking? I think you should get some rest.'

'None of your business. Don't call me again.' He hung up.

Raj needed a whiff of fresh air to clear his mind. As he walked out to the car holding Amelia's hand, the cold gust could not dissipate the hot flush of his cheeks. There was no point in calling up Arjun; Roy hardly kept the police in the loop. He heard the roar of an engine; a blue-coloured van passed them fast, splashing them with muddy water from the road's potholes.

Back in his quarters, Raj traced his thumb over Amelia's forehead gently as a faint smile spread on her face. As he drew his finger over her nose to her lips, Amelia opened her eyes, the gaze stirring a tingling sensation through his body. He took a deep breath. Her fingers twirled the curls falling over his face.

His look wandered, stopping at her belly button showing through the transparent nighty; his mind flashed Dorothy's image. There were no signs of violations, nor did her clothing have any creases.

A sense of dread threatened to crush him, but it passed as he looked at the most beautiful face resting on his lap. Her lavender perfume smelt divine. Enough of conversation—Raj quickly slid down beside her. They were tired and sleepy, but everything wore off as their bodies came together in a tight embrace. Raj's hand ran over her smooth back underneath the nighty. He planted a kiss on her parted lips, and soon, they were immersed in the frenzied discovery of each other's body—a night-long journey, losing track of time.

A phone rang; the ringtone was unfamiliar. It kept ringing while Raj buried his head into her bosom. It rang a few more times, the rings getting drowned in the increasing moaning of two bodies on fire.

'Raj, somebody is calling Dorothy's number.' Amelia made Raj stop as she extended her arm to collect the phone from the bedside table. The name 'Sir' blinked on the screen. 'Raj, it is your director calling Dorothy,' Amelia almost shouted, pushing an unrelenting and panting Raj away from her body. 'I think it must be an emergency. He would not have called at this hour.'

Raj, gathering his senses, clamoured to find something to wear.

'He does not know that she is dead,' Amelia said, covering herself.

'Can you please call him back?' Raj said.

Amelia dialled back the number. But no one picked it up. 'Raj, there is something wrong. Your director is not at home. He is going somewhere,' Amelia's voice was tense as she kept a steady stare on the screen.

'How do you know where Ajay sir is?'

'Raj, gather your men. We need to rush. Dorothy's phone gives your director's location. I will explain it. But I think he is in some soup right now.'

Raj had never driven so fast in his life. The speeding trucks and night buses with their high blinding beams on the highway could not slow him down. Almost all the guards and foresters of the camp followed in other vehicles. He had asked for reinforcement from other rangers nearer to Vulture Hill. Arjun was already on his way after receiving the frantic call from Raj.

Within half an hour, they were on the unpaved road leading to Vulture Hill, the car lights piercing the foggy darkness. Amelia's eyes were glued on Dorothy's phone. 'Yes.'

Her close-fisted hand pushed against her mouth. 'He arrived at Vulture Hill half an hour ago.'

Raj pressed hard on the accelerator. 'How do you know?' His mind was still befuddled by the fact that they were all headed towards the place where it had all started.

'Both your director and Dorothy—the two love birds, have this app called Life360. So, Dorothy's phone shows where her lover is.'

Raj was about to say something but stopped; the dark shadow of Vulture Hill loomed ahead. The hillock's grassy slope, lit by the headlights of numerous vehicles parked haphazardly at the base, revealed armed personnel running about hither and thither. Raj got down from the car. A few policemen directed a torchlight beam towards the silk-cotton tree's top canopy.

Raj caught Amelia and jostled through the guards and police in the dark towards Arjun, who was barking out instructions, his eyes gleaming like a ferocious cat. He wiped beads of sweat from his creased forehead with a hanky and pointed to the top of the tree to wonder aloud, 'How the heck did he climb the tree to get to that branch?'

A lifeless body swung like a rag doll from the tree's tallest branch. Arjun flashed the light on the face. In the darkness, the face was not visible. In the beam of the torch, the eyes had the cold, vacant stare of death, and his head tilted to the side at an odd angle. Raj tugged Amelia away. 'Please don't look up,' he said, aghast.

The scene at Vulture Hill was like something from a war

zone. Burly Forest Battalion soldiers stood ready with their automatic weapons around the rangers alongside the short, tough men from Arjun's police station. On that freezing, frosty night, the men impatiently sniffed the air for the scent of the intruder who came after the life of not rhinos, but their director.

His other colleagues did not hold back; they arrived with their anti-poaching crack forces at lightning speed as they were much nearer to the location than Raj's range office. All dressed in their official khaki uniforms gathered around the hillock's base, slowly marching towards the desolate camp. The mood was of excitement and trepidation; the armed men had no idea of the kind of adversaries they could meet inside the locked house.

'They had already fled when we reached here.' Arjun's breathing was heavy.

'Did you see them? What was the vehicle?' Raj asked.

'We saw a blue van passing. My man said this was the same vehicle parked in the resort when that incident happened in Amelia's room. I think that is the van of his assassins.' Arjun was a raging inferno. 'If only we had reached a few minutes earlier.' He shook his head, panting and heaving.

'How did he ...?' Raj stared at the body hanging from the branch. 'Where is Ajay sir? Is that him?'

'By the time we reached, the man was already hanging from the tree. No signs of your director.'

A strange scent of burning incense wafted through the foggy air.

'He is still here. That's what Dorothy's mobile indicates,' Amelia joined the conversation, pointing towards the camp bathed in a misty smoke. They ran to the top of the hillock, Arjun running out of breath, beaming his torchlight at the door of the camp. It was locked; a brass lock hung there. An orange halo bathed the back of the camp. The group rushed to the rear of the house. They could not see through the smoke of burning incense and coconut husk as they stood under the silk-cotton tree. The backdoor was closed, and a small fire was lit in a makeshift earthen pedestal decorated with flowers, red and yellow cloth pieces and various paraphernalia required for religious rituals.

Arjun directed his beam to the ground and screamed in fright and disgust. Raj felt like vomiting. The place was littered with headless pigeons. A black goat, tied to the tree's trunk, circled it, bleating in panic. On the pedestal rested a large sacrificial sword smeared with a vermillion mark or maybe with the blood of the birds already sacrificed.

Raj dialled Ronald's number. 'Where are you? We are in your camp.'

'Sir, Vijay babu asked us to evacuate the place and go to Riverside camp,' Ronald said from the other side; his voice was heavy with sleep. 'Why have you gone there at this hour?'

'What time did you leave?' Raj had to cut him off.

'We left at around nine.'

'Did Vijay come here?'

'No sir, he called me on my mobile and ordered us to vacate the place.'

'You guys come here as soon as possible.' Raj hung up as the armed forest guards and police officials surrounded the house, and a few policemen, at the behest of their commander, let off a round of blanks into the air. Once the lock was broken, the men rushed inside, opening the door. There, they all stopped and gaped.

A stark-naked director—his forehead smeared with bright red vermillion marks and head as bald as a coot, with the floor littered with his freshly shaven hair, seemed to be blissfully asleep in foetal position on the cot where Raj had found Dorothy's body ten days ago.

★★★

Chapter 36

Day 11 (Morning)

It was well past midnight when the ambulance sped away with the unconscious and seriously ill director.

'We will come again in the morning to get that body down,' Arjun said. 'What are your plans? Are you going back to get some rest?' He sounded tired, his eyes thankful.

The eerie darkness of that night could not hide the silhouette of the body that hung from the branch—the witch's fork. Raj stared up at the sky and studied the moon's silver glow, which appeared from the cloud. Was it swinging to the breeze? Who was it? It could have been the director, or it could have been him. He shook his head. He would not spend the night where a body was hanging from a tree and another man was about to be beheaded in a bizarre ritual. 'Yes, I need to go to the ranger quarters.'

Dorothy, Asha madam, the unknown body and then an

unconscious and shaven Ajay sir and that sacrificial sword—Raj did not think he would get any sleep when he finally reached his campus just before dawn broke. But he slept like a log until his eyes opened to the bright sunlight seeping through the ventilator.

There was a loud knocking on the door. Raj hurriedly put on his clothes. He pulled the shawl over Amelia who had curled her body into a ball, before opening the door. It was noon; a warm, bright day had replaced the freezing night. Vijay stood on the veranda, shaking with excitement.

'Have you heard, sir? There was a raid in the director sahib's bungalow. One tiger skin, many kilos of bones, and a leopard's hide have been found,' his deputy blurted out in one breath.

'Raid in the director's bungalow?' Raj felt a chill up his spine.

'Yes sir, there have been simultaneous raids in the houses of top forest officials—six places altogether,' the man panted, his eyes gleaming.

An uncanny sense of heightened activity gripped the campus. Across the lawn, near the kitchen, groups of people talked excitedly, huddled around smouldering embers of the morning bonfires. Amelia joined him, dressed in her denim jeans and a sweatshirt. 'What is it?' she asked.

'The wildlife crime people raided the houses of many forest officers, including our director's house,' Raj said, his head reeling under confusion.

'Raid in your director's house?' Amelia's face creased in

bewilderment. 'Is that why he ran away?'

Raj shook his head, thinking of his maverick senior who could initiate a raid amid all the chaos. How did the director land in Vulture Hills? Were the superstitious villagers planning to make a human sacrifice? A shiver ran through his spine. He dialled Roy's number.

'Sir, just heard about the seizes at various places.' How had he convinced the CID and the wildlife crime detectives to search the most 'sacred' place—that of the residence of the director of Kaziranga National Park. How did he manage it? 'Sir, Ajay sir's place also has been raided?'

'Actually, we didn't plan it. I don't know how it happened. Switch on the television. You will see what our boss was hoarding with his partners in crime.'

'But...?'

'Don't be surprised. I am not take the credit. However, if the sleuths had better insights, why would I complain?' Roy sounded euphoric. 'My God, who will believe a rhino horn was in the Kaziranga director's residence.' There was a massive burst of laughter. 'I have to congratulate these guys. They took a huge risk. You can see the results: six raids all over the state—eight big cat skins, pelts of rare felines; can you even imagine—parts of a black bear! Do you know how much cash they found? Thirty-five crores! I expect more will be unearthed.' There was a sigh from Roy's side. 'I can retire in peace.'

'Sir, what about River View Resort?'

'Hmm.' Roy paused. 'They didn't find anything in your

friend's place. What do you think?'

Raj let out a sigh. 'Any update on the director's health? Has he gained consciousness?'

Raj could sense suppressed laughter. 'Is it true how you people found him? Who shaved off his head?' Roy coughed. 'Did he run to that place to save himself, or did someone take him there?'

'Don't know, sir.' Human sacrifice in today's age, Raj shuddered. 'Congratulations, sir!' Raj said, but it came out half-heartedly.

'Don't congratulate me yet. My wife is not back; she refuses to take my calls. I hope she is watching this drama unfold on TV. I am now going to see the natural history museum that our boss has created.' Roy hung up abruptly.

Almost immediately, Raj's phone rang again. It was Dev. '*Dada*, have you seen the news?'

'Yes, I did.' Raj felt like a deflated balloon.

'Incredulous, unthinkable!' Dev thundered from the other side.

'Yes, it is a huge slur on the department.' Raj hoped Dev would not find out who instigated the raid at his place.

'They raided my premises also, but didn't find anything. Yes, I admit I accepted many poachers into my NGO. I made sure they gave up what they were doing and contributed meaningfully to conservation. The sleuths arrested five people from my organisation, including a few workers from my resort. I won't deny there were some suspicious characters,' Dev said.

'It's good that they have been busted. I would never allow the name of the Rhino Warriors, for which I toiled for the last ten years, to be sullied by these bastards.'

Dev went on and on till Raj cut him off, 'Dev, I need to go to the director's residence and then to Vulture Hill. Will talk to you later.'

As Raj's vehicle reached the road leading to the bungalow, a vast crowd had surrounded the house. People shouted in excited voices. The few stick-wielding police personnel posted there were facing a tough time controlling the restive horde. The security forces had cordoned off the whole compound. Looking like a warrior who had vanquished his enemy, Roy stood at the doorstep of the bungalow shouting instructions to let Raj in.

There were spotlights, and the room was full of police personnel and photographers. On the floor were the pelts of one tiger and one leopard and dried body parts of various animals.

Roy grabbed Raj by the arm. 'Can you imagine these poachers masquerading as forest officers wiped out the entire feline population from our parks?' He pointed to a corner of the room where a few police personnel were grilling the director's servants. 'Surprising! I didn't expect this.' Roy bit his lower lip.

Roy's phone rang. He received it and hung up seconds later. 'Let's go to Vulture Hill,' Roy barked abruptly in a business-like manner and vanished from the scene. Raj took Amelia's hand and pulled her towards his car through the hordes of policemen, forest guards, and curious onlookers. The media persons, the cameramen and breaking news anchors wound up their equipment and rushed to their waiting vans with gaudy logos and round jutting antenna dishes.

Roy's white Ambassador had already zoomed out of sight. A cavalcade of cars with sirens screaming and red beacon lights blinking overtook them at high speed, presumably going to Vulture Hill. The unpaved road to the place was lined with a motley group of villagers, mostly bare-bodied, wearing a small cotton towel around their waists, but all were armed with their mobile phones. Most of the faces were devoid of emotion; they were just in a mad rush to reach the spot and capture on camera whatever spectacle was unfolding there.

Raj touched Amelia's hand. 'Are you all right?'

Her eyes welled up, and a teardrop escaped down her cheek, which was flushed pink. Raj gave her hand a reassuring squeeze.

When they reached Vulture Hills, Raj saw that the department men had successfully positioned a ladder behind the cottage against a branch. It was proving to be a logistical nightmare—how would they get the body down before dusk, given the short winter day.

A hesitant rotund Ronald armed with a machete fastened to a bamboo pole was standing precariously on the top end of the ladder resting against the branch from which the body hung. Varied instructions from colleagues and from the ground below compounded his confusion. The ladder creaked under his weight.

'Who asked him to go up?' Roy asked, exasperated. 'He is too slow. And look at his body. The whole thing might break; he is so heavy.'

'Don't worry, Sir. He is a strong man; he will do the job,' Raj tried to reason.

'We don't need a wrestler to cut the rope!' Roy shouted again, flustered. 'A lithe young boy,' he said, pointing to a thin boy in the crowd, 'like him would have been the right choice. Look at your man, it looks as if he has got all the time on earth to climb to the top.'

Ronald's ascent, indeed, was agonisingly slow. The branch from which the body hung swayed. Ronald shouted that it would be difficult to cut the rope if the body kept swinging like that.

'Where is the cover?' Roy screamed at his men. A dozen men scampered to take a position under the canopy of the tree, holding a tarpaulin sheet.

'Watch out.' There was a shriek from a terrified Ronald as he clung dearly to the ladder while throwing his machete. The branch broke, and the body came down with a creak. The men laboured to reposition the sheet below the fall. But they were too slow; it fell straight into the water tank below it—the same water tank where Dorothy had spent one whole freezing night.

Everyone rushed to see the body. The confused faces revealed their dilemma—it was not someone they knew. Raj shoved his way through the onlookers. The guards lifted the body out of the tub and laid it on the ground. The man had a round face and a bald head with a goatee. His eyes were closed. He looked peaceful despite the long hours the body had hung from the branch.

'He is Victor, ACF, Hill division.' A cold shiver ran down Raj's spine.

***

Chapter 37

Day 11 (Evening)

'Raj, the hide of the other cat they found in the director's place, is it a clouded leopard?' Amelia asked, her eyes inquisitive.

'Hey, you know a lot about big cats.' Raj's brows creased. 'I was thinking about it. That is an exceedingly rare carnivore. The pelt seized at the bungalow was an old one. I am sure no such leopards have been poached in Kaziranga since Ajay Mathur joined in the last three months. In fact, I am not sure whether we have that species in Kaziranga.'

Raj took a deep breath, eyes spying on her.

She is fantastic; she knows more about the region's cat family than the forest department.

He held the gaze a bit too long, and that distraction made him swerve the vehicle to the side, bringing out a shocked cry from Amelia. A convoy of police vehicles masked by dust heading from the opposite side would have almost collided with their car. He braked and apologised profusely to Amelia.

Raj opened the door and came out; he needed a whiff of fresh air to clear his mind. A cold, moisture-laden gust hit his face as the rain clouds gathered above in the sky. A mourning husband led to a desolate location by his former deputy to meet his lover. Someone had killed Victor and was about to harm the director in a strange way, in some macabre sacrificial ritual. An innocent Australian girl who spent her hard-earned money to get relief for the guards was abducted to be murdered gruesomely. He took a deep breath to steady his nerves.

Amelia was still inside the vehicle, her hand resting on her chin. The evil men could have slit a vein of her beautiful hand to let the unconscious girl bleed to death. A few strands of her golden-brown hair flew out of the car window in the breeze. They could have cracked her skull with a rod and thrown the body in one of the east Kolkata water bodies. Her neck was bereft of any necklace or jewellery. The bastards would have strangled her with their ring-wearing dirty fingers.

Raj thought of the director, a handsome, immaculately dressed, well-mannered, modest officer. He realised he had never met a senior as gentle and efficient as him. The forest department was full of uncouth, boorish seniors. Ajay Mathur was not one of them. He shuddered, thinking of how that beautiful man was lying senseless on the cot without a trace of clothes.

'When is he going to get well enough to talk?' Raj wondered, knowing he could not afford to wait till then. He had to act fast.

Police jeeps with sirens blazing and the red beacon light burning bright, followed by the ambulance carrying Victor's dead body, passed them, leaving a trail of dust obfuscating Raj's vision and mind.

By the time Raj and Amelia approached the ranger office campus, a curtain of rain had swept across the vast savannah of Kaziranga. They hurried inside the quarters as an explosion of the evening birdsong erupted from the dripping trees. The sky started pouring at that very moment.

Raj inhaled the air heavy with moisture. The grey clouds gradually moved in. It seemed the heavens were not done yet. The croaks of red jungle fowls emanated from the bushes. It was not a typical Kaziranga evening; a nameless sense of dread engulfed him. He remembered the gunshots that echoed through the campus just a few days back. It could happen anytime again.

One may have the best guards, but what could one do if there were traitors within. The park was too big and too porous and surrounded by too many people. Now they not only had to deal with sharpshooters from the neighbouring hill states, machete-wielding stubborn hunters from the local communities, or groups of poachers of suspected nationalities armed to the teeth, but there was also a new breed of villains, one who committed crimes in a stealthy manner, there were no gunshots and no sounds of chopping off of the horn. Just clicks of a mouse, a sound too subtle, too sophisticated to be heard by rangers like Raj.

He felt a light tap on his shoulder. Amelia handed him a cup of tea. He stood there, blowing steam from the hot mug cupped in his hands, held close to his chest to ward off the morning chill. He shook his head unconsciously; the world he knew, the people he believed in, everything had evaporated like vapour into a realm of implausibility.

Amelia took out Dorothy's phone. 'It has many calls and messages from the 'Sir' number, your director; the last call was at 12:45 at night. Your director texting Dorothy so often means he did not know about her murder. As per TV reports, the raids took place in the early morning. We found him in Vulture Hill just after midnight. How did he go there? Where was his car?' Amelia asked.

Raj remembered seeing the director's car in the courtyard with all its seats ripped off—the raiding army had not taken any chance.

'If he had gone to Vulture Hill to meet her, he could not have walked to the place. He would have taken his car, but his car was not there. He went there with someone else.'

That someone used Victor to lure him. And then killed him once the job was done.

'Victor might have told him that Dorothy wanted to meet him. That's why your director called the girl's number. When we returned the call, he did not receive it; maybe his abductors stopped him,' Amelia said, lightly clenching Raj's arm with her fingers.

Those butchers first took care of Victor.

'I don't know. But I am surprised that the sleuths would raid the director's place,' Raj said.

'Why don't you talk to Arjun and check if they have any leads?' Amelia said.

Raj dialled Arjun's number. It was not received, but a message popped in. 'I am preparing for my handover. He arrives tomorrow. Call me later.'

Raj shook his head and got lost in his thoughts. He felt like he was walking out of a stupor when his phone rang again. It was the same unknown number.

'Please don't disconnect, sir,' on the other side, the child pleaded, the voice much clearer than the last calls. 'Do you remember me? I served you in our restaurant when you came to the forest office.'

The boy from the hill town eatery. What does he want?

'*Malik* said you came again looking for me. He gave me your number.' The boy almost sounded breathless. 'I have something to say about Dorothy *didi*. I called you many times earlier too.'

'Yes, go on, I am listening.' Raj was all ears.

'One schoolboy came to meet her. They sat here in our place. They fought, shouting at each other.'

'Schoolboy?' Raj was confused. The boy called to tell him a schoolboy visited Dorothy; he felt exasperated, his initial euphoria of getting a new lead disappearing quickly.

'Yes, he wears spectacles, and he drives a big car. It has a picture of a rhino head with two spears.'

So, Dev had gone to the hill division office to meet Dorothy.

'What did they talk about? Did you hear anything?' Raj's interest returned, feeling thankful to the nonchalant owner who had handed the chit with his phone number to the boy.

'Yes, sir,' the boy also sounded excited, 'that's why I called. Dorothy *didi* said he was wrong in asking for donations from foreigners.'

Raj's head spun. 'What did he say?'

'He was trying to pacify her. She said something that got the schoolboy mad. He grabbed her by her wrist and almost dragged her to his car and drove off.'

'When did that man, umm, the schoolboy, go there?'

'He came just a few days before you came here with the memsahib, say three weeks ago.'

Raj felt the crack of thunder, a flash of light in the sky. The campus was strangely quiet—even Daju's kitchen was devoid of any activities. Raj took a deep breath, his head reeling under the latest revelation from the child. The child would never lie.

'Thank you very much for your call. When I come to your place the next time, I will get a good gift for you.' Raj was about to hang up when he remembered something. 'Hello, are you there? Do you remember anything else about that schoolboy? I mean, did you ever see him with Victor?'

'Sir, both are good friends. I have seen them talking with each other many times.'

Dev said he had not met Dorothy for six months. Raj hung up and excitedly narrated the conversation to Amelia.

'You have known Dev for years,' Amelia said as the campus was slowly covered by a dark carpet of night. Raj could see smoke coming out of the kitchen and the frantic movement of Daju's helpers.

'Yes, ever since I joined the department.'

Raj's heart started racing. He felt a hot flush. 'As per Roy, Victor was well aware of the raids. The deal was that he would give information about the places to be raided.'

'But you said the man was equally corrupt.'

Raj was at a loss; how could he explain to Amelia. 'Victor had made money, but far too less than some of his other colleagues. His loot came from timber, minor forest products and illegal stone quarries. Roy and the sleuths were after those involved in smuggling wildlife products. Well, the wildlife crime detectives took him into confidence so that he could lead them to the others engaged in more heinous crimes.'

'And Victor knew both, Dev and your director?' Amelia's forehead creased in thought.

'They had worked together for almost five years in the hill division, and I think they had their secrets. There were some scandals about mining leases. Though not directly involved, the director might have turned a blind eye.' Raj looked across the open courtyard at one of the staff quarters.

'You stay here,' Raj said to Amelia as he went inside his bedroom and bent down to collect the golf club he always kept under his bed. 'I will be back.' He walked out of his quarters, gripping the club. Two foresters came running to him. 'Get some ropes,' Raj ordered them as they headed towards his destination. Raj returned after around fifteen minutes, his heart pumping as he dialled Arjun's number. Arjun received the call immediately. They talked for some time. 'Yes, come now. We need to act soon,' Arjun said before disconnecting.

Raj pressed hard on the accelerator of his SUV with Amelia by his side. A mini truck having a tied and gagged captive followed them as apocalyptic clouds laden with rain hovered up above, hiding the sun. His pistol rested in the gap between his seat and the passenger's seat.

No, he would not use it. A 400 m range INSAS would be better; the man should get a taste of his own medicine—how hard he had tried to force the government to supply the rifles to the park guards.

★★★

Chapter 38

Day 11 (Evening)

The highway was a long grey stretch of emptiness. Streaks of lightning lit up the landscape with thunderous assaults. Amelia had never seen a more ominous sky before. Is this what they call the Indian monsoon? A draft of cold moisture-laden air hit her face; Raj's eyes were steady on the road. She felt the car drifting; with the coming of the evening, the breeze, bouncing back from the green hills, started unleashing its fury on the trees and the savannah of the park. Raj reduced his speed a bit, his jaws clenched as the mini truck following them tried hard to catch up. She shivered briefly, seeing blood on his hands and knuckles. Raj did not speak.

His mood reflected what the day had turned out to be—dark and angry as the tall trees of the hills glowed with a mysterious sheen. Raj's foot pressed on the accelerator on the empty street, and within minutes, they parked the car and rushed inside as a cold, relentless downpour started battering against the tin roof of the house.

'How come they didn't find anything at Dev's River View Resort?' Raj blurted out, seeing Arjun.

Arjun sat on his office chair behind his desk, all tidied up. His unbuttoned shirt revealed a hairy chest glistening with sweat despite the chill as he shook his head. There was a tired smile on his face as if asking, have you ever met a more brilliant adversary. 'That does mean River View Resort didn't have anything. Dorothy saw the animal pelts at Dev's place.'

'How the hell did they get permission to raid the director's bungalow in the first place?' Raj's breathing was heavy.

'Amazing, isn't it? The wildlife detectives daring to search a senior IFS officer's place!' Arjun smiled. 'There were a few allegations against Ajay Mathur when he was in the hill division. The man had been a mute spectator, which can be called complicity; maybe he did receive some cuts. Dev exaggerated that; he convinced someone higher in position that the man was into wildlife smuggling. Dev was sure that Dorothy might have told the director about the things she saw at his place.

'So, as far as Dev was concerned, the girl had to be eliminated, and the director had to be incriminated.' Arjun sighed, his face dark with rage. 'Our clueless Roy had no idea that he would be used like that.' Arjun looked at both Amelia and Raj and continued, 'Still, how did they find those things in his place? They were put there at the last moment.'

Amelia and Raj looked at each other. They did not

feel vindicated; nothing surprised them anymore. The deluge of inconceivable revelations, one after another, had numbed everything.

'One of the sleuths told me that they got a last-minute tip-off that the bungalow was the place of storage. Who did that?' Another cryptic smile. 'They went ahead and raided the place. The discovery surprised everyone.'

'Arjun, we have a lot of evidence against Dev.' Raj narrated the call from the restaurant boy. 'I have got Vijay. I gave him a thrashing. He admitted everything. He had the camp in Vulture Hill vacated as per Dev's instruction. They took the director to murder him. Can we arrest him?' Raj sounded breathless.

'On what charge?' Arjun asked, his hands clasped against his chin. 'Your deputy is a slimy bastard. The likes of him change their statements very soon.' Arjun remained cool as a cucumber. 'It will not hold any water in the court. The phone call, Facebook, all these things. And then he...' Arjun sighed. 'Do we have any time to pursue anything against him? Who will do the follow up even if I arrest him? Who will believe us after all these raids?' He bit his lower lip. 'The new person will be here tomorrow. Vijay will get bail within days.'

'You knew about Dev, didn't you?' Raj asked suddenly.

Arjun's jaws were clenched. 'Well, your director told me about an informer who had seen big cat pelts and rhino horns at Dev's place. He didn't tell me that it was his lover. We were flummoxed. We were in perilous territory. Who would believe Eastern India's biggest nature NGO is actually into these types of activities?'

'What did you decide to do?'

'Nothing! We were clueless, seriously. Dorothy, perhaps unsure whether we would act against Dev or not, decided to get in touch with you. But your friend moved amazingly fast. He is an expert in cleaning trails.' A sneer showed on Arjun's face.

'How come Ajay sir never pointed Dev to me? He never suggested that we should bring him into our radar.'

'Well, you know. Ajay Mathur is new. He is unsure what sort of relationship you had with Dev and how deep it was. That made him cautious. Well, he didn't confide in me directly. Our SP sir, I think, gave him the assurance that I could be trusted.'

'Are you going to interrogate Vijay? He is a departmental employee. I didn't have the right to bring him to the police station.' Raj looked at Arjun.

Arjun chuckled. 'You are a suspended ranger. You can do anything now.' He paused, tapped the table and said, 'Don't worry. We will make him clarify everything. That bastard thinks he is on Dev's payroll. He had asked the guards to vacate the camp on two occasions.' Arjun leaned forward, his palm resting against his cheeks. 'We will use him tonight. This time he will arrange the venue for his boss.' He gave Raj a side glance with a smirk on his face. 'Remember, a suspended ranger and a thoroughly pissed-off police officer can do anything.'

Raj took a deep breath, stretching his arms. The look on

his face said—time to take on the region's most prominent face of the conservation movement. Enough of activism!

Arjun turned his attention to Amelia. 'Dev hired those goons in Kolkata to kidnap you and maybe...' He paused and turned to Raj. 'He knew by telling his dirty secrets, Dorothy wanted to stop her from coming here.'

'Have you got Dev's call record?' Raj asked.

'I have had a mobile phone company ping his phone in real-time. But he has been using pre-paid sims for talking to his henchmen.' Arjun's gaze returned to Raj. 'You were lucky. The water tank saved you. The villagers led by Dev's goons would have finished you off. They would have set the camp on fire. Those people wouldn't have realised the girl was not the one from their village. For Dev, it would have been killing two birds with one stone.'

'Why did you remove the body? We could still have tracked the culprits,' Raj asked.

'No way.' Arjun shook his head. 'That bastard had the minister, as well as the press lined up. The moment a body was discovered there, all hell would have broken loose. The media would have convicted you there and then. The minister would have been quite happy to dismiss a rapist and murderer-ranger.'

'Whether you committed it or not—rape and murder, you would have been despatched to jail. You would remain there forever as an under-trial. That would have been the end of ranger Raj,' Arjun said in a matter-of-fact way. 'It would have been worse for us. It would have derailed our investigation against Dev. In no way would we be able to prove the allegations against Dev once the park ranger had murdered the girl who made the claims.'

Raj shook his head. 'How did he get those things in the bungalow? Roy was convinced that it was the director's fault.'

'That impulsive joker!' There was a sneer on Arjun's face. 'The raid was bad timing. He instigates the sleuths, and then this unfortunate thing happens. The wife commits suicide. They had already finalised the date. Victor leaked the information about the raid to Dev, who acted quickly. He had his man stationed in the bungalow—that Nepali cook. We have nabbed him too. He was the one to receive the animal pelt and other things after the director was led away.'

'Dev was coordinating all this when he told me a cock and bull story.' Raj's breathing got quicker. 'Why did Roy have to talk with Victor?'

'To be honest, it is all because of your crazy boss.' Arjun started fanning himself with a newspaper. 'When you suggested Dev's place to Roy, he might have discussed that with Victor, thinking that Victor knew more about the clandestine dealings of the Rhino Warrior. The madman didn't know that the wild night warden was Victor's buddy.'

'Dev asked Vijay to evacuate the camp. His friend goes to our distraught director and brings him to Vulture Hill. With all the bandits he had hired, it would not have been much of an effort to hang the poor man from the tree. They took off the director's clothes, shaved his head and were going to kill him in a macabre ritualistic way after killing Victor.'

'Why?' Amelia felt a shiver run down her spine.

'Well, some people are superstitious, and if you can attribute the killing to some witches or things like that, you can derail the investigation. Sensationalism pushes down all attempts of logical investigations.' Arjun came over to Amelia. 'Thanks to you. If you had not kept track of Dorothy's phone, we would have lost him.' The big, brawny man made an awkward attempt to thank Amelia by touching her shoulders with his shaky hands.

Amelia could never forget the moment; it was quite an effort to get to the phone, pulling herself away from that moment of just-to-occur bliss. A few seconds later, she might not have heard it ring with Raj's grunting, the brittle stubble of his growing beard rasping over the skin of her cheeks. Amelia turned her gaze on Raj, but he looked like an entirely different man—a Raj she had never seen before, blinking his eyes rapidly, twisting and curling his fingers as if ready to start a fight.

'Why didn't you tell me about Dev?' The sternness in his voice was quite unlike what she had heard before.

'I only came to know just a few days back when your director told me. Before we could formulate our strategy and take people like you into confidence, the warrior went on a killing spree. After that, we have been playing just catch up.' Arjun started hyperventilating.

'Dorothy saw things. He thought Amelia also knew his reality. But why me?' Raj asked, exasperated.

'Dev is fine with all your campaigns against poachers. He

wants rhinos to be conserved. But then most probably, he also instigates the killing of one or two rhinos now and then so that he can continue with his activism charade. But I think his focus items for trafficking were tokay gecko, pangolin, and smaller felines. They get killed and trafficked; nobody notices. When you started stopping all that, he didn't like it. But was it enough to provoke him to kill you?' Arjun paused for some time. 'No,' he said, shaking his head.

'The bastard has bought that piece of land in village eight, hasn't he?' Raj shook his head.

'Yes.' Arjun banged his thumb on the table. 'You were the biggest stumbling block for the scenic resort he had in mind for that spot. His partners, some businesspersons from Delhi, had offered the money for the plot. You, a bloody ranger, you wanted to append that area to the park. What are we calling it? The Eleventh addition?' Arjun gave a sarcastic laugh.

The wireless set crackled in the next room. Arjun hurried to receive it. When he came out, he was a different man, all pumped up. He signalled Raj by moving his brow. They stared at each other, exchanging a look that only those who have fought together many battles earlier would understand. A look that said the unsaid, as if something that they were planning had got into motion; they both nodded.

★★★

Chapter 39

Day 11 (Night)

Sultan was an adamant fella, very stubborn. Nobody knew what he had found in that relatively open area at the park's fringe region that he never bothered to venture back to the safe interior so bountiful in grass and water. All that the beast needed was a mud pit to wallow, and to stand on the riverbed, drying his skin coated with baked soil, away from the prying eyes of elephant-borne tourists and the noisy jeep safari travellers. That had gone on for decades. Authorities had failed to bring the animal to the safer areas of the park.

The frontier camp at Khaspur had the onerous task of looking after Sultan, the biggest and the oldest rhino of Kaziranga.

Standing almost seven feet tall and weighing nearly four and a half tons, the old bull was a giant among the giants, the hidden treasure of Kaziranga that ordinary tourists did not get to see. Only the department people knew about Sultan. And what they dreaded most was Sultan's death, either natural or by poacher's guns, because they knew one man was keeping an eye on the rhino to take his activism to the next level.

Once Roy had jokingly mentioned, 'Dev would have Sultan killed if he didn't like the director's face.'

After adopting Khaspur as its grazing ground, the gentle giant Sultan established its own tunnel-like paths through its tall-grass habitat along the Brahmaputra bank. As some part of Khaspur was technically outside the park's boundary, this had been a constant headache for the department to keep the beast safe. Poachers had tried many times to sneak into the forest to get that one and a half foot of the horn off Sultan's head. Those attempts had been foiled by the elite sharpshooter guards stationed at Khaspur camp, which had the most diligent anti-poaching commandos group. They knew what was at stake. They never hesitated to shoot.

The shootings and killings were rarely reported as encounters were far too frequent, and the place was truly inaccessible. One would have to drive miles through the central range's inviolate core zone to go there, and the last section did not have motorable roads. If anyone dared to go there secretly to get Sultan, he would disappear without a trace. The gunshots did not travel to the villagers as the park was in the south, and the wide Brahmaputra was in the north.

The men were ordered to shoot, always and without fail.

Away from the prying eyes of the elephant-borne as

well as jeep laden tourists, Sultan had led a solitary life till that day, or precisely till that evening when Raj and Amelia huddled with Arjun in the police station. Meanwhile, another daredevil guard joined the occupants of the camp at Khaspur. Immediately upon his arrival, the man transmitted a distress message on the wireless.

A call to the ranger of the central range conveyed that Sultan had been killed. Someone in that office then leaked the information to the Rhino Warriors. As expected, it did not take a moment for Dev to call the officer in charge. The man denied it, and that got Dev started. The rest of the plan unfolded in the police station through a bruised and battered Vijay under Raj and Arjun's threatening eyes.

'Yes sir, Sultan is dead.' Vijay had to make it look real. 'It may be a natural death, but I think some guards heard gunshots. Roy sahib has instructed ranger babu to bury the animal at Khaspur only.' Vijay's tone was low and husky as he looked at Raj for approval. A thumbs up from Raj, he continued, 'Sir, I think it will be good to go there and check.'

The phone was in speaker mode.

Dev knew the park's rules; he couldn't enter the core area after dark. 'With all these things going on, I don't think I will get any permission to go inside.' There was a pause.

Raj shuddered. Has the bastard smelled something?

'The ranger denied any such incident. My men have heard that they are trying to hush it up. What do you think?'

'Sir, with the director sir in hospital and his bungalow raided, poachers might have thought they had an opportunity. So, they sneaked in and got their prize. Or maybe the beast died of old age.'

Dev did not say anything; his razor-sharp brain might be working out the possibilities. Raj muttered a silent prayer. He looked at Arjun's chair. Tomorrow, a new man would be sitting there. The suspended ranger may not even be welcomed to the station.

'You can talk to Raj sahib,' Vijay said.

'I don't think he will allow me to go there. It is not his range.'

Khaspur, situated in the park's northern boundary, entailed an hour-long ride on an unpaved road through the core area. There was another way, longer but quicker.

'Sir, no need to go through the park,' Vijay said. 'You can enter from the north by crossing the river.'

There was some hesitation from the other side. 'I will need some escort to go to the place.'

'Sir, I can come along,' Vijay almost whispered.

'What happens if Raj finds out?'

'He is busy with the Australian tourist. I am on sick leave. I fell in the bathroom. The floor was very slippery.' Vijay paused; the beating surely hurt. 'After the raid and what they found at Vulture Hill, most office people are clueless and demoralised. I can come with you. With so many things going on, nobody will notice.'

Raj marvelled at Vijay's histrionic capability, amazed that he had withstood the conspiracies of his deputy all these years. There was a pause from Dev's side. 'Okay, we can go to the north bank. I can ask my man to keep my speedboat ready. We can be at Khaspur before dawn before your people reach there to bury the beast. If it is a poaching case, I will do directly live on Facebook from there.'

Vijay headed towards River View Resort within no time, but not before having a one-to-one session with Raj in a closed room. The next part of the plan would hopefully go as per the script. After crossing the Brahmaputra by boat, Vijay would lead Dev to the spot, which was the morning foraging ground of Sultan. There would be guards with sullen faces directing the duo to the place where supposedly Sultan's body was lying. As they reached the rivulet, which was the park's core area boundary, the grassland's tall tracks would allow Vijay to slip away. Dev, with his camera, would rush to the lowland, the old bull's usual wallowing spot, but he would not find Sultan.

Raj stared at the backyard as dark clouds hid the moon. Winds jarred the doors and windows of the old building.

The sky lit up as heaven-sent lightning illuminated every nook and corner of the park, though just momentarily; soon after, the entire police station shook in a brazen thunderbolt from heaven. Then it fell dark again. The absolute blackness of the night had drowned the whole place in a sea of sorrow and anger, betrayal and loss.

Amelia had slowly got at ease inside the old, decrepit police station. The police personnel were no longer curious about her. As the men got busy preparing for the mission, Raj could feel his cheeks heat up. He knew his face showed mixed hues of relief and nervousness. On the other hand, Arjun was either yelling on the phone, talking in the walkie-talkie room, or giving his men instructions.

After Vijay departed, Raj's heartbeat almost doubled. Despite the tenseness and a sense of unknown expectation which perhaps Amelia could not fathom, her deep blue eyes revealed some amount of happiness when their gazes met; was it because of what had happened the night before and the continued proximity to him, if he dared to believe it that way; or was it because she saw a closure to her friend Dorothy's saga. Raj was not sure, and he didn't care.

'Get some chai,' Arjun's thunderous shout brought him to the present. As Arjun settled on his seat after a long time, Raj joined him, sitting next to Amelia. His usually busy table was all cleaned up.

'Will the bastard go?' Arjun said, looking at his watch. 'The storm is not showing any sign of abating. I hope he does not cancel his plan.'

'Vijay will make sure he goes. I swear I will kill him if he fails to take our warrior there.' Raj clenched his jaws as he took a deep breath; it was going to be a long night. He looked at Arjun. A load of pain and anguish pierced his heart—the man would be gone tomorrow. All the missions they had undertaken together flashed through his mind. Those were nothing like what they planned to undertake in the next few hours.

Yes, he was edgy; he had never faced a more brilliant adversary. He was taking on his childhood icon, the state's green heartthrob. After what felt like a long night, Raj glanced at his watch. It was three-thirty in the morning—Dev and Vijay should be in the north bank by now. Rain still battered the tin roof of the police station. With every passing minute, his restlessness soared. He had to distract himself. 'Why did she kill herself?' Asha madam's beautiful face flashed in Raj's mind.

Arjun's frown showed. He leaned back and said, after taking a long breath, 'If you ask the servants, they believe their madam got possessed by an evil spirit in the evening. I think it is a case of what psychiatrists call dissociative identity disorder. Her symptoms had been waxing and waning. Her husband cared for her, but didn't go for any aggressive treatment. So, he allowed none of the men to stay with them at night. He took all the brunt himself.'

'People with such condition,' Arjun continued, 'are prone to depression, substance abuse, self-harm, all those terrible things. It had to happen one day.' He shook his head. 'Well, remember the sister we visited in the tea garden? As she said, much tension was going on in the bungalow. The director's wife knew of her husband's infidelities. With that knowledge and her state of mind, what else can you expect?'

Amelia's eyes welled up. 'When do you think he will be able to talk? How is he doing?' She asked, looking at Raj.

'The last time I talked to Roy, he said the doctor in charge called him to inform that the director had gained consciousness. He is too weak to talk, though. Hopefully, tomorrow he will be in a position to speak to us,' Raj said, his palms clenched against his chin.

Raj's phone buzzed; it was a message from Vijay. They had reached Sultan's kingdom. Raj suppressed a smile, thankful for the old bull's one and a half feet horn.

★★★

Chapter 40

Day 12 (Dawn)

Raj gave Arjun a knowing look as the red junglefowl's call heralded an impending breaking of dawn. Arjun picked up the crackling transceiver set and vanished with a never-seen agility into the next room; Raj followed immediately after. Amelia could hear nothing as both Raj and Arjun went inside the wireless room and banged the door shut.

Arjun appeared from the room after a minute or so. The anxiety on his face was gone; he looked at peace with himself as he announced, 'A poacher is holed up in the forest in the northern section of the park. He is playing hide-and-seek with our men, refusing to surrender. There might be an encounter.'

Amelia looked at him, puzzled.

'As you know, we can't allow anyone inside the core area. If the person runs away from the guards, his intentions are not good. We will have to go and check,' Arjun said in a mechanical way, picking up his service revolver and gesturing with his hand to the men waiting outside his room.

'Where are you all going?' Amelia managed to ask, looking at Raj after Arjun had already dashed off like a rocket.

'Khaspur,' Raj said, his face red, eyes avoiding contact.

'That's the place where you said you wanted to take me. Who would go there on a night like this?' Amelia asked. 'Can I come?'

'Do you want to go?' Raj said. 'There could be firing. Poachers are armed with automatic weapons.' For the first time, she saw him gripping a pistol in his hand. She knew she had no business in being a part of the missions of the park authorities and the police, but she found Raj nodding to her request. He was distracted and unsettled. His warm brown eyes burned with despair and anger, his face shedding the hues of betrayal and revenge.

'You go with Arjun,' he said softly.

Soon after, she was in Arjun's jeep on a patrolling track, bumpy at some places and muddy and slippery at others, traversing through a section of the park out of bounds for ordinary tourists. The headlights shone fleetingly on small, unknown animals crossing the deserted road. The car occupants were silent, drowned in the numerous calls emanating from the dense forests.

Raj climbed into another vehicle together with a group of men armed with automatic firearms, their faces covered in balaclava face masks. They drove for an hour or so. Arjun's jaws were clenched; the slight joviality of his face that Amelia had got used to during the long hours at the police station was replaced with an unfathomable sternness. The palpable nervousness in him manifested through the constant tapping of his fingers on the dashboard. Had she crossed the barrier by embedding herself in an operation that they did not want outsiders to see? Amelia made a promise to herself. Whatever was going to unfold, she would keep it to herself for the sake of these men who devoted their every living hour to save the animals. Especially for the sake of these two men who had taken a significant risk by allowing her to accompany them on a mission, which by now she had realised, was not officially appropriate, but was very much required to nurture the red hungry grass of the floodplains so that the rhinos, tigers, and buffalos could roam freely, without fear.

Amelia jerked to the present when the driver braked hard, and the vehicle skidded on soft, muddy soil. As they came to a halt, Amelia could make out the frantic movements of shadowy personnel in army fatigues. An owl hooted from the tree's burrow under which the police jeep stopped. The road ended at that spot. Everyone from the half a dozen or so vehicles got down and started trekking through grasses as tall as elephants, on treacherous mushy ground. Raj's tall frame loomed large over the short, taut commandos around him. The heavens began to pour, and the whole park seemed to be immersed in a weeping melancholy around what was going to unfold. Arjun followed Raj's party with cat-like stealth despite his bulk with a platoon of armed guards and policemen.

Amelia trudged behind them, her boots soggy and pants ripped by thorns. It was a slow and laboured walk for the sleep-deprived bodies through the tall elephant grass. She heard the footsteps of those ahead of her treading on bent reeds and the dismay of francolins at being disturbed by the sudden intrusion as they indulged in their pre-dawn activities. A lone Bengal florican flew high above in disarray.

Suddenly, from the forest ahead of them, the sound of gunshots ripped through the air, as loud as thunder. The group hastened its pace, excited whispers among the trekkers, to step out in the open onto the bank of a small rivulet that wound its way through the reed bed towards the vast expense of the Brahmaputra.

A new day broke as they were greeted by the morning songs of birds, and the Himalayan mountains rose silently in the distant background. Across the stream, in the grey and pallid pink of dawn, Rahman stood tall among the red grass with his INSAS rifle, fiery-eyed and resolute. A bloodied body lay at his feet.

A shiver travelled through Amelia's spine when she saw a pair of rimless glasses lying in a tiny puddle. The gun placed against the body's bullet-ridden chest, with the boyish face, looked incongruent. Over him, the executioner standing erect heaved in excitement. The thoroughly drenched guard's image—one that brought her to the park with the raincoats, drifted in front of her eyes. Yes, he was the same man on the website of Rhino Warrior, Rahman. But that day, he wore a yellow raincoat. Raj stood there looking at the body, both hands on his waist. He shouted to the guards, 'The body is still outside the boundary. We need to bring it inside.'

He then turned to look at Amelia, his eyes teary and face shedding hues of emotion. Did she see a sea of relief in his eyes? A smile seeped through his lips, and his clenched jaws loosened as he pointed his finger to a foggy opening that showed through the grass. Through the mud and the mist arose a primitive mammoth giant.

Was it Sultan with his long pointy horn, just like Kifaru?

★★★

Glossary

Dada:	Elder brother
Dhaba:	Indian roadside eatery
Didi:	Sister
DFO:	Divisional Forest Officer
IFS:	Indian Forest Service
Nimbu Pani:	Lemon juice and water